W9-BWI-335

Marshland Brace

Marshland Brace

TWO LOUISIANA STORIES BY

CHRIS SEGURA

Louisiana State University Press
Baton Rouge and London   1982

MIDDLEBURY COLLEGE LIBRARY.

PS
3569
.E46
M3

11/1982
am Lit.

Copyright © 1982 By Chris Segura
All rights reserved
Manufactured in the United States of America

Design: Patricia Douglas Crowder
Typeface: Palatino
Typesetter: G&S Typesetters, Inc.
Printer and binder: Thomson-Shore, Inc.

LIBRARY OF CONGRESS CATALOGING IN PUBLICATION DATA

Segura, Chris.
   Marshland brace.

   Contents: Tranasse (March passage)—Les perdues
(The lost ones)
   1. Cajuns—Fiction.   I. Title.
PS3569.E46M3   813'.54   82-15193
ISBN 0-8071-1040-X   AACR2

To the memory of Wallace Lovell, my teacher, and to John Walter McGinn Boudreaux, my friend.

Contents

Tranasse

Prologue

In the last year the marsh was the same as it had always
been, Josef Dimanche poled his pirogue farther than he
had ever gone. The muskrat were plentiful. And though
the channels changed and mixed, though the surface blew
in the wind and drifted with the tides, the intricate balance of earth and water, death and life continued, seem-
ingly omnipotent. In constant change, changeless.

Josef Dimanche was young then, and strong. He held
the balance of the moment in his muscles. Obedient to
each nudge of his feet, to each push of his pole, the pirogue shifted and swung and glided deeper. He had come
this far to experiment, but he had also come this far because his prowess needed exercise. He had learned well as
much as could be taught him, and he constantly observed
and tried to understand as well as he was able. But his true
existence was within his muscles, thoughtless and brutal
and superb.

To this he had attached his woman and the life swelling
in her far behind him. He lived within the marsh part of
each year, and the time he was not within the marsh was
spent preparing or planning to return. All around him
consciousness lived and breathed and fed and procreated
and died, and he was part of that but as a higher species,
not so much a ruling one as one that is indomitable.

The experiment was a simple one but one he knew other

trappers would not approve. It was simply to set traps around the muskrat beds, the domed homes of the chief fur producer of the marsh. To set them in a circle around the homes and not the trails the animals took to forage and feed.

The prow of the double-pointed boat broke from the tight channel and into a network of little ponds. About the curving shores and on tiny islands within the ponds, the rounded, graying beds of grass and sticks rose from the marsh like the sculptured domes of a city. Josef Dimanche believed this was virgin ground, that these animals had never seen a human being.

Against the bank he held the pirogue and planted the pole tight against it for anchor. He took up his forked walking stick and hung the chains of traps across his shoulders, then stepped into the marsh itself. It was a warm day in winter, and swarms of mosquitoes rose up from the grass. They buzzed and clouded thick about his face, tortured by his blood.

Then he saw the snake. And seeing, only then did he smell the odor—musky, heavy, thick. It drew back in tight curves, not coils. Josef Dimanche was not afraid. He knew the snake had neither range nor aim. Awakened early by the unseasonable warmth, it had its winter skin, the very covering of its eyes. The forked tongue licked out to hear him.

"Oh, fat one," he said to the thick-muscled snake, "you have fed yourself on frogs and mice and lived to reach your muscled length by fleeing here where none would go. But I have come and now you show your deadly white and threaten me."

It was not uncommon among the people of the marsh to be bitten by a snake. But Josef Dimanche hated the cottonmouths more than most because of an incident of his childhood. So he raised his stick high. Fishhook fangs drew back, but Josef Dimanche struck first. He broke the snake's back and it writhed and thumped against the floating grass and mud. He did not strike again. He had learned from hard experience the mystery of snakes. He was content merely to kill, so he watched and did not strike again.

"But if I had the traiteur Snake Man's magic," Josef Dimanche said, and the dying snake licked at the words, "I would have ringed you with the toe of my new rubber boot as I once saw the Snake Man do upon the dusty levee top. I, though, would leave you here to die. I would not have broken the circle and let you crawl free. I would have left you here to starve and grow as narrow as a worm."

He paused, then, and pondered, watching a ricebird perch upon a roseau stem.

"Perhaps it only works upon the dust," he said.

The ricebird darted his glance to Josef Dimanche then to the dying snake. Josef Dimanche took from his trouser pocket the flat little bottle. Drinking was still new to him so he was still enamored with the gray, powerful feeling and the glaring tones existence took. It was a bout of strength to him. Josef Dimanche needed testing. He tipped the bottle back, let in the biting taste. Through squinted eyes he watched the ricebird, through grimaced lips he spoke to him.

"What a strange ricebird," he said, "to sit upon a roseau stem and watch a dying snake when there is so much grain to gather to your craw. What care you who feeds on grain if meat dies writhing in the marsh?"

The snake flexed, curling one more great slow time, showing the lighter gray of the belly, and was still. Josef Dimanche walked on and found a low-scooped trail where otter and mink slide through the marsh beneath the bending grass. This is where he would set his traps if he were not experimenting. But instead he walked on to the domes and set the traps around them. He had set almost all the traps before he saw the child.

The child was sleeping, curled on one of the domes of grass and sticks. He slept in shivers because his clothes were wet. His face was tucked beneath his arms as some wild things sleep to protect eyes from the insects. Josef Dimanche went soundlessly toward him.

About his face, the insects flowed with each breath like a tide. The breathing was a whimper. A small hand brushed at a swollen ear, then settled on his neck. There were large welts on his cheeks.

He was the second son of Vasito Lopez, of those who lived the entire year within the marsh. As one will seek to learn by touch the true nature of a new and wondrous thing, Josef Dimanche reached out his hand. He touched the head of Etienne.

Instantly, the boy was off the dome and running through the marsh. Josef Dimanche overtook him. His great strength overwhelmed the boy, brought him to the cypress pirogue, and by that boat to his home, a shack upon the levee of Bayou Chien, behind two young cedars. The boy said nothing. Josef Dimanche spoke French, and the language of the Lopez family was an ancient form of Spanish. And the father always spoke for them.

The father stood between the cedars as they walked up the levee from the bayou. The cedars and the man and the shack behind him darkened in the setting sun. Etienne walked past him to the shack. They spoke somberly but not of the boy. They spoke of the strange, orange-toothed creature Lopez called *coypu* which had begun to invade the marsh. Lopez cursed the coypu and said it would drive the muskrat away. Dimanche had not seen sign, yet, of this, so he merely listened and did not allow himself alarm. The Americains called the animal *nutria*, but for the rest of his life Josef Dimanche would think of him as coypu.

Finally, Josef Dimanche took to his boat and poled himself away. And then he heard the blows. Josef Dimanche had never been whipped as a child and therefore knew only of victory. And he believed strength carried the responsibility of judicious restraint. And he did not believe children should be beaten. But each man lives his life alone, and each man has his own house. So Josef Dimanche took from his pocket the flattened bottle and tried not to hear the sound of blows that fell without a protest from the child.

He heard also, far down the watercourse and singular and distinct, still rare, the cry of the new animal of the marsh. The coypu's cry is a dying baby's weak wail, though a full-grown male makes the sound. The light failed, then, to a deep, dark blue. A grosbek, night heron, lifted from the water almost at the cypress prow. On dark, purple, wide, and graceful wings, he flew the twisting channel.

The moon rose, then, and lit the way.

Monologue

Quickly I grew weary of the town. As soon as decency allowed, I made ready my return to the marsh. I did not wish to hear more of Etienne Lopez. I did not wish to watch my daughter in shame. And so, as soon as decency allowed, I made ready my return to the marsh.

The night before my return my daughter, for she is a good woman nonetheless, prepared my supper and packed my supplies. I had had my daughter take the kitchen tools, and thus after I ate I sat and saw for the first time in my home how bare is death. My home in town would now have no need of kitchen things. But more than the tools of nourishment had been stripped away. It was my intention to strip away the pain that resides in memory. Instead I was left this bare reminder of her death. I had not had strong drink since those moments of my young man's strength, and yet I craved it now.

My daughter, still washing dishes, spoke over her shoulder to me.

"Papa," she said, "don't go, please? It is too soon, and it is not necessary."

I did not answer. I had given enough time to the ritual. A man can mourn alone as well as in the sight of others. And I had never liked to stay in towns. People who live in towns want silly things. They speak of unimportant and unpleasant things. Now they talked of murder and of murderers as though their talk could bring the terror to them, for what purpose I do not know.

My daughter dried her hands as she sat down at my table. She put the drying rag upon the table. Never in her long years had her mother put a rag upon that table except in cleaning. My daughter folded her hands upon the table before her. Her hands were white and wrinkled from the water.

"Papa," she said again, "please, do not go back into the marsh? It is too soon, Papa."

"What care you for old rituals?" I said, and was instantly sorry I had said it. For it hurt her. Such things, once said, linger in the air like smoke on a windless day. "I have stayed a proper time. And a man has his work."

She looked down at her water-wrinkled hands, probed a tiny cut in one finger. The skin around the cut was dead, lifeless, bland. Suddenly, she looked up at me, into my eyes. Her eyes were like her mother's, dark gray with fine black circles around them. But her mother's eyes no longer saw. My daughter's eyes studied mine and I refused to drop my gaze.

"Papa," she said softly, "wait until they find Etienne Lopez? Papa? Just until then."

"No."

She dropped her eyes again. It was growing late. My grandson would need her. I did not like the thought of the man with whom she lived giving comfort to my grandson, Little Josef. That was a wicked thing to think, I know, for comfort with affection is far too rare a thing to have denied. But there were certain proprieties.

"Go home to your son," I said, and this time her eyes filled with wetness but did not overflow. She knew I would have liked to say, "and to your husband." This man with whom she lived was good, a man I would have chosen, but he was not her husband. Such things bring scandal and worse.

"Stay, Papa, until they find Etienne Lopez. Little Josef and I will stay with you here, in this house."

And then, you see, I was both angry and weary with sorrow. The anger welled inside me strong, for she had bribed me with her virtue. But sorrow welled inside me like the depths of the great sea.

"Go home to your son, daughter," I said, "and leave an old man to live what life remains."

My daughter wept, then, with sobs she tried to hold inside her. Even as she left the house, she wept. I, too, was filled with sorrow, and took her tears to bed with me. That night I dreamed of water running, and of rain, but when I awoke the land was dry.

The aged pirogue was still sunk and the water inside it had become as clear and green as rainwater in the cistern. The edges of the pirogue's sides rose and fell as if in greeting, as I poled the flatboat beside it. The other boats, also, were moored correctly as I had left them. The boat of LeBlanc, the trapper, was not there.

It was late in the morning to be running traps, but perhaps as I suggested he was setting a new line along the levee by Lac L'Onion. I unloaded the supplies onto the little pier. The cypress pirogue's lines above the water were perfect. It was good to think of the water keeping the cypress pure from drying cracks. The cypress, like our people, is born with his feet in water. Only closeness to water can sustain him, even after death.

Not all I saw was good that morning I returned to the marsh, however. Near LeBlanc's little shack was a pile of trash. And the big house had been used. The wood stove in the bedroom had not been properly watched. A board cut too long had been burned in it, and the end had fallen to the floor, scorching the worn old planks. With houses old and dry, intelligent men take much care with fire. And the bed was soiled.

The northern room had not been used, but I unlocked the door and checked it nonetheless. A musty coldness rushed from the door long locked and closed. It enveloped me with the chill and scent of houses long abandoned. Carefully, I locked the door shut once again.

The rats, smelling flour inside the cabinet, had tried to chew through the wood beneath the screen. I put the flour into a can and patched new screen upon the tooth marks in the wood. Then I put my supplies away and went outside.

The wind blew from the north. Far to the west, it carried smoke heavy like a plume. The fire was near Bayou Cocodrille. Across my line. DesHotel was having a bad year, to come so far east and burn so late in the season to find new trails for traps.

The smoke rose heavy and black from the fire I could not see. Then it curved southward, across the great canal, and toward the sea. Its shadow widened a fan across the marsh, and the smoke quickly lightened into gray. So the wind was losing strength. What sort of weather was in the making?

In the east, over the Iberia marsh, the sky sat strangely purple. It was difficult to interpret with the wind out of the north. Perhaps rain if the wind shifted south. Well, whatever came, I'd live with it.

I walked the high bluff of the levee. A butcherbird had hung many kills on the old thorn tree. Lizards and tiny snakes now hung dry and cured, speared on purple thorns. The black-beaked bird flew to the roof of the shack and perched there, watching me.

His head darted so he could see the area I walked. His sharp eyes saw everything. He never looked directly at me, yet he knew my every move.

For many seasons I had watched this butcherbird, and I admired his skill. He was a fine hunter. Indeed, he was a great one. From early spring each year his fresh kills dried upon the thorns and he ate of the cured flesh only in the winter months. He was wise and successful, but I never saw him take a mate. It was a thing I considered very curious.

Near the edge of the marsh on the west side of the house a lark had thatched his nest with goose down. Six steps into the marsh I found the pile of feathers hidden beneath marsh grass. Field mice lived beneath it. So many geese would only have been killed for the market. The new gamekeeper would bring charges if he knew. I replaced the grass.

I ate my noon meal, then buried LeBlanc's trash. There were no more good young marsh men. It required a wildness and a courage that was no longer approved. And there were, now, other ways for them to make their money. I tried not to plan what I would say to him.

The gamekeeper came in mid-afternoon. We took our coffee with us from the kitchen and sat upon the dried gray clay of the high levee bluff. This new gamekeeper, although an American, was interested in the marsh. He would learn if he was given time. He knew how to speak politely, which was important, and he spoke in French, though of the other kind.

"Monsieur Josef," he said, "in all your years have you ever seen the marsh so dry?"

"Oh, yes," I said. "There was a time once when deer came to drink from our cistern, for salt had backed up with the tides and the low water and made the very bayous unfit to drink. Before the rains, salt formed upon the low mud banks."

"But this dryness is severe, is this not so?"

"Oh, yes, but we will live."

He smiled. This gamekeeper was a rare one, one who listened well and so heard many things. The marsh fires worried him. This winter, he said, he had seen for the first time how in a dry marsh the fire can fly across the tops of the grass.

Once, he said, Uribe, the trapper at Lac Blanc, had set his fire with a northwest wind to burn toward Bayou Noir, and there to cease. But Bayou Noir had been dry so long the fire crept across dead bottom scum. It left behind a blackened, smoldering carpet, and lit the grass on the south side of the bayou. It had burned all the way to the lake, he said.

And at the lake many small animals had been trapped. He asked if in my many years in the marsh had I ever seen a deer trapped and killed by fire. I said that I had not.

Deer, he said, were plentiful. But because of the dryness of the marsh, the ducks had moved across the sea. Many geese had stayed, he said, and asked why this was so. The goose is more a bird of habit than the duck. He will starve before he changes his ways.

The new gamekeeper said, indeed, the geese were starving. They were, he said, as thin as if they had only just completed their great flight into our land. They were thin and weak, now, and eating the roots of grass. The marsh would not recover in two years, he said, and hunters plagued the geese terribly.

And then there was a silence between us. I thought he would now speak things he had come so far to say.

"Monsieur Josef," he said very seriously, "you knew Etienne Lopez?"

"Yes," I said, and nothing more.

"This is what they told me in the town. It is thought Etienne Lopez will now come into the marsh."

I said nothing.

"It is said if this is so, only you will know the way to find him."

Again, I said nothing.

"They have asked the gamekeepers to watch for him. Will you help me in this?"

"Yes. I will watch, but Etienne Lopez will not come into the marsh."

"Why do you not think so?"

"What kind of place is the marsh for a man who must shun other men?"

"A good man can hide here forever. A man such as yourself could live out all his years and not be seen."

"Yes, this is true. But what kind of life would he have? For when the winter chill turns warm and other creatures rule the marsh, he would wish he was in the prison again, or dead. Oh, some have lived here all year long, but they had special powers."

This Americain was different, for he did not smile at special powers.

"Then, Monsieur Josef, in this matter of Etienne Lopez, you will watch and tell me what you see?"

"Yes. In the matter of Etienne Lopez, I will tell you what I see."

I said this carefully, because, like the butcherbird who seems to look everywhere except where he is seeing, I was even then watching LeBlanc unload and hide his illegal kill.

"But I think in this matter there will be nothing for me to

see. It would be better for a man like him to lose himself in a forest of other men."

"But in town, they say that Etienne Lopez always shuns other men."

"What do people in towns know of the people of the marsh?"

I was growing tired of this talk. It had pursued me to the marsh. But this gamekeeper was polite.

"You knew those Lopez well?"

"As well as any man. They came into our marsh and trapped for my papa. They came after the Trapper's War in the Saint Bernard. Eustis Lopez, he still had wounds not healed. They were a hard people, but they trapped well and kept the marsh clean."

"Where did they trap?"

"The Iberia marsh."

"If, as they say in town, Etienne Lopez would come back, would he return there?"

"No. Nothing remains. A great storm took it all. Even the marsh is changed."

LeBlanc came to us, then, sat heavily and uninvited before us. He was heavy and always dirty. He had the eyes of drink, watery and red-rimmed. I knew those eyes well. I had stared back at myself with them many mornings of my young manhood. I had never made my peace with drink but only used my will. LeBlanc lacked that sense of will. He brought a bad taste with him. I adjusted my hood, for the north wind was at my back and blowing cold. After some more talk of the marsh, the gamekeeper said:

"I wish I knew what Etienne Lopez would do."

"Mais, Etienne Lopez, you say?" LeBlanc said in English. "That man, him, he crazy, yes. A crazy man, po yi, you don't know what he do, him. For to do what he did? Man, he have to be crazy, him. To fuck, piquer, something, yes. All right. But to kill it like that? And him brother wife, him.

But they say she was his woman, too. I don't know, me. That what they say. But if it true, them kids, them, was for him too, some of them, nobody knows. He cut that woman like a calf."

LeBlanc's big dirty finger jabbed up into the air above his head.

"And for to shoot him own brother in the head, him. . . . Pop!" LeBlanc's finger struck his own head.

The gamekeeper and I looked away, then, in distaste. I looked into the south, where the plume was very white. A ricebird settled, wings beāting backward, upon the tip of a roseau first bending to the wind, now bending to his weight. Balanced so well on such a weak perch. Yet, what cared the ricebird? If the cane should break, his swift wings would carry him away.

"What they call them, them people from the Saint Bernard? What speak that Spanish?"

"Isleños."

"Yeah. That's what. Them, they all crazy, them."

"No, they are men as other men. Their life in that land has not been easy. And in the Trapper's War they took their land away. It is why Eustis Lopez came to this marsh."

"And you don't think it was a crazy man, him, what done that to that woman over there? And them kids, them, too, yeah."

"I do not think of things I cannot see, things I cannot understand. Some things though known are not to be believed. My own wife died. I buried her last week. I waked her and let them put her in the ground. Yet I do not believe her death. The deaths of wives and the murder of children sleeping are things better not believed."

There was a little silence, and then LeBlanc said, "Huh! Them from the Saint Bernard. Me, I think they all crazy, them."

Then all of us were silent. The ricebird flew away, the

roseau springing straight and then bending again with the wind. The smoke plume grew even whiter and less thick in the south. Polite small things were mentioned, and then the gamekeeper went away.

So tired I was of talking, I did not reprimand LeBlanc.

Only a small bit of yellow light came from his shack as I stepped out into the cold night. The moon was already high. He was like a curved bowl balanced on his edge and spilling stars into the west. There was a partial shadow where his nose would be and a full shadow at the eye. Before he set, he would turn and move below, toward the sea. At almost midnight he would set a little south of west. A nightly search for all his parts, to find them in the days and lose them again, poor man.

He was reflected in the water of the cistern. Ice already formed around the iron edges of the tank. I sank my bare arms into the rainwater and felt for the best of the traps. I pulled up six, and stood there dripping water on my boots. The kitchen was so bright against the night.

The old wooden steps bowed down with my weight. Rusty water dripped upon her floor. Her floor. She is no more. And yet I took the mop, dry and stiff from little use, and wiped away the trail. The rainwater was clear upon the boards, and the rust inside was like little veins the color of old blood.

I sat at the table and rubbed my leg through my trousers and heavy stocking. I had been standing long, cooking and working, so the little veins were bulging. The white beans were boiling in the pot. One by one I took the traps up onto the table. I dried them and then oiled them well. I worked their springs, spread wide their jaws, set the latch, then sprang them with the handle of a spoon. They were still taut and fine. I put them in a sack.

I put my breakfast beans into a jar and left them on the front porch to cool. The moon had hidden himself behind the roof of the porch, but the marsh, lighted silver, lay cold before me to the east. North wind had cleared the air before it died. I could even see a town beyond the Iberia marsh, glowing like a glass bowl turned over.

The bits of wood I gathered were already frosted with ice. I made the fire in the wood stove of the bedroom. The blackened tongue of the wick rolled down, the kerosene lamp went out. In the darkness of the lonely room glowed only the orange-blue streaks of light from vents in the old iron stove. A winter hand of loneliness gripped at my heart. I breathed the dark, vacated air, stripped off my outer clothes, the stocking for my veins.

I got into the sagging bed, beneath the weight of blankets thick and old. The hand about my heart now squeezed so that I turned my eyes against the streaks of light, then turned them back again. Part of me could not bear to see the loneliness in there. And yet, I had to seek the warmth, light licking at the truth.

In time I slept.

How bright and warm it is this day she first comes with me into the marsh. The marsh stretches rich and flat and golden in the autumn sun. The southern breeze holds north of us great clouds of mosquitoes newly hatched by the heat.

We are so completely alone. I put my arm around her. She is such a tiny woman. One might think her waist would break in our embrace. Her eyes are gray with black rings along the outer edges. I tell her something of the marsh, something of the tides, of how the moon's tides bring life into the waiting marsh.

My arm outstretched points to something in the south.

She smiles and holds her cheek against my chest. My shoulders bulge the brown cloth of my shirt. I lead her to the door. She is shy, but finally obeys.

In the hard new bed, brought to the marsh with so much waste of precious bateaux space, she clings to me to keep my sight from her. For the room is filled with daylight, and she is shy and though well married I have yet to see her nudity. She clings to me. I kiss her lightly. I kiss her braided hair. Her muscles are so taut. Her eyes glisten with tears, and yet she smiles again. She is smiling gently at herself. I kiss her lightly. I pull the blanket over us and do not try to look at her.

Expended in the night, I sleep. And while I sleep the winds change and blow, now, from the north. I pull the blankets over us. I try to stretch a cramp from my leg, but still it aches.

The northern gale winds slap the windows, slap the doors that bang against the house, and cold rushes in with gusts that rattle at the cabinets, rattle beneath the bed. I gather her to me for warmth, for now she must be cold.

And cold, she is. And lax and soft. Her skin, now puffy white hangs loose about her jaws. Wrinkles rim her eyes in lunar curves. She stares at me, not seeing. I shrink from her. I sit up in the bed.

And there was nothing. No wind. No woman in my bed. The stove's fire smoldered. There was no longer any moon. A rattle of rats in the kitchen. Soft, encroaching cold and an old man's dreams.

Yet, in the morning, the beans I had put upon the porch were gone. A back door had been left open to the night. Rats ran from the opened cabinet as I entered the kitchen. And my newly oiled six traps were missing. How bold. My six best traps.

Far down the bayou, LeBlanc poled crudely as I walked to the high point of the levee bluff. Once, he almost dropped the pole, and a curse carried to me from across the marsh, for sound travels wonderfully across the marsh. I did not call him back.

Inside the house, I pulled the shotgun from its case. I wiped away the heavy oil and took three shells I had reloaded with light shot. Two of them I slipped into the chambers of the barrels. One, I put into my shirt. Then I put the house in order.

The veins in my leg ached terribly, even with the tight stocking holding them.

I left the old one resting in her water and took another pirogue. Before I entered the marsh, the sky was blue in the way a teal wing patch changes darkly in the sun. I took the old trail Antoine Mestayer had built that year to reach his special pond, but turned from it on the first natural channel that I came to. Twice, flights of ducks came from my back to cross my head and linger over water to my front.

When I was close enough to reach the lovely water, I hid myself and the third flight—these of canard noir—came over and then circled to the pond. I rested in the grass while they grew easy. It was a fine marsh, still.

Papa would have had me set a trap for ducks in that little piece of water that probed for a new channel. Poor ducks, they have only their wonderful eyes and almost no intelligence. Wonderful eyes and wonderful wings, but almost no intelligence, no defense for treachery. A baited corridor of wire will snare a dozen as they crowd into the trap and then cannot turn around.

Once, as an experiment, I left a poule d'eau inside the trap each morning as I gathered the ducks of the night before. A poule d'eau is not a duck, but he stayed three weeks until I released him. Papa, he would have been angry to see me release the poule d'eau, for he considered it a waste of both my effort and the bird. But it did not matter, for the same poule d'eau was inside the trap the next morning. He was well cooked by noon.

Using a point of high grass to hide me, I pushed the pirogue silently ahead, then, toward the three canard noir. I got so close I could almost strike them with the pole. I fired high, so only a few pellets would strike them in their heads. All three were dead in one shot. It was not sporting, but I was not hunting. I was gathering meat, and there is a difference.

I hid myself again inside the grass and feathered the ducks in the field. Other ducks flew peacefully over me and settled in the pond to talk and feed unmolested. I listened to their happy, curious talk. I also heard two otter pups playing, splashing in the sunlit water not very far off to my left. Were they older and I younger, I'd walk the marsh and gather up their pelts. And, though otter pups in play are a joyful thing to see, I made no move. I had the sight of their uncles and ancestors as pups playing stored up in my mind. So I only listened and went home.

Harsher sounds greeted me as I moored the pirogue in the slip behind the house. It was the sound of chopping. A sound like that of an axe biting into driftwood still soaked with water from the sea. And mixed with it was the sound of bone splintering.

The legs were extended over a wooden block, a block already patterned with many cuts. The hatchet fell. The furry dead feet flew, toes curled by severed sinews. Flesh and fur stuck to the bit. The hatchet fell again and the forelegs were severed. Bone splintered.

Then he shifted the corpse, positioned it so that the

head rested on the block. This time the blade smashed jaws. White back teeth for chewing broke dully, and orange front teeth for biting hung limply from the gashed flesh and skin.

So these were the inheritors of my marsh and my profession, a brute with dull, stiff, and ugly ways, and a beast, it seemed, designed to destroy all that we knew. A brute who tried to do a surgeon's job by using an axe with a dull bit, and a beast that devoured all, that seemed to reproduce itself each morning before rising. Even its hides were almost impossible to cure. They were well suited to each other.

The brute did not even notice as I crossed behind him and went to hang my kill upon the rafters of the porch, so dull he was. I sat, instead, upon the porch and leaned against a post. My rubber-booted foot I set upon the boards. I stroked the swollen veins.

My God. Once, I battled frost so thick my feet crunched four inches deep into the lacelike cold. That winter of the great ice storm. I killed the muskrats in their traps and skinned them on the spot. Their pink-white bodies steamed as the skin peeled back and as they tumbled to the icy marsh, tossed clear of the trail.

My thin skinning blade slitted them with an artist's deft, swift strokes. And they were gentle, worthy, even dainty creatures who ate only of the three-cornered grass that grows in bunches by the ponds.

I took only skins, and food was so scarce that winter that predators stalked behind me, waiting for the leavings of my trade. At first they went before, and killed the squealing rats that fought as any creature would, cornered by death. But the meat-eaters of my marsh soon discovered this was wasted work. They let me do the killing.

I forced my cramped leg straight, then stood. I knotted

the canard noir, the dos-gris heads together with a piece of twine, and hung them from the rafters. Their gutted bellies gaped, gashed open to their tails. Flesh split and forced apart, the holes were like three women's parts, but jagged, bloody, unfit for looks of love.

My mind was foul. I grimaced, spat, and went into the house.

I boiled coffee as my blood cooled. The sounds of hacking stopped. I took my coffee out to talk to him. He was seated at the scraping bench. The pointed scraping board was covered with the stretched tight coypu skin. It jutted up between his thighs.

He held the knife incorrectly, and as he scraped he cut the pelt and patches of fur burst through. Inexcusable. I wrenched the knife from his hands. Coffee spilled across my fingers and I dropped the cup to the ground. He looked up, disbelieving, and I stuck the point of the knife into the bench between his thighs.

"If you cannot but waste the hides," I said, "cease stealing traps to catch them and go into some other marsh to plague the starving geese."

His lips then formed obscenities, English ones.

"Mais . . . you old bastard," he said. "Old men . . . I could kill you . . ." And he stood and drew back his fist, broad and hairy, as if to strike me. But then he calmed cunning. He even smiled.

"Monsieur Dimanche," he said, now in the French, "did you not say when I came here that I could use your traps to set my lines? I only took a few. And you get a share of all the hides they snare."

"What worth is a share of worthless hides? Ripped through carelessness and chopped from carcasses. No. You hunt for the market. I found your kill. I hunted at a

time when it was right. I did not slink and hide my kill,
nor did I worry starving geese."

He tried to speak, but I would not give him time.

"It is no longer justified. Now, it is a sin. And the traps,
yes. Yes, the traps stored against the rust in the water of
the cistern, those are yours to use. But do not invade the
home in which I sleep to steal from me those I have oiled
and readied. Is it your great ignorance that makes you
have to steal your traps? Do you not know how to care for
them? Better that you shoot your starving geese."

He smiled, then. His teeth were yellow and brown.

"The geese," he said, "the geese. I would not have mentioned them. I would let you have your old man's way. But
who are you to speak of stealing and of geese? You, who
creeps like one of your precious rats to where I hid my
game and takes away my plumpest bird."

"I do not know of what you speak."

"Nor I of your 'stolen' traps. 'Josef Dimanche, Josef Dimanche, grand old master of the marsh.' Ha! Old and
wasted and wilting for his dead woman."

"I . . ."

"Enough! Enough of you!"

He took one step toward me, and I knew that he could
strike me then. I knew by virtue of his years he was much
stronger than me. But I did not step back and he crowded
on me, shouting.

"I thought at first it was a fox, some other scavenger
than you! But then I saw the prints, shoe prints. You
wanted one of the geese and so you stole one to hide the
fact that I am as good at hunting as you ever were. Then,
like a child, you make up this tale of other thefts. I'm used
to it, this type of thing. I've had it all my life! I could kill
you, old man! Out here, I could kill you!"

All around the levee bluff the marsh was silent. No bird

calls. Only the ever present and uncaring swish of wind on grass.

"Ahh, old men and children," he said, and went into his shack.

Crimes and countercrimes, but I knew my reality. The thing of which he accused me was a trick of his own, one that he used even as he accused me. Could it be that, as with old Desormeaux, the wind has blown away his reason? Regardless, LeBlanc must go.

I went into the house. I took the empty shotgun shell and loaded it with heavy shot. Shot designed to drop a deer five times as far away as a fast-flying teal can fall. I put the loaded shell into the left chamber and propped the gun out of his sight, inside the back door of the house.

I did not knock at the door of the little shack because it was no longer his home. He looked up from the table. He was drinking. Yet another offense.

"You are no longer welcome here," I told him. His face became red, then suddenly went pale. I understood. The marsh was his last place to go.

"But, Monsieur Josef . . ." he started, but I did not let him continue.

"You say that you have heard of me? Then do not waste more words. You are not welcome here."

"Monsieur Josef . . . I . . ."

"No. Go now. No, go in the morning. I would not like to see you lose your way in darkness. You are not a marsh man, that's not easy to forget. Before day, though, you be gone."

I turned and left. He called to me from the door, but I did not turn around. I heard him curse me loudly. Things slammed and broke inside the little shack. I went to the scraping bench and removed the damaged hide. Disgusted, I threw it on the ground, took up another pelt.

This hide's ends were jagged, butchered, but I stretched it pink and cold on the scraping board before me. The knife was an old one of mine and I had not noticed that before. Carefully, I began the scraping. The bits of fat and inner skin came smoothly off. In time, the sounds inside the shack subsided, but LeBlanc did not come out. I stretched my leg before me to let the blood run smoothly through the swollen veins. I scraped hides until the sun began to fail and cold crept in his shadow. LeBlanc, probably drunk, did not emerge to make his afternoon trap run. I would have to find them in the morning. The animals would suffer all the night, be stiff and dead by daylight, and that was wrong but could not now be helped.

The scraped hides I put on stretchers and hung them from the rafters of the porch, near the dos-gris which were now cold. They would be frozen by morning. Once Le-Blanc had gone, I'd make the shack a drying shed. It would be like when I first began to trap without my papa's orders. Except, of course, that now I was old.

The moon rose high in the sky to the south of east. Thick and nearly round, it seemed he had been hovering there, high, waiting for the sun to hide, hovering high over the Iberia marsh to cheat in the race for his last part.

He lustered, and his lower rim was bright like silver finely tooled but as yet unpolished.

When I awoke there was no silver light beyond the window. The moon had set, and a black stillness had settled on the marsh to aid the night, wind-sniffing hunters. Yellow light and shadows came through the kitchen door. They came with whispers. The whispers were my name.

I reached beneath the bed and pulled the gun within easy reach. The shadow of the man danced with the lamp wick light into my room.

"Monsieur Josef? Monsieur Josef?"

And still I lay and did not speak. The man had stopped inside the kitchen door. He would be holding the lamp behind him to cast light into my room and not blind his eyes to darkness. Slowly, quietly, I drew the shotgun into the bed with me. The cold barrels slid down my leg, the hammers tugged at the thick stocking for the veins.

"Monsieur Josef. Monsieur Josef. I have seen him. He is here, Monsieur Josef."

And then his reek came to me through the door. A reek of drink and sweat stale and foul. But the smell of drink, even on his foul breath was to me delicious. It made me long for forgetfulness.

"Stay where you are, LeBlanc," I said, then sat up in the bed, my feet upon the deerskin on the floor, the shotgun still beneath the covers, pressed close against my thighs. I put on the cold old jacket. "Come in."

He came swiftly, then, bent closely to my face so that I smelled the foul, tempting breath, saw each woolly whisker. Suddenly, I, too, stank, felt dirty. His eyes were red with drink and fear. Drink gives fear to some men, to others it gives a kind of courage.

"Monsieur Dimanche. I cannot leave you here. Not now that I have seen him here. An old man like you . . . I cannot leave you here alone, not now."

"Seen who, LeBlanc? Sit you down, there. Seen who?"

He made to sit, but no sooner had his soiled trousers touched the stack of firewood than he was up, then kneeling, leaning toward me. The lamp shook in his hand. The kerosene splashed inside. I took it from him. I placed it safely on the floor.

He bent his watery eyes downward from mine, covered his forehead with his hand as if he were shading light to see a long way off. It is a liar's trick, a childish liar's trick to hide the eyes' truth against the words. He was a failure at lying, even at lying in his desperation.

"Be still, now, and tell me what you saw. What was it that you saw? Monsieur Satan and his nine friends? The Caller of the feu-bête? He did not singe your beard."

I should not have used the Caller's name. I well remembered seeing him as a boy. Across the marsh he rose and beckoned with his yellow, fiery arm. I pulled the blanket close around me.

"No. No, Monsieur Josef. Lopez! Lopez, I tell you! He leaned over my bed. I saw his face, his mouth, his teeth. He had a knife, Monsieur Josef!"

"Sit you down, man. Sit you down or leave right now."

He settled back, eyes wide, and waited.

"You see only the stuff inside your belly," I said. "Your drink is seeing for you, and thinking for you as well. Go, now, and get some sleep. But leave my land while the morning is still young. Your demons and you are not welcome here."

The Curé d'Ors, it is said, was tormented by demons in his sleep. Once, the devil set his bed on fire. The Curé was a holy man. I, too, have been tormented in my sleep. I, too, have known holy men, and not all of them were priests.

LeBlanc was suddenly standing above me, shouting. His breath called me to drink. He had the lamp in his hand. My fingers touched beneath the blankets the barrels of the gun.

"No! No, no, Monsieur Josef! I cannot go! You cannot stay! He is mad for blood. He killed his own brother. Cut him up! Carved up his brother's wife! He . . . shot those children where they slept. And he's come back into the marsh. Into my shack, Monsieur Josef. He came into my shack!"

"Good," I said, my fingers closing on the chambers of the gun. "He can have your shack when you are gone. All the Lopezes, they were fine trappers. They kept the marshland clean. True, they rarely spoke, but sometimes this is a blessing."

He came on me quickly. Before I could bring the barrels from beneath the blankets one hand had me by the shoulder. But his face was filled with fear, so I held back the barrels pointed at his chest. For strength I held my breath until he knelt again before me. I worried about the lamp.

"No, no, Monsieur Josef. No, no." His voice was now a whisper. "I do not lie. No, no. I do not lie. It was him, Monsieur . . . He stood beside my bed. His face was as close as mine to yours. He breathed upon my face, that breath." Spittle dripped from the corner of his mouth, into his beard.

"Go now," I said, very angry, now "Do not compound offenses with your cowardice."

He sat back on his heel, then put his open hand before him, as if to keep me away. He sat against the stacked firewood, which scattered, fell around him. His other hand was held against his eyes.

"Monsieur Josef . . . I . . ."

But I could stand no more. My own voice rose, now in a shout.

"Go, man! Go from my marsh. Go! Get out! Leave now! Drunk or not, leave now! Let the twisting bayous confuse you even as the drink has set your mind on fire and shown you terrors for children. Go! Go!"

I shouted as his face turned hard, I pulled the shotgun from beneath the blankets, balanced it across my legs, then took my hands from it. I did not move. I did not give him cause to rush.

His eyes followed the lines of the gun, caressed it.

Breathing coarsely he rose, and behind him his shadow was huge, blotting out almost one whole wall. He filled his chest with breath and seemed enormous. His eyes then glared with hatred, and I could see that I had been correct. Of course, his tales were lies.

He brought the lamp to shoulder level. His bloated shadow coursed the room, like a ghostly dog pursuing game. The lamp was poised. He looked down on me with hate. My hand went to the ridged hammers of the gun. I caressed the aged metal. He turned and left. His shadow followed slowly, filled the door then vanished.

For a long time I sat at the edge of the bed, listening. Then I sat back against the old brass bars at the bed's head, still with the gun across my thighs. In time I fell asleep.

There was numbness in my leg from the weight of the gun when I awoke. And there was the smell of smoke.

I pulled on my boots, went toward the back of the house, carrying the gun and expecting to see flames in the kitchen. But the flames were behind the house. LeBlanc's shack was burning. Sparks swirled into a graying sky.

I called for LeBlanc, but there was no answer. As a man will do, though there was no hope, I took the pail and went to the cistern for water. The cistern had been drained. The lumps of the arms of traps stored beneath the rainwater level now stared back at me with rust. All around the iron tank, the clay was slippery wet. The spigot was open.

I leaned the gun against the outside wall, took some old sacks from inside the house and went to the great canal. I soaked the sacks and returned in time to beat away the fire at the edge of the marsh. Bats and swifts hunted in the churning cinders above me.

The shack burned quickly, and soon there were no

flames. There was only the drifting smoke rising above the marsh and hanging like a dark rain cloud against a bland, gray sky. High, rainless clouds, blown from the sea, sat upon the marsh in all directions. They seemed to hold the smoke down to the marsh.

The marsh was very dry. My body was soot-covered from keeping the fire from the grass. I found a spade and raked the ashes into a pile. There were no bones inside the rubble. And no bottles of the whiskey.

I went down to the boats. His boat was gone and all the others had been sunk. Each keel had been split through.

Holding my breath, I bent and grasped the bowline of the old pirogue, the ancient, one-piece cypress boat. I pulled the line and the bow rose lightly. The water skimmed between my fingers from the line. The pirogue was undamaged. Perhaps it had been moored awash so long LeBlanc thought it was ruined.

I had no water to drink, but I had food, a boat and protection from the cold and rain. And I had most of my traps. I could still make the season work for me.

From a pond inside the marsh where the mud had settled, I took enough water for cooking. I set it upon the cooking stove, and when half had boiled away I knew it would be safe.

The sudden warmth would bring out dormant snakes and mosquitoes. I went onto the porch. The breeze was cooling, pleasant. Already, near the edge of the marsh, clouds of mosquitoes hovered.

The canard noir, dos-gris, were unfrozen. I spun the ducks, inspecting. Only the heads and backs remained. Something had torn their breasts away. I checked the posts for recent clawmarks. There were none. There were no signs on the rafter, either.

The dust at the edges of the house revealed a three-footed raton laveur had crossed from the rear, exited at the front. The raton laveurs are skillful climbers, wary and intelligent scavengers. But no raton laveur with one foot curled and dead inside a trap can climb a post, cross upon a rafter and lean down to eat a man-sized meal of dos-gris breasts.

And on the north side of the house I found dry three-cornered grass which had been cleanly cut, stacked beneath the wall and burned where a north wind would fan the flames. But the shifting winds had put out the fire, or something had. Only part had burned.

I got on my hands and knees and tried to find the match. I found none. But atop the dirt beneath the house were tiny, blackened specks. Like tiny seeds turned into coal. Specks from sparks of steel scraped on flint to make a fire.

Squatting at the great canal, I washed my face with cooling water. I put the swollen leg into the great canal, and water pressed caressingly through the rubber of the boot. One of the crabs with deformed limbs had been crushed upon the bank. His larger claw had been untouched. It still raised itself in terror, but now from a flattened, jellied mass against the mud. The foot that had crushed it had hovered and then struck.

I followed the print backward, toe to heel. He must have walked along the water's edge in hopes the tide would submerge his tracks before the fire was seen by someone far away, if it was seen at all. There were no more tracks except a slit where the bow of his pirogue had pushed into the clay. It was a pirogue like my old one, with extended keel dipping downward. I did not know of one such other boat capable of use. Very, very rare and not LeBlanc's.

I took a trick from the butcherbird and searched the shore while pretending to merely gather wood for my old bones' fire. But there was only that one print, as if he had left a sign to show me something I, alone, would find.

I decided, then, to stack the wood and rest. Sometimes with rest, the answers easy come.

But answers did not come. The tide came in, instead, and washed all prints away.

I stood above the great canal, holding my plate of dos-gris bones and watching water lap against the smoothly mottled clay. I stood as if as an old man finally alone I cared for nothing but my peace, understood nothing but my loneliness.

I saw nothing, though, across the great canal or on the far banks of the bayou where scrub oaks choked to the water's edge. A marsh hawk perched a rifle shot away, peering with his yellow-circled eyes in his search for game. Had I his eyes, I would have believed everything that I saw. Had he the wits of men, however, he would build a house, make money, wage war, and would not be here, watching with me.

I left the dos-gris bones at the marsh's edge for the three-legged raton laveur, a gift for his lost foot.

The gray clouds had sapped all color away, as water will do to flesh too long submerged. The western bayou levee seemed a brown tangle of lifelessness. Even the yellow-dun of the marsh grass seemed without color, flavorless.

A movement near where a tiny channel from the marsh merged with the bayou. I did not look directly at it. I turned my gaze away but kept unclear sight of it. A man.

He stepped clear of the roseaux and stood near the bayou water, leaning on a staff. As if I hadn't seen him, I slowly turned and went into the house. I stepped into the shadow of the door. He remained standing, leaning on what I could now see was a long pushpole. He was not LeBlanc, but I could not tell if he was Etienne.

I looked into the chambers of the gun. The heavy load
was in the left barrel. I closed the gun and my thumb caressed the hammers. Still standing in the shadow, I looked
at the man across the water, and I wished for the eyes of
the marsh hawk. He seemed to turn his eyes toward me,
though surely he could not see me in the shadow. There
was a sort of smile, I thought, and then he stepped into
the roseaux once again. The man was Etienne.

The gun grew heavy as I watched, but he did not come
back in sight. I went behind the house, into the marsh,
and got more water. Frogs were out, and green snakes
slithered from me. Back in the house, I set the water on
to boil.

When I came again onto the porch, he was sitting again
where the little channel touched the bayou. He still held
the pushpole, old and gray, in both his hands, and it stood
straight before him like a reed marking where a trap lay
set. I looked straight at him and he looked straight at me. I
could see no feeling in his face.

While the water boiled, I sat with the gun across my
thighs and watched him, but he never moved. He did not
even move to brush mosquitoes from his face. The trousers were dark green, like his shirt, and wet up to the
knees. He wore no boots. He wore shoes of the kind men
wear in towns.

I made coffee and drank it while the water cooled. I held
the cup high before me, offering it to him, and then there
was that look of a smile. He seemed to smile without moving any parts of his face. And it was not a smile from
friend to friend. It was like something I had never seen
before.

I was the first to grow tired of the game. I grew eager to
begin. I searched for something strong and found wire to
build duck traps, to keep fowl behind. I took this, the gun,
and the water to the old pirogue. The bottle of water I put

into the pirogue still awash, to let the bayou water cool it.

A point of land hid me from Etienne. And, when the pirogue was drained and loaded, Etienne was not in sight. I stepped into the stern. The feel of the cypress pushpole, smooth from long use, was like an old friend's clasp to me.

I poled across the bayou, gliding softly, smoothly, silently. The old pirogue was as perfect as a violin. The bayou's ripples sang at its sides, and my heart beat as fast as spring. We entered the channel carefully, but Etienne was far ahead.

Across the high grass I could see him from his waist upward. He poled quickly, setting very hard his pole and leaning very heavily on it so that he lifted his whole weight on it. His shoulders jerked very hard between pushes of the pole because the blunt end buried itself so deeply in the marsh with each stroke.

Yet, though he seemed to work so hard, I poled smoothly, and during the first hours we kept the same distance apart. The old pirogue obeyed instantly each nudge from my leading, guiding foot. Together, we easily navigated each twist of the winding channel. Etienne did not look back at me. He knew I would be there.

It had been a long time since I had poled so far so steadily. But after the first aches, my muscles gave in to my will, and as the afternoon wore on I seemed to grow stronger. I had not followed this channel this deep into the east in years. I saw much sign of mink. And there was wild rice on the edges of one of the great ponds, though for some reason there were no ducks.

I did not halt my poling, but I searched as far as I could see for sign of duck. None was there, and when I looked again ahead Etienne was gone.

I poled on slowly, waiting for some trick, but very soon he was in front of me again, but closer. Again we began that strange pursuit. By now, it was almost as if we were hunting friends, one leading the way to a great pond he had found deep in the marsh. And then I saw his filth.

It was on the point of the sharpest turn the channel had yet made. The gray grass had been blown down in a thick mat a man could stand upon. The filth was in thick, dark links like sausage or like red boudin made with rice, meat and the blood of pigs. It was shiny with the fluid from his bowels and already green flies buzzed about it.

When I looked up, Etienne had stopped and was watching me. Then he turned again and bent with the push of the pole.

The afternoon grew long. The light seemed to be fading. The clouds would allow no shadows. I grew weary of watching Etienne's straining back.

Those Isleños of the Saint Bernard, though I never knew too many, seemed to like the strain. As with the horses at the festival in the fall. The Frenchmen raced the horses. They liked the horse to run without care for obeying the rider, or they liked the horse to be calm and obedient to work their cattle. But the Isleños, they made their horses obedient but somehow kept the wildness in them.

Sometimes it seemed to me those horses they rode, with their muscles gathered taut, and white always showing in their eyes, were always ready to kill their riders. And the Isleños were happy with this. The horses always seemed more tame when the men were not around them. But I never saw magic in a horse. I would rather walk if it was not too far. And a boat, that is so much better. That is the best of all. A boat like this pirogue to flow smoothly with my least effort, that is a true pleasure.

Then, as I watched, Etienne sank beneath the level of the grass and I saw him no more.

I was alone in the marsh, now, with the snakes and the mosquitoes and the deerflies. Or so it seemed since Etienne had disappeared again.

At each turn, I expected to see his filth again, but I did not. I had long ago poled past the point where he sank down out of sight, and still there was no Etienne Lopez. And I searched the edges of the channel but could not find sign of him pulling his pirogue from the channel. It could only mean he was poling sitting on the stern, for what purpose I did not know.

Then we entered that time of quiet before nightfall, and I began to be concerned. Some trap, perhaps. Perhaps he would leave the pirogue and walk back to surprise me in the fading light.

But with so many snakes, awakened by the heat and beginning their first night's hunt in months, I would not do this. Especially without boots. Another strange thing. Though lizards and snakes and insects were out, I had not seen one turtle. It was very strange.

I watched for a trap and wondered, and then I turned a bend and there was the pirogue of Etienne Lopez before me empty in the channel. It rode high and light upon the water, and I put my pole into my pirogue and took up my shotgun as the bow of my boat nudged against the side of his like the nose of a horse against another's flank.

Away to the north a coypu cried like a baby cries and above my head bats hunted in the twilight sky. The mosquitoes overtook me, then, and I breathed slowly, mouth closed, so I would not suck them in. There was nothing, no sign of his leaving the pirogue, no grass wet where his foot had pressed it beneath the water. It was as though he had burrowed beneath the grass like a duck crippled by a wing shot. There was no other place to hide . . . except a growth of roseaux that had somehow found land solid enough for its roots to the south of our channel.

I wedged our pirogues together to lock them in the channel. His was smaller, even older, gray with tempered age and absolutely dry inside. The marks of the ancient carving tools were unmistakable. Stern and bow were the same except for the worn, fire-hardened bowline hole. Etienne had taken the bowline with him as if I might tow the pirogue away. But I had not come for the pirogue. I had come for him.

I took a drink of water, put the jar back into the pirogue, entered the marsh, hid myself, and waited.

There were only different shades of blackness. I could no longer see the roseaux. Water and the rotting grass pressed coolly at my rubber-coated, blood-swollen leg as I leaned forward, resting on my knees. I waited silently, not even killing the mosquitoes that sucked at my skin, but no one came.

The marsh, now, was alive with hunters. Snakes, owls, mink, and otter and me. I began to move. Places where I would sink up to my neck were lighter patches of water before me. Solid stepping places were dark lumps. And with no walking stick and the gun cradled ready, the way was very slow and very hard but I made it silently. The roseaux loomed dark before me, then became light as I got closer until I stood beside the reeds and watched their paleness against the night, as I listened to the rustle of roseaux leaves in a breeze I did not feel.

I waited there, listening. My blood pulsed at the stocking on my leg, pounded in the veins of my head, tormented the mosquitoes whose tiny wings fanned around my eyes. I heard no sign of him. I heard only a night-hunting hawk above me and the delicate hands of a raton laveur in water somewhere to my left. I entered the close cluster of the roseaux.

I eased my body around the roseaux stems and the

pointed leaves caressed my clothes like dry fingers. There was no way to move without the rustling sound. So I waited again and strained my eyes at the darkness. My eyes must make themselves as wide and dark as the great duck hawk, the great peregrine. But I could see nothing beyond the first gray, ghostly roseaux.

Then there came a tiny sound. I thought it was from a creature small and shy of men. The sound ceased. I waited, then took a step. The sound again, louder, larger. I took another step. It bolted huge and loud into the marsh.

I ran to the point of the roseaux, breaking the dry stems and leaving a swath behind me. I held the gun with hammers cocked before, but when I reached the edge of the marsh, there was nothing but the sound of my own blood within my ears.

It could have been a deer, but there was no sound of pointed hooves upon the marsh. No ghostly flicker of his white pointed tail. And deer do not make their beds on hard earth in the center of sparse cover, on the seaward edge of a dry stand of crackling, lonely roseaux.

Back inside the roseaux I found where he had been sleeping. Roseaux had been uprooted. The earth was warm where he had curled and slept as I was waiting, crouched in rot, and as I was creeping cramped and bitten to him.

From the north came the sound of water pouring. Then came the sound of glass smashing. Then other water sounds. Etienne. Etienne, and so quickly, so silently. Etienne.

I walked back, hands ready on the gun with hammers cocked. Only one pirogue, mine. And in the bow were two bottles, now, one smashed to shards, one shiny, intact, and new to me. LeBlanc's whiskey, pecan-brown and potent-sloshing as I lifted it. I could almost feel its power by contact of my hand against the glass. The other bottle had been emptied before smashing. He had poured the water into the marsh and left me only whiskey to drink. He had not even left me the chance to lap the water from the bottom of the boat. And he'd taken the wire. I should have poured the whiskey out, then, thrown it into the marsh. For the whiskey to me was the wire to him, something to bind, to hold. But I could not.

Etienne had eaten. He had water to drink. He'd slept calmly while I hunted him. And he was young. And he was strong. He was fresh and rested and poling now with silent laughter far away from me.

I sat upon the stern. My chest swelled with despair. I put my hands upon my face and smashed the bulging mosquitoes on my skin. My hand came away all smeared with blood and blood in wide streaks began drying on my cheeks.

Etienne had strength and food and water and youth. And purpose. He had some purpose. Etienne was rich. He owned the world. But I had time. And I had resolution. I would buy some strength with time.

I lay down in the bottom of my pirogue, rolled the whiskey to my feet, pulled the collar of my hunting coat above my face and tried to calm my rage, to sleep. I was in no danger here from Etienne, not now. Etienne would not come to me again. It was clear I was to go to him. But, if I could make him come to me . . .

Weariness burns intelligence away, so I must sleep and leave all thought for morning. My body's aching muscles fitted into the curved cleft of my boat. I made myself breathe easily. The mosquitoes' buzz became a roar.

If there were just a tiny wind to blow mosquitoes from me. Just one marsh wind from north or south to blow mosquitoes from me. I did not sleep. All around me were insects searching out my blood. A wind to blow them from me. My blood tormented them as LeBlanc's whiskey tormented me. For I could almost feel the whiskey enter me through the glass of the bottle and the soles of my boots and feet, up the leg with swollen veins. The mosquitoes' starving, buzzing, never-ceasing cries were mine. Their starving, buzzing cries became a roar. My hands were swollen from their bites.

No wind. I huddled in the bottom of my pirogue. My world was crushed into the stifling space between my collar and the cypress of my boat. I waited in the screaming demand for light to drive the mosquitoes beneath the grass.

Wind could save me. I could stand up in the wind. Put my bloody face into the wind. Where had the ever-blowing marsh wind gone? And could I find a cleansing wind within me?

Old Desormeaux, old Desormeaux. His yellow and gray hair ragged, his pale blue eyes watery and faded, his once great muscled arms turned flabby, his insane taunting laugh against the wind high-pitched and wailing. Even old Desormeaux, himself, his brain blown addled by the wind, would pray as I did for the air to move.

Perhaps not, though, for Desormeaux lives in madness with the wind where the great canal and the river meet and the channels bring the wind from all directions.

Something heavy and alive brushed the side of my pirogue. I felt it nudge the length of the boat on its course up the channel, ever eastward. Coypu, otter, mink . . . whatever, ever eastward like Etienne. A creature of the water, of the marsh.

Old Desormeaux was bred of a people of the sea, from a place called Brittany. A wild people who fought with axes, he said. And yet, he was so gentle with my daughter and with my lost son Jean.

My Jean, my Jean, my lost son Jean. My forever baby son, now dead. Oh, God, his straw hat floated on the brown, warm-moving river as I turned around. Such a sunlit day, Good Friday. His mother warned us not to go.

"The Good Lord is suffering," she said. "The crown of thorns is crushed upon His head. His back is scourged. The nails are driven into his flesh. Even now the holy Stigmateaux suffer in flowing blood His Sweet Agony. Stay home, do penance, make this Easter well."

But I had drink inside me on that Holy Day. It meant nothing to me, then, the fact of its holiness. I argued, who put the fish into the river but Our Lord? Who fed the masses with fish and loaves? And wine, do not forget the wine. Wine for saints, strong whiskey for a man of flesh and blood and earth and water. I took my children to the river. Yes, I took them. As I believed my right. A river swollen in the sunlight. Fertile, green-choked with life upon its banks and beneath its silty surface.

The whiskey inside me did not dull the sunlight, it made the sunlight brighter, made shadows darker, made my very movements exaggerated, made the solid ground of the town a floating marsh to me. Made each sound into something else.

Oh, God, the screams. I shivered in the hot night, sweating into the mosquito roar for my blood and my own blood's roar for relief, relief in drink. And in the screams from years before. The child's scream to me was like her squeal of deep delight. Until I turned, laughing as I turned, until I saw her mouth misshapen, red and dripping with terror. Squatting and reaching for the bright new straw hat her brother had worn. It floated on the still, brown, swollen river. Oh, God, I dropped the line. Contrition, worse than sorrow, filled me. And I knew in that instant it was hopeless.

But I pushed my daughter back and tried to dive deep

down in the river. But my legs, my arms had lost their strength. They had betrayed me to the drink. My own clothes buoyed me, mired me on the surface. I fought for sense inside myself as I fought for depth and finally stripped my clothes away and choking in the silty red, then brown then blinding dark I dove. I, God, I do not know how many times I dove and plunged my hands into the mud at the river's bottom, mud impossibly soft, far softer than any baby's, any mother's skin. I could not tell where river ended and riverbed began.

Each time I hit the surface empty-handed, her wails drove me back down. Her wails. Her cries from that misshapen mouth. They filled my ears as I drew breath. Her wails became the screaming within me and without that long night in the pirogue. She'd lost her brother to the brown, gaping river, and now the river sucked her father back again and again. That day I dove until I almost drowned, myself, and clung to the wharf without the strength to raise myself. Her little hands tugged at my shirt. Then, still screaming, she went for help.

The others found me on the wharf. They brought us home. I never saw my Jean again. They found him three days later and buried him at once. There had been the leeches and something else, who knows?

Something then ceased between me and my wife. Grief-madness came to live with us. And guilt. Loneliness filled all our quiet moments. Something other than our child had died. I never drank again, but whiskey's slave is always whiskey's slave.

Old Desormeaux, he visited us and our grief-madness, and he understood. Old Desormeaux, who lives with madness all his days, he understood. My little daughter crawled upon his knee to eat. Upon the table their plates were side to side. His great muscled arms encircled her and he ate around her curly head.

Old Desormeaux, bred of vicious people, men who fought with axes, men who taunted nature, sailing men who laughed at seas whipped by winds into mountains of water higher than their masts. My little daughter led him like a puppy, ruled him like a princess with a slave. Ruled the man who when the wind was up and his brain boiled with the sound of it in his ears he'd make magic by rushing from his cabin and hurling his well-honed axe into the wind.

Old Desormeaux, where was your magic when I needed the wind to rid me of the mosquitoes? And of my inner torment? Why did your magic not send wind to rescue me? No prayer, no magic, would help me. So I endured the night.

The graying finally came, a morning without sunrise because of the clouds. I walked to the bow of my pirogue and flung my yellow morning piss in his direction.

The yellow-white bubbles, barely visible in the gloom, welled up and flowed toward him. I wished in my misery that he would be ignorant enough to drink of the poisoned water of the marsh. And I had such thirst, such thirst. I kicked the bottle to the bow but I could not throw it away.

I looked into what must be the east, though no sun rose in it. And I saw the Caller truly, exactly as I had seen him in my sickness inside the traiteur's shack that day.

He rose up from the marsh, a yellow-blue-orange flowing cloud. A bright ball that hovered and flowed and melted and shot up a peaked arm to me, to me in my old age as he had done that day in my youth's sickness. That time I nearly died in the Snake Man's shack.

The leg, it is inflamed. From dead yellow-circled fang holes near the ankle, red streaks trace a path. Below, my foot is blue. An orange band swells my ankle and a dead yellow encircled the holes. My papa carries me into the

Snake Man's shack. He lays me on the bed of sacks that still smell of the feed. He leaves my life in the care of the Snake Man.

"I will pay you anything if you will save my son," he says.

"Then, go now," the Snake Man says, "for to watch it is forbidden. My power would be taken from me. Le Bon Dieux, he is strict. Go, now. To watch it is forbidden. Go."

"But, Monsieur Le Traiteur," my papa says, "I have seen many snake bites. Never, Monsieur Le Traiteur, have I seen . . ."

"Go, Monsieur Dimanche. Go quickly so that I may work."

My papa kisses me, leaves me afraid and alone with the traiteur. My fever makes me writhe. He ties me down. Such heat upon my leg, such heat. Words I know are prayers but do not understand. A fire makes his dark face shine above me.

The snake around his neck, then, fills me with great fear. His hand is stroking, cool upon my face, sliding on my face. He brings the snake, thick and black and deadly, down onto my face. I try to scream, but I cannot. I try to scream, but I cannot. The snake's wedged head upon my cheek, so near my eyes. I scream, but no sound comes. I scream inside my head, but the only words I hear are words of prayers. Words of prayers I cannot understand.

The wedged head, now, at my leg, upon the swollen ankle. The short, thick body coiling around the blue and swollen foot. The prayers I cannot understand. The prayers, low like Latin in the mass. The fire's smoke like incense. The wedged head tracing streaks of red upon my leg. Tracing streaks up to my crotch. I jerk and tremble. Snake Man again stroking, cool hand at my head. Wedged head, deadly head, again at my face. Again upon my leg. Again around my foot. Again up to my crotch.

My papa, finally, again.

"Go to the town, Monsieur Dimanche."

"No, no, Monsieur Le Traiteur. It is too far. I do not want my son to die alone . . ."

"He will not die if you go to town. Go to the town. Go to the church. A candle for the Virgin, the one who crushes the serpent's head. And one, one of the biggest, for Saint Medard. Saint of our people. For this is not entirely of the snake. This is not entirely of the snake. Go now."

"What is it then, Monsieur Le Traiteur, which does this to my son . . . my son . . . Oh, God, my son."

"I do not know, monsieur. But go, leave him to me and Saint Medard. He will not die."

My father's worried eyes. My father's worried kiss. And he is gone. I sleep, and then I wake. But I wake as in a dream, to some other place, a place of gray, dim light. My fevered eyes stare across dry needle points of grass and see the Caller rise up from the marsh. A yellow-blue-orange flowing cloud, bright ball that hovers and flows and melts and shoots up a peaked arm to me . . . I try to follow but cannot, a weak and feverish boy.

Then the Caller was gone. The light was much brighter under the gray dawn. Weak and throat-parched, I picked up my pole, began again to follow him. After a little while, Etienne rose up from the marsh and glided along before me.

Saint Medard. Saint Medard. S'il pleut le jour de Saint Medard, il pleut quarante jours plus tard. If it rains on the day of Saint Medard, it will rain forty days more. But Saint Medard was in summer. Parched throat, parched marsh, dry needle points of grass. Could not this day have been summer? Could it not have been Saint Medard?

Etienne. Etienne. Ever ahead. The way narrowed, straightened. It was a tranasse, marsh passage into nowhere. The grass was brown and dead with dryness. It overhung my pirogue's sides. A lover dipping to the cleft of my pirogue. I pushed. The crowding grass wedged at the cypress sides of my pirogue. I pushed.

A turtle's head with bright red ear patches broke brown water before me and scurried to the grass. Frogs leapt the trail, the tranasse that bound me to Etienne. I could not see well, but Etienne was always there, dark green against the high, brown grass. My throat. I could not swallow. I had no spit.

My muscles ached. My leg now burned with swollen veins. My ankle swelled against the boot. My leg. My ankle swelled against the boot.

I saw a deer across the marsh, toward the sea, toward where the sea should be. There was no sign of direction. There was no levee of a great canal. There was no bayou's line of scrub oaks. And the sun rose and set beyond the clouds.

The deer trotted as a horse will sometimes trot. Why did deer never sink into the marsh? Once, long ago, old Desormeaux killed a buck with our steel trap still caught upon his leg. There were scars upon his tawny skin from hoof to knee, and the trap was worn thin from miles of grass. It was shiny, lovely, thin and delicate as though it were some silver ornament wrought and carved for kings. It was beautiful, his painful ornament that we took from him in death.

The pirogue tranasse was now a straight, long brown thin line of spittle from me to Etienne and then beyond. I pushed. My leg ached. My throat was dry. I could not swallow. I had not the spit.

And then the snake was there again. White-mouthed. A thump upon my cypress boat, and then the snake was there again. White-mouth. My faded, flowing, waving eyes beheld the snake, once more . . . again . . . with me inside the boat.

He struck. His eyes. His sightless winter's eyes. I brought the blunt pole's end into the boat. He struck again, again with me. He struck. I felt his weight against my boot. I hit him with the pole. I pushed my pole into his thickness now against my foot. His thickness at my foot. I struck my pole into his thickness at my foot.

And fell. And fell upon him. My leg betrayed me and I fell upon him. And upon the whiskey bottle. Upon his writhing, fat, thick, stinking form. I fell. I fell and fell in slow . . . I saw it slow, how I fell upon his writhing form. The pole across the bow, I fell. I fell. He coiled and writhed about my foot, but did not strike again. He was dead. We were dead.

He writhed about my foot, so dead at last and writhing still. And smearing blood upon the bottle. A smearing of blood thinly on the bottle. And writhing against my foot. I drew up my legs away from him but grasped the bottle sticky-slick with the blood of snakes. I breathed mosquitoes in and spat them out. My breath was harsh. My throat was parched. I reached also the coiling tail. His body lifted heavily. He writhed. His head was gone. His head was crushed. A bloody, streaming mass of flesh, black-brown and white. I swung.

A scream. A scream. My own, my own deep-throated scream of rage and of despair. My own deep-throated scream of deep despair. I threw the coiling body far from me. I fell. I fell again into the pirogue.

And lay, my leg, my throbbing swollen leg. I lay. I lay. And breath came in, a harsh, dry-throated burning rasp went out. The cap I tore, then, from the bottle. The blood of snakes adhered my hand to the glass. I tilted it and drank the fire of the feu-bête. It burned my mouth, my throat, opening me with fire, a fiery post shoved in the marsh. But my stomach would not take it. My stomach threw it back at me, back at the marsh, back at the writhing snake, back at Etienne, back at the feu-bête. I was lost. It was my only hope, my only escape. I gave the bottle to the marsh, lay hopeless against the blood-smeared wood.

My hand dangled to the water of the tranasse. The water flowed to some thing I did not know. Cool. Cool. Coolly flowing smoothly. I reached and cupped . . . my face now cool, now wet. My throat now wet. The taste of mud and sulphur born of hell inside the taste. Inside the taste.

I lay and sucked the water of the marsh. My pirogue shipped water and wet my clothes. I lay in wetness. And then I stood.

Etienne had stopped. He stood above the marsh and watched. I pushed again. He turned and led the way. I felt the pain before the light began to fade away.

Full dark and vomit. Pain high in the stomach spread both ways. Leeches on the bow as I bent over. Shaking cold. Full dark and vomit. Roaring in my ears. Jean's bright straw hat. Thick fingers in my guts.

Leeches on the bow as I bent over. Cold in the slow-moving water. Thick fingers in my guts. Waves of pain inside my bowels. Face numb. Face numb against the wood.

Full dark and vomit on the pirogue's wood, worn raised grain like ridges leaving ridges on my skin. I drifted in the pirogue trail. Needle points of grass so dry against my skin. I drifted slower than the stream. Then stopped.

All stopped. The dark. The vomit on the wood. The needle points of grass. The drifting. All stopped. There was my mouth all slack and limp and open on the cypress. Then all stopped with ringing silence. My head a huge deer bladder filled with air, to hang above my body, above the marsh, to float and hang but not to see. It stopped.

Ringing slaps. The whole marsh shook. Ringing slaps. The whole marsh shook. Water, wetness, cold and damp.

And ringing slaps. Gray shape. A cry. A whimper cry of anguish, pain. Gray cry of anguish, pain.

Etienne. Ears pointed gray against the black. Etienne. Ears stuck out and pointed gray against the black.

Snake man. Fire in a rounded earthen hole. Snake Man. Fire from your packed mud dome. Snake Man. Your ancient words. Snake Man. Etienne. His cry. Snake Man. Etienne.

My papa's stroking hand. Etienne. Etienne. Snake Man. The whole marsh shook again, and then. Etienne. Snake Man. My papa's stroking hand. More ringing slaps.

I choked. Water in my mouth, I choked. Bitter, bitter mouth. I choked. I spat. I drowned. I died. I slept. Etienne.

Jean's hat, bright straw. My woman's sobbing in the night so deep it shakes the bed, and flows. Flows deep brown silt that sucks. Jean's hat, bright straw.

Old Desormeaux, where is thy wind? Where is thy wind, old friend? Old violent, gentle friend, where is thy wind? Thy wind for sweet Celeste. In candlelight, friend, where is thy wind? Broad madness smile. Sweet smell of holy incense smoke.

Celeste has gone, old Desormeaux. She eats not at my table, to sit between your muscled arms. She writhes in bed. She pants. She bleeds.

My sweet Jean's hat. My honeyed son. We flow.

Full gray and bright. We flowed. A shadow on my face. Snake Man. Snake Man has died. We found him in his shack, Snake Man. We went with sticks. His charges crawled. Full fat with rats. We went with sticks. Full gray and bright, we flowed. We went with sticks. Full gray and bright. We flowed. We went with sticks. His charges crawled. About his thick, duck down featherbed, his

corpse. We flowed, with sticks. A shadow on my face.
We killed the charges coiled. We struck. The stench. We
struck. We flowed. The stench. We killed the snakes with
sticks. In cracks upon the walls. Coiled upon dead coals in
his earthen hole for fire. We struck his magic down as he
lay dead upon his duck down featherbed.

Old Desormeaux, he struck the thick black deadly one
upon the Snake Man's chest. It thumped. It writhed. He
struck again and laughed. Two feet wedged at my shoulders. He laughed. We killed the snakes then left the shack.
Breathed deep the fresh marsh air.

I breathed deep the thick marsh air. I raised. His knee
against my shoulder forced me down. Old Desormeaux,
he laughed to kill the Snake Man's snake upon the Snake
Man's chest. He laughed. Etienne.

A dreamy, cold bright marsh. A boat like a pirogue, but oh
so big. With gun muzzles linked together and tied upon
the bow. Such guns, with huge smooth bores, they fan before me as I lie in the boat and let it drift to where the
ducks are feeding. There are so many ducks they seem to
be a huge dark island in the lake.

We flow toward them, the muzzles fan. One duck rises
from the flock. Fingers in my guts. Fingers in my guts
tighten.

Orange flashes from the muzzles. The large boat jerks.
My guts are twisted. Muzzle flashes. Muzzle flashes. The
boat, it jerks and pitches. Each great muzzle flash sends
the great boat reeling, my entrails soaring, bloating wide
with pain.

Orange muzzle flashes, blasts. White and dark gunsmoke hangs before the bow. The ducks cannot be seen,
and still the muzzles flash. The ducks cannot be seen but

their pointed wingtips in death must crowd the lake because beneath me the water is pink with blood.

The gunsmoke obscures the marsh, the world. All sight,
all sound, ceases.

We flowed. Again we flowed. The needle points of grass
were moving, draped across each cypress side.

Feet at my shoulders. Leather-covered feet beside my
shoulders. The world was reeling. Reeling. Needle points
of grass caressing. Close pressed, caressing.

I raised. I breathed the thick . . . the sweet marsh air.
My papa's stroking hand. Etienne. The gaping, now cold
earth fire mound. A gray-black woman's hole, now cold.
Etienne. My papa's stroking hand. Etienne.

Bitter in my mouth. Water bitter in my throat. My papa's
stroking hand. Etienne. Above me, Etienne. Full gray and
bright and needle points of grass, we flowed. I slept.

Full dark and cold. A grinding swish upon the marsh. A
pirogue, empty, pushed upon the grass. A ghostly pirogue,
shining in the night. Dark trousered legs drove it forward
in the night, across the grass. I lay back down.

My papa's stroking hand. Water on my face. My face.
Cold water on my face. My neck. My hand was forced
. . . my arm ached at the cypress side of my pirogue. My
hand was forced down against . . . down against . . . Tiny
cold things crawled. Tiny cold, hard things crawled and
pinched my fingers, cutting them.

I pulled my hand away. It was forced down again. Tiny
cold things crawled. They crawled against my fingers,
pinched them. I tried to pull my hand away but a steel trap
grip kept it there. They pinched like needles . . .

Needles of gray-yellow overhung the cypress sides of
my pirogue. The day was bright, but still full of gray. I lay
back down and slept.

I awoke truly cold, without the fever. I lay for a long time blurry staring at the worn cypress. I huddled in my coat. There were no mosquitoes. The smell of death was with me.

I stretched my cramped legs. Glass grated at my feet. The clouds were low and dark. I tried to sit, but a ringing in my ears and dizziness would not let me. Instead, I wedged my back against the stern. The death smell came strongly to me. The shotgun was propped, breach open, in the bow. All my shotgun shells were scattered around its stock. And there was another bottle, this one unbroken and filled with water clear and beautiful.

I ignored the ringing and crawled through dizziness and broken glass to the bottle. A roseaux stem was wedged into the narrow neck. I was so weak I hardly got it out. The water was bitter as medicine, and tasted of copper. My stomach moved. I drank more slowly.

The broken glass had cut my hand, and blood smeared on the bottle, thin and streaked red against the clearness of the water. The little cuts were not deep, no deeper than the other, older ones.

I thought at first the shotgun shells had been fired. For each end was puckered open. But they had not been fired. They had been pried open. The light bird shot, he left alone. But the buck shot was gone. The powder, wad were still in place, but the heavy shot was gone.

I settled in the stern and sipped the water. My world had become that cypress slit of boat. The pushpole had been sunk in the mud before the bow, holding the pirogue in the channel.

I sipped water and then I saw the coypu, small eyes almost closed, orange teeth arching from his mouth, all in death. His bowels had been slit open, staked apart with sharpened limbs, and his entrails crawled with écrevisses.

Tiny écrevisses, some not as long as one joint of a finger. Half of the coypu was staked beneath the water, but under the water or above, écrevisses swarmed like bees among his fish-white entrails.

Their tiny bristle feelers, pointed snouts and black protruding eyes sought out the tender parts of the coypu's bowels as in death he lay spread wide by wooden stakes and seemed to smile with his orange tusklike teeth. His half-closed eyes now had a humor squint. The écrevisses were frightened by the sight of me and scurried away into the safety of the water. I saw my reflection in the channel and knew, then, they had reason.

My face was swollen, blood-streaked, and muddy. I watched my face in the water until the pirogue stopped rocking. I was quiet, still, and the écrevisses came back. Their flat-based, curling, jointed tails churned the quiet, death-stilled water in their gorging. I harvested them.

Handful after handful, I plucked from the coypu's guts. I crushed their bony-shelled, skeletonless bodies between fingers streaming with marsh water. I chewed them whole, sucked their juice, spat out their plated armor.

I ate for strength until my bowels moved like a tide in from the sea. And then I sat upon the stern and overhung the marsh, let down my clothes and let the poison flow from my body. When I was done, I felt my strength returning.

Beyond the pushpole anchor, the channel widened to a lace of ponds. Duck and poule d'eau sat feeding on the water. An otter climbed into the marsh at the far edge of the first pond.

Dizziness assaulted me. I sat back down upon the stern. I sipped the bitter water. I pulled the shotgun back to me and checked its working parts. All were in order, though rust had formed at the bases of the hammers. If we were near the sea, the air might have carried salt to rust my gun. But this was not salt marsh. Near me grew the three-cornered grass the muskrat love.

I molded flat the puckered ends of the shotgun shells and slipped two into the chambers of the gun. My thumb caressed the ancient twisted pattern of the steel. I propped the gun near me in the stern, thanked the dead orange-smiling coypu for the feast, pulled my coat close about me, lay down again, and slept.

I did not dream.

The heavy coldness of the air awoke me. I could see lines between the layers of the clouds. Lines like jagged cotton streaks between clouds bulging, black.

The channel behind me was no longer a man-dug trail. It was twisted. Twisted as the snake's body writhed between the marsh and the clouded sky when I flung him headless from me.

The clouds were moving. They coursed the sky from my back toward the east. A breeze from Saint Medard fanned cold upon my face. It fanned a hunger in me. The push-pole had been sunk so deep into the marsh that I almost sank the bow to pull it out.

As though released from some deep yearning, the aged cypress pirogue drifted from the channel into the open water of the pond. I poled across the net of ponds, studying closely this new marsh. Such beauty as I'd never seen before, I thought.

The ponds were deep enough, but not too deep. The channel still cut through them, but all the silt had settled. The bottom could be clearly seen. The only mud was in a line of puffy clouds thrown up behind us by my pushpole. The bottom was carpeted with food for ducks and for the tiny young of shrimp that tides would carry here to nurse in richness and in safety.

Duck food was everywhere. Wild rice grew along the shores. Sweet-rooted grass in clumps dotted every pond. Duck weed was in the shallows.

I saw mink and otter—one otter bloated with his fresh kill of warm-weather-released snakes. And then I saw the beds, the houses.

The muskrat homes—dried domes of grass—dotted every shore and rose from every grassy island. Gray and high and round, they made up a village, a town of muskrat in that last refuge from the all-consuming coypu in that basin of the marsh.

And now I saw them swimming, fearless. The sight of a man in a pirogue swiftly gliding, powerful, faster than they could swim was simply not of interest to them. They did not seem to know that men control all that they can see.

A female with a mouthful of grass and sticks climbed to the roof of her thick grass house and patched a place, then slid swiftly into the water, dived to the submerged entrance of her home. Like monsters in a children's tale, hiding their entrances beneath the water. All around me, muskrats fed while in every other marsh I knew the coypu had pushed them out, devoured everything, killed the three-cornered grass. But I saw no sign of coypu there. There was only the breakfast chef coypu, which had in death given me lécrevisses.

Now the water seemed alive with muskrat and mink. Their tiny swimming heads and shoulders traversed the water everywhere. I ceased my poling, let my pirogue drift. It slowed, then stopped, then the bow slowly drifted around. A dancer turning gracefully. My gaze over the prow scanned with it, sweeping circular, seeing all the beauty, all the hope.

The pirogue came to rest against an island of grass, another little island crowned by a high gray muskrat bed. I sat with the pole across my knees, the gun propped at my feet. Across the marsh two tiny dots rose and fell in flight. Swift flight coming to me. Swift teal coming to me. Teal was the perfect meal for me.

They rushed upon the lacelike ponds as swift and pure as bullets in the night, their red throats and chests shining now, so close they were. I raised the barrels swiftly as their flight paths crossed, brought them both down with one shot.

All around me water churned with fleeing life, like trapped mullets in a pothole swarming at the surface for a crust of bread. They swam in fear and chattered squeals. I thought I heard inside the muskrat bed beside me a scurrying of tiny bodies packed against the sides of grass, squirming to the narrowest niche.

Then all was silent. I felt ten thousand angered, fearful eyes upon me as I poled to where the teal had fallen. One wing fluttered slightly as my pirogue ripples reached it. But both were dead as I pulled them from the water.

And in that silence of death and fear, I again let the pirogue drift, and sat in the bow, plucking the feathers from their breasts. Feathers the color of dried blood from the Savior's thorny crown. I ate them while they still had the heat of life inside their tiny bodies.

Then, packed with strength and meat like a lion content and sleepy, I set what was left of the carcasses of teal upon the bow and lay down in the boat. I stared up into the heavy, pregnant sky. I had no direction, no landmark and no sun to guide me, but I began to feel the channel still flowed from west to east. We had surely come at least as far as the Iberia marsh. We had surely come at least as far as that line they drew on maps and charts, a line of ink across a page, separating men from men. How vain. A line upon a page.

And then, in a movement lovely, graceful, and smooth,

two layers of clouds parted and I saw a long, twisting line of purest blue. Break! You clouds, you break! But the blue was covered by heavy cotton clouds.

But then I *knew*, I knew without reason just where I was and where was Etienne. I looked, then, past my feet and the bow and the now silent muskrat town and wondered what I would do. I raised my head higher and gazed earnestly into the east. If I knew things I could not know, then why not see things I could not see?

Black wings hid the marsh, the sky. Wings with long, curved feathers like fingers stretched black in silhouette, spread wide before me while sharp black curved claws gripped, bit into the cypress of the pirogue bow. I lay quite still while the hawk settled, curved ebony beak parted in a threatening scowl, upon the pirogue bow. He folded in his wings and he was no longer huge or black, but gray with compact fierceness.

A comic, tragic, awkward step with each claw and talons gripped the carcasses of teal. He was a duck hawk. His eyes had not the bright, yellow circles of the less vicious marsh hawk. He was a peregrine, a swift and deadly hunter who preyed on the same animals men preyed upon. We were hunting competitors and now he had swooped down to take, not steal, part of my kill from me.

His eyes were totally black, filled with pupils for seeing things I could never see. They looked straight into mine as his taloned, serpent's feet adjusted their piercing black control of what was left of teal. His eyes looked straight, deep, black into mine above his curved and deadly beak. And then I knew which way to go. And then he, too, was gone.

I felt the wind rush from his wings. His booty nearly touched my head as he sailed over me. I twisted, turned to see him straining low over the marsh. And then he began to soar, in circles widening higher, farther from me in the sky, until he was no longer with me in that little world.

I took the spent shell from the gun and put a fresh one in the chamber. I looked into what I knew now to be the east. A mink ventured into the water. I could feel in the quiet the eyes of the others watching to see if he would survive the booming voice. Then others came into the open.

The blunt end of the pole I planted into a knot of grass and my first push took me almost to the little channel which I easily found and followed to the east.

I would not defile again this place, nor would I tell another of it. This was the muskrat's little kingdom and refuge. Here he would grow strong and fat, to overflow his boundaries and again populate our trapping grounds with animals we understood better than the monstrous, orange-toothed coypu.

The muskrat haven was alive again. Again it was not disturbed by my meager crossing.

I had not reached the first far shore before I saw the line of fires. They rose singly from the sea of grass, then flowered with dancing petals, then arched their handless, pointed arms. Quickly before an unfelt wind they grew and crackled, roared and swept toward me, spreading from their starting points and leaving blackened talon shapes behind them on the tawny land until they joined in one fiery wall.

Etienne was there, of course, how far I could not tell. I strained my eyes for sight of him but he was not to let himself be seen. He moved so swiftly. The fires rose quickly, like warriors sprung up from the ground, to begin their march toward me. I watched for Etienne from the basin's edge until the flames towered before me, a wall of screaming fire that heated all my front like a shirt scorched beneath a metal iron.

Two does and their buck, his rack lowered in fear and flight, plunged into the pond so near to me I could have hit them with the pushpole. They glanced at me, with childlike fear before the panicked monster roaring toward us, then ran on. The water foamed white at their legs as their pointed feet churned the bottom chocolate. The does were swollen.

I retreated from the fire. Already, sparks from the burning edge ignited muskrat beds on the islands of the ponds. They stood beside my path like lighthouse beacons of destruction.

Flights of ducks rose through the smoke. I heard the piercing rabbit screams. A family of raton laveur escaped with their swift, aloof style of swimming, their masked faces just above the water and their thick, plumed tails floating delicately behind them. Hawks hunted on the edges of the smoke, bringing confused birds down.

A muskrat crawled smoking from the water at the foot of his burning home. He looked all about him, as though he were confused, lifting first one foot and then another upon the smoldering grass. No others swam up from the water to meet him, and the muskrat bed burned on. He went into the water, swimming insanely toward where the fire had come, confused in swift destruction. But the far bank was no longer lined with spirits roaring, bright orange, and with searing pain.

Now there was no line of fire, only smaller ones that burned with angry crackling growls, impotent after their lavish, wasteful jaunt across the marsh. The homes of the muskrat tribe, though, burned with high bright tongues of flame. I lost sight of the singed muskrat's head against the reflected line of charred marsh.

In time, I poled behind him, entered the now barren channel of the marsh. Without the grass, I could now see its twists and curves before me, all the way to where the tawny claws and blackened claws interlocked as in a bout of strength. But precious little life I saw.

Smoking corpses like lumps of dirt were everywhere. Animals of feather and fur who did not escape the fire. A flock of the foolish poule d'eau, who do not like to fly, had perished in one group together.

Etienne. Why? This fire would not stop me, he knew. And suddenly in the way I knew direction without sign, I understood. And I pushed on, through powdery soot that smelled of death and coated my clothes the color of the darkness now descending with twilight and cold and dark clouds low above me. I poled on, and with my one look behind me I saw the mounds of red-blue glowing coals and ashes that had once been rounded dwellings.

Etienne had left no place to hide until I reached the tawny claws.

Marsh grass chest high. A cold wind whirling with the clouds. I stopped when, as I expected, the channel drifted right, toward the sea.

My coat was already buttoned up to my neck and the collar was around my ears. I wished for my hood as the body heat from the poling left me. The bayou would be in front of me. The channel's new direction would run with it.

I left the pirogue and went into the marsh to cut the grass. I went far enough away so that the stubble could not be seen from the channel. With my sharp skinning blade, I cut a great sheaf. I bundled it with twine I kept inside my hunting coat.

Placing the sheaf in the bow, I smelled rain. It would come soon and I wanted to be ready for it. I fastened my boot tops to my belt and uncoiled the bow line. I walked the marsh until I found solid footing, then pulled the boat to me. Like me, old age had made it light and smoothly it slid through the marsh grass behind me. The bow would come to me, parting the grass again, like a happy puppy glad to come when called.

I stood upon the ancient border of Bayou Chien, and looked at how the great storm had changed it, blending it with the surrounding marsh. Yet, one who knew the art could pole it in a good pirogue.

Upon the highest point of bayou ridge, I turned my pirogue over, stowed beneath it the grass and my gun, and crawled under its protection to await the rain. It came quickly. I lay in darkness like a turtle in his shell and listened to the heavy drops. Such sound would make good cover for my hunting, but an old man in the marsh must use wisdom. A wet skin in the winter marsh is foolishness unforgivable.

And so, his fur removed from him from fire, he came to me for protection from the wetness and the cold. He came with sounds I almost did not hear. He lay in stealth beside the pirogue at my head. I clearly smelled the singed and burned fur. He must have heard my breathing, for he crawled low in the grass down the pirogue's length and entered at my feet. He burrowed into the sheaf of harvested marsh grass. We both lay still, savored what warmth there was and listened for the movements of each other. I heard nothing.

So long I listened and heard nothing that I began to think I had been mistaken. I thought, and in my thinking I did not understand. For his race is timid. It does not move. The coypu pushed them out, of course, but did not change their basic ways. I had seen that inside the fertile basin. There, they lived as muskrat always lived.

But this muskrat had followed me. My mind told me

this was not so. It said the muskrat was not there, burrowed at my feet where he surely was. And so I did not think. And once again in not thinking I understood. And as I understood, the world beneath the pirogue was lighted bright with a flash from without. A blue-white flash that startled me. And startled him, because I heard him nervously shift position in the sheaf.

But there were no booms to follow the flash, no treading footsteps to haunt its ghost upon our minds. It must have been a break in heavy clouds, which meant the rain would soon end. And from the brightness of the flash, I knew the moon had found his parts.

He would now be strong above the clouds. He would be pulling at the tides with arms as muscled as old Desormeaux' in youth.

Oh, pull your tides, you Ancient One. Pull them in with life to me. Flood my marsh, his marsh, with seeds of life to populate the sea and earth. Let your muscles pull the tides, let them bulge with silver blood and pull your tides. Pull your tides into the marsh, into the crippled Bayou Chien. Give my pirogue better draft, more silently to move upon our destiny, your destiny. Pull on, Ancient One.

Another blue-white flash. Another, and the rain was done.

I left the pirogue carefully, to not disturb my guest. I lifted the pirogue at the stern above my head, and quietly crept from under it. The tide was coming in. My leg no longer ached. Another blue-white flash showed me the swelling channel of crippled Bayou Chien.

My pirogue in the flash was like the turtle's shell. Cypress shining in the moonlight, rounded and sloped to shed the water, keep the water from me. I lifted it easily, and gently set it in the sparse but rising water of the bayou. I loaded into it the pole and gun and the water Etienne had given me. But I did not want to move the sheaf of grass.

Perhaps I'd cut too much marsh grass, I reasoned with myself. I must hurry, now, but perhaps I cut more than enough. Perhaps I could leave some behind to help him this first cold night of his destruction. But he was gone from the sheaf when finally I inspected it. He was gone, for both of us knew I needed all the grass. I lifted the sheaf and turned toward my boat. There, from the bayou ridge, I looked across the marsh. Powerful moonlight shone through breaks in heavy clouds, casting upon the Iberia marsh a silver system of blue-white veins, even as the Ancient One was pulling tides with blood and seed into the grassy paradise of life.

And now my time was short. I set my feet well in the boat and pressed the pole against the ridge. I pushed myself along the bayou bank, pushed myself southward toward the twin cedars and where I knew, outside my thoughts, Etienne and I would meet.

I rubbed my leg again, to satisfy my thoughts the ache was gone.

I leaned against the cedar and covered my legs with what grass was left from hiding the pirogue. Then I covered my chest and let my head rest back in the shadows.

An angry moon, a boastful moon exploded light upon the marsh in waves and spurts. A mighty worker drunk with power in his muscles, grumbling darkly and then bursting into song. He was a warrior of life and death and not to be looked upon. I looked upon his completed self once, coming down the crippled bayou, and now his shimmering face nearly blinded me in the time that I most needed sight.

The marsh wind whirled in gusts from all directions in

no order of their turn. The sky would darken, then burst with light that made the floating marsh a work of art, a carved and chiseled platter on which to serve the supper of a king, or of a god. I waited.

Old Desormeaux, what does your axe do to my wind? Snake Man, have I paid? That flash again of angry moonlight as wind blew swiftly, cold, through my grass shelter and I shivered. Old Desormeaux, what does your axe do to my wind?

I waited and prayed my boyhood prayers as one would say the rosary and plan the next day's trapping in the same moment. To mellowly and lovingly say the words of the *Notre Pere, Je Vous Salu Marie, Le Confeteor* and the others, and yet see the line of trail where one would set the traps, see even the marking reeds stuck firmly in the marsh and bending slightly in the wind.

I waited and prayed and could not help but think those last few moments before our meeting. The ones outside the marsh who wanted to cage him for their fear and for his punishment, what duties were owed to them? What right has a man of God's creation to choose to live like an animal? And if he kills again, after one has the power to end it, will that sin go with two men to their graves? Such questions are for holy men, priests, with little else to do but sift back through their thoughts.

But thoughts now merely wearied me, and so I waited, with only what I heard and saw and felt to guide me. Grosbek lived upon the crippled bayou. I heard their talk, and in a surge of mooonlight I saw one of their silver crests like the gray hair of a man as old as me, brushed back and bristly. I saw the crest as the male passed very close to me. And that grosbek was silent. Could he know that I was there? I checked my camouflage and it was perfect.

And then came Etienne. Low to the marsh and groping,

formless, like a darkened pool upon the grass, a shadow of some giant bird cutting the air between the moon and marsh.

I was silent. I was still, and yet not far from me he knew that I was there. He knew that I was there before I cocked both barrels of the gun, for he had crouched and widened himself as a raton laveur will do when he is frightened. But at the hammers' deadly clicks, he began moving to the side as a fox does with a wounded prey.

He knew me, where I was, and then fear welled up in me exactly like the tide. I moved then. I rose up from my hiding place and new-cut grass fell about me like a winter coat of fur dropping from a man-beast at the first fine hint of spring. I braced my foot behind me on the cedar roots and extended the gunbarrels toward his head, tucked tight against his shoulders. Like some great cat, he sprang.

I kept the barrels pointed at his head, my fingers firm upon the triggers, and he came as though drawn to the light that glowed upon the barrels and made them twin moonbeams. He struck the barrels full upon his head and yet he came, he still came on me. His heavy black body came full past the barrels—now wrenched without explosion from my hands—and crashed into my chest. My body bolted backward from the blow. A searing pain shot up from my ankle. Then all was still.

All was still except my breathing, which shook my body, and I scrambled on my painless but broken ankle for the gun. The moon in angry boasts first showed it to me shimmering as himself, then hid it in the darkness of the clouds. But I finally grasped it and turned it again on Etienne. But he lay still, one leg drawn up against his chest and his arms spread upon the bayou ridge, one hand upon the cedar roots.

I watched his unmoving darkened form until moonlight

flooded the marsh and no longer teased with darkness and with light. For a long moment we were bathed in silver moonshine and I looked upon him close, not in a dying fog, not back among the ghosts of years.

His beard was grizzled, darkening on his face. The skin was covered with welts from the insects of the warm weather. His eyes were closed as if in sleep, and he was breathing fitfully. One of the gunbarrels had put upon his head a mark, the image of the moon still missing some of his parts. A circle with one part rubbed out, so it was not complete. The Snake Man's broken circle to let the snake go free. The whiteness of his skull shone through the cut, blood trickled darkly to the bayou ridge.

I began to remove my boot before the ankle swelled to press it tightly. My decision had been made, and even as his eyelids began to flutter with his consciousness I drew the cold gun up to me, placed it between us, caressed the cold steel rounded chambers, watched his legs begin to stir . . .

Epilogue

Ted Johnson, who was the game warden, and Harvey Spurlock, the seaplane pilot, heard the first shot as they walked out onto the screened porch. They had just finished a late supper and were full and content and warm as they walked outside to take the fresh night marsh air, so they were surprised by the cold. Inside the State Camp the stove had been going, and the two men had been talking and cooking and then talking and eating, and they had not noticed the abrupt change in the weather. They looked at each other in amazement twice, first for the weather and then for the shot.

A strong, erratic wind gusted whistling through the screens and around the supporting poles of the porch. A little rain had fallen, and when the moonlight broke through cracks in the ceiling of the sky the water beaded silvery on the tips of the marsh grasses and railings and beams of the pier. The wind carried to them the sound of the first shot, almost like a polite cough for attention, a tiny, muffled cry. At first they thought it was someone spotlighting deer or shooting ducks by walking a levee. But then the shots came spaced so they knew it was a signal.

They took the airboat and followed the sound, going straight across the floating marsh. Behind them the airplane propeller and engine roared, but they sat high above the boat and the marsh and skipped across the grass and loam at a high speed. They stopped often and listened for sound and adjusted their direction exactly as one would on the open sea or in the air. Harvey Spurlock was terrified. He was aware the vehicle they were using was similar to the airplanes he piloted, but he was not in his element. He had a natural inclination to trust Ted Johnson because Johnson had the training and the experience in that boat and in that marsh, but Spurlock expected disaster.

Then they reached an old bayou levee, and Johnson slowed down and found a tranasse and entered the bayou very carefully and turned the bow north. He shut the engine down. The bayou had been plugged up and was turning back to marsh with hardly more than a twisting tranasse to mark where it had once flowed freely. Johnson ·spoke softly, listening for the signal.

"This used to be Bayou Chien, he said, "Dog Bayou. Hurricane plugged it up long years ago. Before I ever came into this country. Now nobody calls it nothing anymore. You can still find it marked on old maps, but nobody uses it for nothing. Not worth calling it nothing, I don't guess. Not worth fooling with. I wonder wha . . ."

Then came the shots again, and Ted Johnson marked them by sound very close and dead ahead. He cranked up the motor again and they followed the ruined bayou's path. Both men had an eerie feeling. It was as though they were the light, floating ghosts of a boat and crew on the specter of a bayou, a remnant, that which remains to mark a passage.

Eager, now, Johnson stopped once more, and the shot came immediately and very loud, and Johnson gave a blast on the airhorn and some ducks got up close to them from a pothole of the plugged up bayou so that they both marveled that the ducks had not bolted from the marsh at their approach but waited for the airhorn. The sound of the airhorn reverberated across the undulating waves of marsh grass for tens of miles, another sound as frightening as the nutria wail but magnified one hundred times.

Neither man was ready for what they found. The old man was propped up against one of two large cedars. Cedars are strangers to the marsh. They had to have been planted long ago. The old man's broken ankle was resting on his other leg. Even with the sock still on, the swelling indicated something serious.

The old man was speaking incessantly in that broken English the Frenchmen of that country used with the outsiders, the ones they called "les Americain." He was babbling all the time they were tending to him and installing him in the airboat, talking about a daughter of his and her son and the man she lived with and about his father and about his wife when she was very young. They paid no attention to him, realizing he was delirious from the pain.

He was in great pain, but he seemed happy, even jubilant, and he did not stop talking even when the motor drowned his words. Each time Johnson swept the light and lit the old man's face he could see the words forming on the old man's lips. He had no boots or jacket. Johnson said nothing to Spurlock or anyone else, but it was unlike the old man to be in the marsh without the proper equipment. He could read weather better than a meteorologist with satellites and all the rest of modern technology, so he hadn't been deceived by the elements. Johnson gave him his own jacket, and the old man gathered it around his shoulders, holding it at the neck so that it draped across his back like a cape.

Johnson took the Intracoastal Canal for speed although the wind was churning the canal into a choppy sea. And they put the old man into the seaplane and buckled him tight, and Harvey Spurlock took them up into that lively sky and to Abbeville and the hospital.

Ted Johnson had an eerie feeling after that blinking white light and those two little wing lights, one green and the other one red, had disappeared with the old man and Harvey Spurlock into that sky churning all around. He had the feeling it had never happened. But he knew it had happened, though he was never going to understand it, and he knew the bad weather was about to happen.

And he was right. He was right about the bad weather and he was right about never understanding all of it. The weather broke on him with fury and whipped the marsh into frenzy. Ted Johnson was glad to have a warm, dry place to sleep that night.

He was never to see the old man in the marsh again. He never came back. And all the trouble over the Lopez man was for nothing because he was never spotted, not in the marsh, not anywhere. The old man spent the rest of his time sitting on the benches of the wide veranda of the courthouse in Abbeville, telling stories to whomever would listen. Telling them to children, mostly. But that morning after the storm, Ted Johnson didn't know the old man would never come again into the marsh. He could just wonder what had happened.

He wasted the first two hours of the morning watching ricebirds perch on the beams of the pier, preening their feathers the way they usually do in the spring. After the storm, the day dawned bright and cold so that everything in the cleaned-out atmosphere stood out as though seen through binoculars. The air itself had that rare quality of being charged with ozone, which comes after an electrical storm. And everything, every living thing seemed to be at peace.

Les Perdues

It was raining hard outside, and this should have made him sleep. But he woke up in the night, and it was one of those times he could not sleep. The house had a tin roof, but it was tin over a layer of good seasoned cypress. And the space between the hard slant of the cypress and the ceilings in the house was insulated with a thickness of bagasse. So when it rained hard, as now, it had that deep drumming that should have put him to sleep, like the vibrating motor sounded as he came in from the fish traps after a long day, deep in the bow beneath the foredeck, alone in the somber shadows and cuddled into the feather-bed, cushioned against the hull rising against the swells, the constant, deep motor sound all around him. The rain on the roof.

It was almost time to get up, anyway. The house was in perfect order. Everything in a well-established place. It was as though each night they set the house as a shrine to sleep, in mellow, unconscious darkness, to exist for the pleasure of shadows. He needed no light to find his way around the tables and chairs, sofa, television set, gun cabinet to the hall.

But there was something else in the house. All around him in the house every day but more noticeable at night. When the rest were asleep. In the darkness of silence, where small sounds can finally be heard. A pressure about him. A pressure at once a goad and a bridle, or at least a halter with no bit.

He stood outside the open door to the room. The room where his uncle slept. The door to the room was always open. The room was bare and white. It contained only a narrow white-painted bed, a small stand for a lamp near the pillows, and a chest. There was nothing on the walls. His uncle used it only for sleep. The boy had never seen the door closed, and he somehow associated this with the unspoken pressure of the family, and with himself. All the other doors were closed at night, closed on whatever was within, against whatever was without.

The boy stood for a time without, then silently stepped inside. Throughout the house there was at night the feeling of a presence, but it was greater here. As though the presence somehow combined with his uncle's sleeping form. Antoine Viator.

There was no clock inside the room, and the uncle wore no watch with glowing dial such as the boy's father wore. So the boy did not actually know how long he stood inside the uncle's room before he moved closer to the bed. But he was conscious of the thin fabric of his pajamas as it swished with his walking, like tiny whispers with each step.

The gun was on the table beneath the dark lamp. The uncle carried the gun always, somewhere on his person, no one knew just where. He showed it to no one. But the boy knew it well. He knew it from his darkened visits. It was a .41 caliber derringer, handmade and very old. With two barrels over-and-under. And it had a nickel finish and ivory handles on the tiny grip. Finally, of course, the boy knew it was always loaded.

He reached two fingers and touched the cold, hard twin barrels. The pistol rocked, the handle lifting lightly and then knocking slightly on the tabletop, and he knew his uncle was watching him. He did not know how he knew it. The uncle had not moved. He had not even turned upon the bedsprings in sleep. There had been no whispers. No sign. Nothing. There had been nothing except a subtle change in the presence of the room. No longer was it a sleeping presence in the room with the boy, but an alert one, watching.

He took his hand from the pistol and stood looking toward the bed, expecting, even hoping for some sound, some movement from the dark space that was his uncle's face. But there was nothing except the feeling, the unmistakable and indefinable knowledge. The uncle was watching him. The boy waited, longer than he had waited just inside the door to the room. So long he waited that it seemed it would be noon outside and the household up and moving around them and breakfast eaten and the chores done and the schoolbus gone down the long paved highway between the huge water-filled ditches without him as he stood beside the bed in darkness. But there was nothing. Nothing happened.

So, as quietly as he had entered, he turned and left. Crossing to his own room, he became aware, again, of the rain on the roof. Not a thunder, but a heavy, deep drumming. He slipped between the sheets and blankets. The sheets had grown cold and this was pleasant to him. Winter was approaching and during the winter he liked to slide into a cold bed and make a part warm to his body. In the night, in his sleep, he enjoyed the knowledge that he was sleeping in a space warmed especially for him. And when he strayed from the space, he liked the knowledge that the outline of warmth was changing to suit him. He liked sleeping best of all in the fall and the winter. Then, in what seemed no time at all, his mother was waking him. There was no sound of rain on the roof and she was shaking him. Speaking to him in English.

"You got to get up, you, yes boy. It late, yes. You going to miss your bus, yes. Antoine, him, he already went to the barn. And breakfast almost on the table, yes."

She was making the bed before he was out of it, smoothing the sheets and blankets into proper place as each part of him made it out of the bed, his feet to the deerskin on the floor. He could not understand how he could have been sleeping.

"You wash your face and hands before breakfast, yes, you," she said. "And you better hurry, you, yes. Antoine, him, he already went to the barn."

Throughout the house was the strong smell of coffee. His mother had already picked up from the floor the socks and blue jeans he had discarded the night before and put out the brown slacks, belt, and sport shirt that was required wear. She had put the blue jeans folded on the edge of his desk and had draped the school clothes over the chair. On school mornings the boy had to dress twice, once for chores and once for town. He pulled on the soft good-feeling blue jeans. He hated school mornings and Monday school mornings more than the others.

His father and grandfather were already seated at the table. His father had removed his boots, and the bottoms of his khaki trousers were splotched with mud. Already he had made his rounds of the pasture. They were talking together in French, already drinking coffee even as the various smells of the general breakfast aroma were beginning to rise and blend from the skillets on the stove.

"He makes rain today, Pa-Paw?" his father asked of the old man. The old man did everything with solemnity. There was a kind of solemnity even to the jokes he told, though everyone laughed when he told them. It was as though everything he said was a ceremony, a celebration as mass is a celebration. He considered the question as though there were a thousand answers from which to choose. His face had a chewing motion, the chin going slightly up and down as now, when he considered the question of the rain. He spoke only French, and if English were spoken to him in his house, he pretended he did not understand. If

English were spoken to him anywhere but on his own land, he looked ashamed.

"Possible," he said. "Possibly he makes rain in the afternoon."

The father noticed the boy, but said nothing to him. He would not speak to Leland until the boy had finished his chores. And even then he spoke only to direct him, to give an order. He was firmer on Leland than anyone. It was his duty to mold Leland, to prepare him. In fact, Leland remembered a time when his father was softer toward him. That was a time when Leland himself was soft. Round and babyish. It had never been a warm relationship, but since Leland had begun to grow lean and angular, to form tall and etched from the unmarked material of infancy, the relationship had grown sharper, more brittle.

"Good day, Papa. Good day, Pa-Paw," Leland said, and as he had known, only his grandfather answered.

"Good day, grandson," the old man said.

Then the boy bid good day to his grandmother and to his mother, though the mother had already spoken to him and the father had already begun speaking to the grandfather again. The boy sat in the chair, stomped his right foot into the boot. The boot thudded solidly because he stomped on the floor above the four-foot-wide cypress beam that ran the length of the old part of the house and still had the marks of the adz that had formed it.

"Then will he make flood this year, this fall?" his father asked of the old man.

"Yes, yes, possibly, yes," the old man said. "We must be ready."

The boy pulled on the blanket-lined blue jean jacket and went out the door, onto the porch, and down the steps to the brick walkway that led to the backyard gate. The clouds were broken, especially in the east where the clear white sky of morning, tinted rouge, ran the length of the horizon to the high trees of the Mont Blanc woods south of the pasture. He did not know why they had called the woods Mont Blanc, since there were no mountains in all of Louisiana, white or otherwise, and there was no flatter land than the coast with its marsh and swamp and rice fields. But sometimes he imagined a mountain in the woods, and today the mountain pushed up into the clouds from the woods. And so the scene was not much different, though the mountain was there in his mind.

It was a cold fall. The rain made it colder. The cattle wanted hay, as in the winter. They milled in the pasture and looked toward the barn. Because of the mud, the hay wagons were crowded into the wide doors of the barn, blocking entrance. But there were no tractors attached. No hay would be loaded and distributed in the fields. The huge flatbeds on double axles were merely parked in the doorways to keep the cattle from wandering in and out and across the soft and muddy entrance ways. The boy had seen the barnyard so muddy the cows sank to their barrels, and even large calves sometimes had to be hauled from where they bogged.

In the days that they wintered their cattle in the marsh, or even on Pine Island, often a cow would bog and the mosquitoes would smother her. Once, his Uncle Antoine had almost killed a good cutting horse trying to pull one out of a bog. His uncle was said to have a strange set of values.

The boy picked his way across the barnyard, stepping on the more solid pieces of earth as one will try to step only on the clumps of grass in a floating marsh. He crouched beneath the flatbed and swung his body over the four-inch pipe welded between the axles. He could hear his uncle ladling cracked corn from a two-quart can into the wooden boxes for the horses. And he could hear the horses' eager stomping inside the stalls, and their great crushing jaws at work on the corn.

"Mais, I got the horses, yeah, cher," his uncle said. "Let's get the calves, you and me."

His uncle was thin but powerful. At his waist the fabric of his khaki work trousers was gathered by a narrow leather belt across a middle absolutely spare of excess flesh. He wore work boots and a khaki workshirt. And in summer or in winter he wore the same felt hat with dents near the point of the crown and the brim turned down, similar to those seen in old movies of the thirties or forties. He was the finest rider, the best man with horse and cattle in the parish, yet he bore about him nothing of the mark of a cowboy. And he was always clean, his trousers creased. Not even the farm work seemed to rumple him.

Indeed, like the strength in his thinness, it was part of his manner that he accomplished things that seemed out of his range. He could trap and shoot wonderfully. A boat or a tractor with rake or plow, or a heavy truck or even a rice combine responded to him as though connected by nerves to his brain. And yet he did not have the appearance of one able to do these things. He was pale and thin, with the blond hair and blue eyes and long face of the boy's father, but without the ruddy complexion and the heaviness of jowls and arms and hips. And the uncle took no outward pride in his abilities. He never bragged or made a show. It seemed he did things well because it was the easiest and fastest way to get them done, finished. He had no pleasure. Fluid, he swung the bulky, hundred-pound sack of feed from the feedroom and in a walking-running gait took it all the way to the long trough. Sometimes he reminded the boy of a spider.

At a side pen a dozen or so feeder calves—half of them steers for sale at slaughter weight and half heifers to keep if they matured with promise—crowded to the gate. Inside the barn the soil was always dry and powdery and the dust now rose from their walking, giving a gray look to the stalls and hayracks and posts and pens. Hardly had the sack touched the ground than his uncle had found the key strings in the sewing of the mouth and was stripping the thread easily away. Seldom could the boy find the proper string to pull, and nearly always his father had to cut the sacks open with the sharp skinning blade of his pocketknife. But the uncle seemed to always have that ability to pick and pull the right string.

Together, they spread the feed pellets evenly in the worn trough. This was something the boy liked to do. He liked the sound of the hard pellets hitting the wood worn smooth and shiny from use. In places, the gunwales of the trough had been chewed for roughage by the penned calves. The boy enjoyed scattering the packed grain, high in protein, watching the pellets roll noisily down the long trough.

Then he unlatched the gate and swung it open as the calves surged through. He propped the gate open with a chunk of four-by-four but stood watching the calves as they crowded, nudging and shoving each other, to the trough. Already, his uncle was in the stall with the filly, sacking her down as he spoke to her softly and blandly in French. As she ate, he caressed her completely, the empty sack in his hand fluttering along her neck and shoulders, down the forelegs to the hoof and down the side to the flank, across the rump, down the leg, inside and outside. At her head, she jolted slightly when the sack passed her eyes. Each day she grew calmer to the touch. She would not resist when she was saddled for the first time. She would never resist the rein.

"You going to miss your bus, you, and catch hell, yeah," his uncle said to him in English but in the same tone as the

French he was using on the horse so it was almost as though he had continued speaking to the filly as Leland leaned on the cypress slats of the stall. When he spoke, he mimicked the tone to not disturb the filly.

"He makes rain today?" he asked in French.

"Today no," his uncle said. "This is the third day and it is the season for clear skies. The great storms have ceased. He should make cold, now."

"Pa-Paw says it may flood."

"Great flood?"

"Yes."

"This he said to you?"

"To Papa," the boy said, then after a pause, "He makes great flood?"

"No. To have a great flood of his experience is now not possible. The water from the north now goes through the Atchafalaya Swamp. He always thinks of the time the house was washed from its foundations and found against Mont Blanc and brought back piece by piece. The time of his boyhood when the family lost all the cattle from Pine Island, washed them out to sea. It is no longer possible. Go to school and forget great floods."

The boy left him gentling the filly, speaking to her in nonsense curses in the special, seductive tones. Inside the house, now, they were already eating. The aromas had blended into that overall breakfast smell dominated by the odor of the thick black coffee. Coffee was the sit-down smell all day long every day, and in the morning it was the sit-down-and-eat smell blended with the scents of broiled pork grillards marinated in vinegar and cooked in butter, cush-cush and cahier, hotcakes, corn cakes, pain perdue, eggs fried or scrambled, buttermilk, and toast. But he did not sit immediately to eat. He went straight to his room to change. He could cut short his eating if the bus interrupted him, but he could not cut short the dressing. The nuns would tolerate a poorly fed boy, but not a poorly dressed one.

His lunch money was already in his pocket, and he found the quarter where he had left it deep in his drawer. The books were where he had left them Friday afternoon. By the time he was done, his father was already ladling pear preserves onto the second stack of hotcakes.

The boy's plate had on it three of the long strips of lean pork now grilled dark gray and curling and crisp on the edges and still smelling of the vinegar. Before the old man was a bowl of cush-cush. He ate his cush-cush every morning, like the other old people, claiming it was all that was needed for a full day's work, though he no longer worked, and he ate the cornmeal fried dry with plenty of salt. Into it he poured cahier, the sour milk thick and lumpy, and a little Steen's Pure Ribbon Cane Syrup, rich and dark so that it all blended in golden, white, and brown swirls.

"You do your chores, you, boy?" his father asked, the tone harsh, carrying the weight of a demand.

"Oh, yes, Papa," the boy said, pretending to concentrate on his breakfast and relieved that his mother chose this time to deposit his eggs on his plate.

"And Antoine, where he at, him?" his father demanded again.

"He . . . uh, well, he working with the filly, him," Leland said. Somehow he felt responsible for his uncle or at least for the criticism constantly leveled at him. Often the father used the boy's statements as wedges to drive home the criticism. It could have been because his father was anxious that he not take after the uncle too much.

"Huh! Always playing with them horses, him!"

The boy knew the uncle never played but said nothing of this. He knew the response would be to mention Antoine's yearly disappearance just before planting in the spring. No one knew where Antoine went, but Leland's father believed Antoine went to New Orleans for the prostitutes. Or at least this was what he used to emphasize Antoine's immorality.

So Leland said nothing and gave great attention to lacing his hotcakes with butter and reaching for the yellow and black painted can of Steen's syrup. Two wedges were punched into opposite positions in the silver top of the can. From prior pourings a rim of syrup thickened at the edges of the top. The boy tilted the can and watched it pour slowly, thickly to his plate. It was loaded with flavor but had only a little of the lush smell of the silver-painted mill in town.

One of the most pleasant things about coming into Abbeville in the fall was the smell of the mill across the street from the church and not two blocks from the school. Cane juice from the mountain of cane fed into the mill by a dragline, the mountain itself constantly replenished by a long line of huge trucks loaded heavily with cane that spilled to the pavement where the double rows of wheels crushed it and the juice fermented in the street and gave the syrup aroma a tang of beer. Town boys stopped there after school and selected the tenderest and sweetest stalks from the inexhaustible supply, then sat on the bank of the river and peeled joint after joint, cutting them into chewing size and spitting the chewed pulp into the water. The boy had only the aroma.

Rabelais, the schoolbus driver, was an unquestioned authority. He was one of them, a Frenchman of the countryside. He understood the tricks of the country children and the nature of their discipline. So the bus was relatively quiet until the smell of the syrup and the sight of the town children on the way to school inflamed them on fall mornings. Then they leaned out the windows to smell the cooking syrup and shout to their friends, and Rabelais ignored them because he knew they'd soon be rid of him and he of them at least for the space of the school day.

The plaza of the Gothic church—technically a cathedral because a bishop was once exiled there because of drinking problems—was speckled with children who crossed it and walked beside the huge brick building and danced and skipped happily between the cement and brick tombs of the old graveyard behind it. The girls all wore brown skirts and white blouses now covered by brown sweaters. The boys were dressed as if for church, though khaki was also allowed.

The school was very old. Decaying, in fact. It was wood frame, painted white or covered with white asbestos plate, drafty, poorly lit, and it smelled like no other place Leland had ever visited. The boy thought the smell was from all the scratch paper they used, or from all the chalk scratched upon the dull, chipped blackboards, or the oily mixture the janitor used on his eternal push-broom, or the forever scent of morality and virtue the nuns carried with them in rigid habit of black and white, their stern and knowing faces framed in a close ruffle of white fabric like cardboard packing or the neckpiece of Sir Walter Raleigh in the history book.

Their teacher was Sister Hubert. The boy knew from one of the stained glass windows in the church that Saint Hubert was the patron saint of hunters. He had noticed the window for the first time in midafternoon of a day in midsummer when the light blasted through the western windows, and Saint Hubert and the deer that converted him glowed and shimmered.

Privately, the children called their teacher Sister Huge-Butt. This was because she carried an immense expanse of rolling flesh beneath the black robes. Her presence was enormous in other ways, also.

She taught fifty-six pupils that year. This was more than

she could handle, but no one knew this except the students. Their class was the last one in Cabrini Hall, an elderly structure that once housed the nuns' convent and extended all the way from the huge central gymnasium-auditorium-cafeteria to Second Street, which ran parallel to the river and close enough so that in the warm months one could smell the hearty odor of sulphur and loam. The relative isolation of the classroom abetted her reputation for keeping order with twice the proper enrollment.

Before class the children lined the thin sidewalks beside Cabrini Hall. One of their own rules allowed them to leave their books in line to mark their place while, like greedy or starving people, they eked out the last moments of play. Sister Huge-Butt was nearly always late for the first class in the morning. Speculation ran that it was breakfast that delayed her. Finally she was spotted just as she turned the corner.

They ran for their places, and at once the talking ceased as they watched her roll toward them. Her books were always held before her, clutched to her ample front by arms that reached their full length to end in fingers laced like a zipper. Her feet swung outward when she walked, slightly slew-footed in the manner of a pregnant woman. And she carried with her all the bulk and authority of an army tank. At the very sight of her the students formed their tight, rigid line.

She surveyed their rank with quiet, somber satisfaction, the satisfaction not of a drill instructor but a commanding general. With a superior nod she sent the class into the room. Once past her, the boys and girls did not hesitate to stomp their way to their seats, which were in alphabetical order. Everything was alphabetical. Fifty-six names were easier to remember that way. The boy enjoyed the sound of the class stomping into the room. It was the last noise they were permitted until recess.

The desks were nailed on two-by-fours to assure their rigid line. The students took out the proper book—they knew the routine—scratch paper and a pencil labeled *La. Schools No. 2.* It was just as well to get math over with first, the boy thought, and perhaps he would not have to read aloud today. Friday the reading had ended two desks behind him. Fifty-four stammering readers were a lot to get through in one period.

Probably he was safe from reading for that day, if he kept his head down into the book and gave the appearance he was keeping the place. Reading was not until after recess, and he still had math and geography to traverse, but he began to fear reading the moment the day began. He knew as little about the other studies, but reading was so humiliating. Now they were on long division.

Leland had no idea how the number outside that little house drawn on the blackboard could combine with the larger number inside the house to make the medium-sized number on the roof. They had names for each of these numbers. They even had a name for the house, itself.

Actually, as he looked at it, the house was more like a one-horse stall or even more like a boathouse because it was open at the back end and seemed to sit in water. The boy could not remember the names but considered vaguely they were Numerator and Denominator. Now he understood they were somehow subtracting figures again and again into the water beneath the boathouse. This was a little clearer. He thought if the huge nun were to ask him to do only this, he would not be humiliated.

If, for instance, he were asked to subtract the numbers down into the water while someone else did the other part —someone smart like Marie Hoffpauir could always juggle the three sets of numbers in a way that made the nun smile until the lacy cardboard at her cheeks bulged outward—then they could together very easily make the numbers descend downward smaller and smaller into the water like in the Gulf. When something is dropped over-board it descends smaller and smaller into the clear water until it is gone. He could do the subtracting and she could do the rest. This was the way the rice farmers divided the work and helped one another during the harvest.

He loved Marie Hoffpauir. But he could not speak to her. He was afraid.

Cleveland Castinet at the blackboard was doing no bet-ter than Leland would do. In fact, he was doing exactly as Leland would do. He was pretending to understand. Part of the deception was that discrepancies in the numbers were merely oversights. His camouflage was that he was overcome with the marvelousness of the concept of long division and this clouded the minor elements of arithmetic.

There were many embarrassing pauses at the black-board after the nun had informed him of a wrong number and asked him to correct it. During these pauses, the back of Cleveland's neck and the tips of his ears grew livid. Fi-nally, at the nun's direction, the class loudly chorused the correct figure. The bright students shouted loudest, and the others such as Leland, gave the appearance of chant-ing with them but used neutral sounds.

Then Cleveland slapped his forehead with the heel of his hand. Oohhh, of course! Why hadn't he seen it? And he quickly erased the number with the soft part of his fist and chalked in the correct number. Sometimes, though, he erased the wrong number.

Cleveland was from Belle Isle. His people were rice farmers, but unlike the Viators they neither trapped nor fished commercially. And, though like most of the families in the country they raised calves for slaughter, they did not run a herd of beef cattle as did the Viators. Still, he was a farm boy, and that meant someone from the country was likely to be called next. There was a certain subtle justice in this, but Leland dreaded the experience. Cleveland settled into his seat two rows from Leland and sighed with relief.

Across the room, near the door, Marie Hoffpauir sat perfectly dressed. Of course, all the girls wore basically the same thing but Marie's dress looked better. The sleeves were always turned up at the cuffs in just the right folds. Her teeth were perfect and the whitest the boy had ever seen. Her hair was a rich brown and curly, though parted on the side and combed straight on top to the rim of short curls that seemed to snuggle to her head. The boy knew the hair to be soft because he had more than once touched it. She was unaware he had touched her hair because he had been very stealthy, and lightly brushed her hair with the back of his hand. Once he had done this as she sat on the floor of the gymnasium waiting for a film to begin; he walked past her on the pretense of having to go to the bathroom. Other times included those when he had passed her chair in the cafeteria, holding his tray at the level of the soft curls. The girls and boys were segregated in the lunchroom, and it was Leland's good fortune that the girls' section was closer to the exit so that if he ate hurriedly enough and were stealthy enough he could look forward to touching her hair each day.

But Leland was not called on to go to the board. They left arithmetic. Leland could always spell arithmetic. John David Latour had taught it to him the year before, waiting in line outside of remedial reading. A-rat-in-Tom's-house-might-eat-Tom's-ice-cream.

They put their arithmetic books away and took out geography. As far as the boy could tell, geography was the same as reading, though not quite as bad. He did not really see the use in having both geography and reading. One or the other, if not both, was a waste of time. In the geography book, for instance, there was a small section on France that really told him nothing. He doubted that it was true. But he loved the section on Switzerland. There was a picture of a man carrying cheese in the mountains with a pack that had a band for the head. That was very smart. The boy had never seen a real mountain, but if he ever had to carry a heavy load in the mountains, he would use a pack that took advantage of all these muscles. And there was a huge picture of men unloading hundreds of cheeses into a net. He did not understand why the cheeses were round, like a small watermelon, and why they had been painted red. He was admiring it, holding his finger in Scotland for the place, when he heard the whisper. Coffeepot.

It was E. J. Simon. He said it again. Coffeepot. E. J. had already been expelled from the public school. He was just waiting for his sixteenth birthday and the end of Louisiana's legal educational hold on him. Already he had failed three times, so each year he was given a "social promotion." He was larger and more physically mature than his classmates and violent. A playground tyrant.

"Hey, Coffeepot. You want some cream and sugar?" E. J. did not care if the nun heard him. He would be put into the punishment room to sit alone on a bench for hours. But there he could smoke.

Leland was silent, immobile. He was not ignoring the taunts, he was trying to stay out of trouble. And he was afraid of E. J. Once the older boy started on someone it meant submit or fight. E. J. had never been beaten in a fight. But he was a town dweller and Leland was a country Cajun so for him to submit was to place the entire group of his peers in the position of reaffirming their ability with fists.

E. J.'s intention then became very clear. He did not use

the term *Cajun* because it meant nothing to the French of southwest Louisiana then. The term they used was *Cajin*, the close derivative of *L'Acadien*, and like the term *nigger* to blacks it was accepted with friendliness and even humor from Cajin to Cajin but not accepted at all from others. He used this term next and the town children around him giggled.

Now came *coonass*, then the Cajun French word from which it was derived, *couyon* meaning country bumpkin or simply stupid, depending on how it was said. And again there was no doubt in how it was said.

When the recess bell was sounded they filed out in reverse alphabetical order. That put Leland ahead by several places. He knew E. J. was coming hard behind him, but he hoped somehow he would be distracted, that somehow he would not follow through on the course that had already been well established with others. So Leland headed for Essey Jeansonne, another trapper's son. Essey was Leland's age but had failed one year. Now he spent his recesses running up tree trunks.

Essey was from Indian Bayou where the gulf wind had slanted trees in growth so that they were easy to scale running. But these trees of town were normal, perpendicular trees. Still, Essey was pretty good at it. He ran at the tree, assaulted it with the soles of his tennis shoes and made it higher than his height before he pushed backward and landed clear of the roots.

First, Leland was looking at Essey running at the tree, then he was looking into E. J.'s grinning face, then he was suddenly pushed backward with force, tumbling backward over Butch Bernard behind him on all-fours. Butch rose quickly to his feet and stood just behind E. J.'s shoulder, grinning a leaden grin of dental braces, teeth the color of birdshot.

"Hey, little coonass," E. J. sing-songed. "Wants to fuck Hoffpauir but going to get fucked now!"

Leland was stunned. He had shared with no one what he felt for Marie. How could anyone have known? The words shocked him so or the blow came so swiftly that he was on the ground before he felt the sting. There was a whirl of the forms of those milling around, and then E. J. was on top of him and Leland made a feeble attempt to connect with his nose, partly because a bloodied nose discourages but mostly for honor alone. But Leland made no connection, and E. J. made many so that the best Leland could do pinned by the larger boy's knees was to cross his arms over his face and keep his eyes from being blackened.

Then there was a shrieking of Sister Bonaventure, an ancient nun, tiny and fierce, who sometimes walked unannounced into boys' urinals to stop the noise and the squirting contests. The wilted nun, not even as tall as E. J. and lighter than either boy, separated them and held them at bay from one another with fearsome authority. E. J. cursed her as she shrieked at him in his turn. But he cursed her below her hearing level.

The judgment was swift, but the interrogation took some time. Leland and E. J. stood, the huge nun towering above them at her desk on the platform, while the rest of the class waited in a rigid and silent line outside, eyes wide as they watched through the window. The inevitable question had been, Who started the fight? Thus they stood before her in silence.

Leland could not answer because of the code of not incriminating even the guilty. E. J. did not answer because he was the center of attention for the three of them and the class beyond the windows. Neither of them was really injured. Leland was scraped and his trousers had been torn on the edge of the sidewalk. But he had been defeated miserably in view of the entire playground. So he stood and hung his head. Finally, the nun spoke.

"Well, I know enough about boys and about fights to know they don't generate spontaneously. Do you know what I mean?"

"Yes, Sister," they said in unison. "Yes, Sister" and "No, Sister" were the first things they had learned at the Catholic school. They were the easiest to say.

"So if you insist to stand together on this, you'll get the same punishment. Immediately after lunch you will begin picking up paper from the schoolyard. You will each fill three wastebaskets and show them to me before you deposit the waste into the incinerator. If you do not complete this task during lunch break you will spend tomorrow's morning recess finishing. And you'll each have an hour in the punishment room this afternoon. Understood?"

"Yes, Sister."

"Good. And do not forget this Thursday at confession."

Leland realized, then, that he might salvage some respect from not tattling on E. J. But immediately he remembered how humiliatingly he had been defeated. And all in the sight of the sons and daughters of farmers and trappers and fishermen. Now the thought of wanting to accept alliance with E. J. to save grace, or face the future of his skin overwhelmed him, and knowing he could not stop he began to sob audibly, openly, pressing his palms against the tears and mucous.

"Baby!" E. J. said.

"That is quite enough, E. J.," the nun said. "Take your place in line. Not you, L. D. You remain here for a moment."

Leland heard E. J. leave the classroom and did not have to look to know he strutted. He thought the nun wanted to say something private to him, but she said nothing.

There were only the sounds of his sobbing in the almost empty classroom, and these sounds seemed to unleash even more of the flood. He, himself, was amazed at the grief that poured out of him. Finally, he began to sigh and catch his breath. He wiped his hands on his torn trousers. "Very well, L. D.," she said. "Go into the bathroom and wash your face. Then return immediately. We've all been delayed quite enough on account of you."

He left the classroom as the others were filing in, and he could not bear to meet their gazes. He avoided them when he returned, also, seating himself as quietly as he could and taking up the proper book. At lunch they played an old trick on him. They distracted his attention by saying there was an opossum in one of the oak trees. Leland should have known there would not have been an opossum, in a pear tree at night perhaps, but not in an oak tree in the middle of the day in town. But it was just the unusualness of the idea that struck him, and when he looked someone unscrewed the salt shaker top so that when he salted the food he ruined it.

Second servings were not allowed, and though he was still hungry, he was relieved to leave the cafeteria alone, take up the wastebaskets, and begin collecting the wastepaper, candy wrappers, and potato chip bags from the playground. After a while, Essey came to help him. Together, they put paper into Leland's wastebaskets. "Mais, he too big, yeah Leland," Essey finally said. "E. J., him, he strong, too, yeah. Mais, when you start hitting, you, I say to myself, me, 'I hope Leland kill him quick, yeah, cause he don't kill him first he get killed second for shore, yeah'."

If the paper was wadded, they loosened it, fluffed it for more bulk. E. J., they knew had immediately filled his more than half-way with rocks or chunks of dirt to be topped with paper. The nuns would never check under the surface. They were brides of God and had dignity. "Essey, mais thank you, yes," Leland said. "But you gone get in trouble, you help me, yes."

"Mais, I don't care, me, no," Essey said. "And anyway we got the tree between us and the school, us, yeah."

They picked in silence for a while, checking the path of their picking over their shoulders from time to time like someone on a tractor pulling a two-way disk to see that the tree was between them and authority. When Essey spoke again, softer because he spoke French, there was a more serious tone.

"Will you go with them into the marsh this year, to Cheniere au Tigre?" he asked. It had been named Oak Island of the Tigers by the earliest French because of the abundance of raccoons there, but Leland's ancestor the Doctor —he thought of him as le Médecin—had once kept tigers there, and other beasts of Africa, Europe and Asia in a sort of garden. Essey knew they would all go into the marsh, so the question was merely to open a statement.

"But yes," Leland said. "We will do well this year. There are many rats. And you?"

"I, no," Essey said, speaking down into the wastebasket. "This year none of us will go. Papa is making too much money in the oilfield, and it is easy work. We are moving into Abbeville. It is better."

Essey had used the English word *oilfield* since English words for new things were always incorporated into French and no longer considered foreign.

"Yes," Leland said, "it is better." The firm decision is always better.

Leland hoped his turn in the punishment room would be during reading, but E. J. took it first. And what was worse, the nun was not moving alphabetically across the room. She was calling random names. Leland tried to keep place with his thumb while scanning ahead, trying to anticipate the hardest words, what principles of pronunciation he had gleaned to those words of many syllables, often glancing back to the place to make sure of it and move his thumb down into correct position.

The worst offense was to be caught reading out of place. E. J. should be there, now, in place of Leland. E. J. made a great show of being unable to master subjects and of not caring to master them. Leland believed E. J. had gone past humiliation, that he cherished his role as an outlander.

"L. D., do you have the place?" she asked.

"Yes, sister," he said. He bent his head to the book. What happened next was inevitable. The boy considered it his own personal failure, as though the language he spoke from birth, and which flavored all his words, was a particular curse. He was not ashamed of his heritage, only of his inability to be like everyone else, to master that which they mastered so easily. French was forbidden, and its remnants in Gallicized terms and accents were discouraged, ridiculed, and displayed as ignorance. All of this so that American ideals might flourish even here, even in these lowlands, even here in this pocket tucked away at the heel of that great overpowering goodness that was the Flag, George Washington, the Constitution, High Wages, and the Church.

He struggled through the words, trying to sound as though he were linking them to the whole they were supposed to represent. He knew by the sly laughter around him that he was failing. He felt his body tense, he even felt his ears redden at the tips. The ordeal went on. One paragraph, two. Another and yet another. He no longer knew what sense, if any, the passage had. Indeed, he could no longer even follow the direction of a single sentence. Each word presented an immeasurable difficulty. Just the pronunciation. He began to suspect each letter of some hidden sound, something disguised and peculiar to that word alone in the English language. Now small words snared him, sent him sprawling, and the long, hard, complex ones were terrifying. Each word stood bright and glaring from the page. He tried to give proper pauses to commas and periods but was confused rather than guided by them. Sometimes he would be shocked at the existence of a question mark at the end of a sentence and would have to go back and reread it to give it the interrogatory tone, having to traverse again that painful ground.

"Thank you, L. D.," she said finally. "That's enough. Lawless."

Lawless Fontenot did not know the place. The nun directed Julie Mouledoux to tell him where to begin and directed Lawless to write five hundred times "I will keep place during reading." Leland knew this bothered Lawless little because he had learned the art of writing lines with three pencils simultaneously. The distraction gave Leland the opportunity to lower his head behind the cover of the book.

When he entered the punishment room the smell of E. J.'s cigarette was acrid and strong. Leland quietly opened the window and let the cold north wind freshen the little storeroom. He could tell by the shadows of the trees in the yard the approximate time. When it was nearly three, he closed the window and waited for the bell. It was supposed to be a punishment, isolation to ponder your sins, but Leland found it pleasant to be alone, in the quiet, with the north wind to make it better. The nun gave him a sealed envelope with his parents' names on it as he left the room. This was a mere complication. Already, he had no idea how to explain the torn trousers.

The bus silenced for a tiny profound moment as he entered. Gazes examined him as he passed the rows of eyes. But the prattle settled about the bus again as he took his seat. Leland, at the window, was relieved when Abbeville melted away into the countryside.

The canals were all filled with water to the brim and flowing swiftly southward with the brisk north wind, blue wavelets sparkling at the tips. The bus flowed southward with the stream. At every bridge Leland checked the rice canals. The water was high, but he knew it was from the rains draining and the north wind pushing it gulfward. The gulf gives rain and receives the flood. But by the following afternoon, or perhaps even by morning, the canals and bayous and coulees and rivers, even the lakes and ponds, would show their muddy, slick sides below the vegetation line.

There had been many minor floods of Leland's own experience. They came in the spring and in the fall. The rainy season was in summer, and if it rained on Saint Medard's feast day in June, it would then rain without fail for forty days. But these were only afternoon showers. Only hurricanes brought floods in these months. In the spring there was the danger of all the drainage of the nation washing through Louisiana. And in the fall it was as if summer, like an old man, were growling in relinquishing to winter in October storms. But the skies of winter were clear and cold.

All the floods that Leland remembered were played against that great flood long ago when land and life were changed by an onslaught of relentless water. Roads first dwindled to strings of firmament then disappeared. Watercourses swelled and deepened, then spilled their banks and joined in a new brown sea across the marsh. All of the family's cattle were at Pine Island, then, when Leland's grandfather was a boy. The flood washed the house from its foundations and against Mont Blanc and when they finally made it to Pine Island all that was left was the carcass of a cow too heavy with calf to swim. The bloated carcass floated in an area of little mounds, hundreds of them not three feet high on the exact highest point of land on the island.

It had been clear that the animals must have gathered ever higher for that final touch of soil before the water swept them away. All this had burned itself so vividly into the consciousness of Leland's grandfather that he had etched it into the consciousnesses of all his descendants. It was as vivid to Leland as one of his own memories.

Now they entered Big Woods, which the Viators had once owned and in which the Doctor had buried the larger portion of his gold. It was here he came "to do his banking" for large transactions such as the time immediately after the flood when he replenished the herd in one huge purchase. Leland watched for the spot where the Doctor used to enter the woods with the gold in a bag tied with a horse pistol from the pommel of his saddle and used to reenter on the return trip with his "change." Farther down the road, closer to Esther, was the spot where the Doctor used to enter the woods on the trip to town and come out with the bag empty beneath the pistol, on the last leg of the trip home.

His descendants had followed him into those woods as stealthily as four-footed predators. But each time he had lost them. He and the horse he rode vanished among the palmettoes and blackjack vines without so much as the track of a shod hoof on the soft, dark earth. He had always emerged from the woods alone and unsoiled as his sons and then his grandsons cursed and hacked their way out of the forest. Leland looked for the spot and found it though it was not marked, just as he felt Augustin Mestayer slide into the seat beside him.

Augustin had entered high school that year. He was the quietest of the tribe of Mestayer, steadfast and kind. He was tireless and uncomplaining in the field. He said nothing at first. Then he slapped Leland's thigh and leaned back with his arms across the back of the seat.

"Mais, I guess you feel pretty bad, you, ainh?" he said.

"Mais, oui," Leland said. "What you think, you?"

"Well, don't let it worry you, no," he said quietly. "You feel bad, now, you. But E. J., he going to get his, yes. And you know who gone give it to him, ainh?"

The boy felt he was on the verge of tears again and did not want to be disgraced yet another time. He did not answer, because he was afraid this would unleash the tears. But Augustin waited as he might wait for a deer to browse its way closer down a worn path.

"No," Leland finally said.

"Mais, you, that's who," Augustin said with quiet assertion.

The boy was shaking his head, no longer able to look into Augustin's earnest face.

"You watch," Augustin said. "You watch what I say, you. You going to see, yeah."

Now they had entered the road through the cypress swamp that the Doctor had originally built by laying cypress logs side by side and filling with dirt. He had marked its course by the sound of a hunting horn blown every fifteen minutes by a slave high in a tree with the Doctor's watch, and the line was perfect. But because the cypress beneath was finally turning back into the swamp, Rabelais might have been powering a boat on a bay with gentle swells, so like wavy water was the road. Ahead in the first row of seats someone was laughing very loud.

"Your papa, him, you think he gone want me to feed the stock for ya'll when ya'll go to Cheniere au Tigre, ya'll?" Augustin asked.

"Mais, oui," the boy said, "j'espere."

"Mais, that good, yeah," Augustin said. "Po yi, the older I get the more money I need every year, yeah, me."

All the Mestayers got off at Esther. When they left the bus it was as though they took something else with them, a feeling almost tangible, an exuberance. The boy saw many hundreds of snow and Canada geese in their fallow ricefield just before the curve into Forked Island.

Most of the settlements, the villages, were called *islands* because they were until recently pockets of people in a vast and remote windswept land as flat as the sea. Pine Island like Outside Island, which was inaccessible, and many others were surrounded by a marsh soft and floating. Of course, there was Marsh Island at Southwest Pass, which was really an island but unpopulated. And there were the chenieres such as Grand Cheniere and Cheniere au Tigre and Pecan Island, which were like solid ridges or fingers permanently in the attitude of waves frozen between the marsh and the sea and held together by giant oaks. Grand Cheniere and Pecan Island were inhabited, and Cheniere au Tigre had been a sort of rustic health resort until the new stretch of the Intracoastal Canal was opened and the beach silted up.

After Cow Island and Mouton Cove there was the pontoon bridge with its central grate that sang against the tires. Only Polycarpe Veazey was left on the bus with Leland. The Veazeys were practically the only true cheniere people left. They had always made their home on Pecan Island, in Vermilion Parish the only cheniere connected by road to the mainland. There they farmed and raised cattle and trapped. The Viators and the Veazeys had the bond of livelihoods. The Veazeys were remarkable cattlemen, famous in the area for devising a type of barge to transport their cattle through the canals from forage levee to forage levee.

And the Veazeys still considered the Viators cheniere people from the days of the Doctor. It was a special distinction of mutual respect, practically unspoken. Polycarpe's father nodded seriously in greeting to Leland when he met his son at the mouth of the road to Pine Island.

Alone in the bus with Rabelais, he took the note from the envelope. When he was sure Rabelais was not watching in the mirror, he crumpled the envelope and let it swish from the window. The note was as he had expected. It asked both his parents to sign it for Leland to return. He could not forge their names, and he would have to find some way to explain the torn trousers.

Johnny DesHotels had had his cousin Maurice Hollier, now ready to graduate high school, sign all of his notes since the second grade. His parents thought he must be an exemplary student. Next year, with Maurice off somewhere, probably in the army, they might learn the truth.

Leland's father detested the reputation Uncle Antoine had for fighting. It was as though he thought it shamed them somehow, though all the parish respected Antoine. Or feared him. Or both. Leland's father was not an overly moral or religious person; it was more that he opposed his brother in nearly everything. So if his brother was well known for fighting, Emile was against it and determined to beat any fighting tendency out of Leland. The closer they came to the house the more Leland was afraid.

But as the bus halted in the driveway and Leland got off, his grandfather shouted for him to hurry to the pens. He pointed with his walking stick, shouting, "Hurry, now, hurry to help your father and your uncle. It is the Brahma cow with the banana horn. Her old malady. Hurry."

So the boy had respite. He did not even enter the house. He dropped his books on the steps and ran around the house to the pens and barn. But when he reached the pens, everything was still. The only movement Leland saw was his father perched on the top wide cypress board of the pen, inching painstakingly toward the gate with a cattle prod in his hand. The handle of the prod had long ago been removed and the curved handle of a walking stick substituted. As Leland approached and the maze of boards separated, he saw the cow.

Pain and fear and frustration had made her immobile except for the head which swung quickly between Antoine and Emile, the rubbery banana horns flopping about her eyes. Her eyes were wild dark orbs filled with suspicion and hate. Antoine was in the open gate to the pen, one arm clutching his coat and the other hooked around the corner post to pull him to safety. He was trying to draw her through the gate with the coat.

Dangling behind her, which the boy thought at first was only afterbirth, was her womb. Like a huge, gnarled dark walnut, about the size of a cantaloupe, it dangled from blue-veined, pale, and opaque tissue that stretched no tauter than a knotted curtain through the shredded slit still with two of the hog clamps attached. The boy knew at once what had happened. It had happened before, all of it.

She was a young cow, bred first not two years before. That calf had been stillborn. The next, last spring, was born dead, also, and this time the womb came with it. They had inserted the womb back into her and clamped her shut with the hog clamps, large triangular staples. But they had removed the clamps when she healed. These must mean Antoine had reinserted the womb once before that day and it had already torn loose again.

Leland's father reached the cattle prod to shock her, stretching the metal cylinder with the two brass electrodes toward the dangling womb, the torn slit, the blood, which had dried down her hind quarters to her hocks.

"Mais, no, don't shock her, don't shock her, man, don't shock her, you," his uncle shouted. So intent was Antoine on trying to draw the cow through the gate that the boy was surprised he was even aware of Emile. He still leaned forward, even with the shouting, coat in hand, waving it gently back and forth.

"And you tell me why not," the father said in his certain, irritated way.

"Mais, open your eyes, you," the uncle said, now quietly, in the same tone he used for the nervous young horses he broke each year. "She looks at me," he continued in French, "and it is me she wishes to kill. And I entice her to me. She is afraid, and she wants to kill and to escape, and I entice her to me. She looks at me and she will come. You, my brother, are an unwanted intrusion."

And she charged. She hit the gate with a dull, heavy crack which sent the corner post against the uncle who had pulled quickly to safety as she went past him into the holding pen. The boy jumped into the pen and ran to shut the gate, but he fell and his father's boots thudded past him, and it was his father who shut the gate behind her. Then the boy made a deception. He rolled on the hard earth of the pen, earth churned into roughness by the cleft, pointed hooves of the cattle. This way no one would suspect it was by fighting and not by working that he had torn his trousers.

Now his uncle and his father were running either side of the chute and blocking her forward with pipes between the wide boards and against the posts. The chute, also, was made from cypress and oak boards and was so narrow the full-grown cow could not turn back, though she tried when she saw the steel trap. She arched her neck back and tried to get her front quarters wedged around against the wood.

Now his uncle and his father were readying the trap, his uncle opening the head-catcher and his father opening the squeeze then sliding open the steel gate.

"Leland, she'll fall, cher," his uncle shouted. "She'll fall in the chute."

Leland knew exactly what he meant. For all her ferocity she really didn't have much strength, comparatively. Sometimes when they fell in the chute they seemed to give up something and the boards had to be sawed and the cattle dragged out. And Leland knew what to do, also. He came up quietly on the right side of the chute, slapped her nose around and and thudded the heel of his hand into her rump, shouting, "Huh-hyah-huh!"

She burst into the trap and the men together in one explosive movement shut her in, caught her head and squeezed her tight in a standing position. Now she could not fall. She could not move.

Antoine unfastened the two pipes, which hinged downward to brand. Leland remembered when they took this trap apart while it was new and reversed all its parts. Only Louisiana brands on the right side. Everywhere else they work from the left. So the trap had to be turned. The old trap was destroyed by a bob-tailed bull now on Pine Island.

Then his uncle went to the storeroom where they kept the refrigerator and the medicines. He came out with a syringe and filled it with milky liquid from a squat bottle with a rubber lid. He handed the bottle to the boy.

"Save that up for me, ainh, cher?" he said.

Leland's father had an exasperated expression. Dusk was falling.

"And, mais, tell me what you doing, you," Leland's father said to Antoine.

"Penicillin for her, that's what," his uncle said rather sharply.

"And her calf, where it is?" the boy asked, then, hoping

to distract the attention and relieve the tension. But it intensified it instead.

"Dead in the ditch," his father said, then to the uncle, "You waste, you. You waste everything. She no good, no. Three calves dead, her. Ainh?"

The uncle didn't answer. He gently pushed the bubbles from the syringe. Then he turned to the cow trussed in steel. He slapped the flat part of the rump once and then quickly inserted the needle and injected into the muscle. The boy walked back into the barn to the tiny storeroom, opened the refrigerator and deposited the penicillin amongst the other penicillin bottles and bottles of anthrax vaccine. Stacked on the floor were the two-quart jars of worm medicine for the spring, the malted-milk thick green phenothycine, and the equally thick white fluke wormer they mixed and inserted down each animal's throat with a large, steel applicator that worked on the same principle as a syringe.

When Leland returned his father was leaning on a post and scowling at the uncle who was washing his hands at the spigot. There was a little rack for soap nailed to a post near the faucet. He lathered his hands well, then rinsed the lather from the soap before he put it into the dish. All the while the boy's father stood leaning on the post, arms crossed, scowling.

His uncle had washed a pair of pliers and the plierslike grips for insertion of the hog clamps. Both of these were in a pail of clear cold water he brought with him to the chute. He positioned the pail securely on the boards of the chute and the flat of a supporting post. Then he got the soap and a bucket filled with water from the faucet. He began to gently wash the entire area around the protruding uterus.

"Mais, man, you crazy, you, yeah. Mais, look. Let's just see, us, what Pa-Paw has to say, him, ainh?"

The uncle continued washing away the blood and the brown plastered waste. He lifted the uterus gently to wash beneath it, as gently as Leland had ever seen anything done by a man or a woman either. Soaping slowly in every crevice, every fold before he began to rinse the entire area with clear water from the pail.

"And Pa-Paw, where he at now, him?" the uncle asked quietly, not taking his eyes for an instant from his task. The simple question had a marvelous effect on the boy's father. He unfolded his arms quickly. His mouth opened in a gasp. He started to speak, glanced once at the boy, then shut his mouth and turned to stride away. But he only took one step before he turned and spoke a little shrilly, now red-faced even in the gathering twilight.

"You know what I think, me? Ainh? Ainh? I think we ought to sell her, that's what I think, yeah, me," he said, and as he spoke he leaned toward the uncle, turning his finger back against himself and jabbing it into his own chest.

"Mais, sure, Emile," the uncle said sarcastically, still not looking at him. "Call Benoit the butcher and make hamburger out of her. And that's business to you, ainh?"

Now Leland's father resorted to French. To him, French was also the language of conspiracy.

"No. We shall sell her as a brood cow. Perhaps at the sale in Abbeville. Her coat is brindled and she has a black nose. Ah-ha! The sale at Carencro. They love black noses at Carencro."

Antoine put the pail on the wooden walk and took up the tools before he spoke.

"Mais, you . . . toi fou, you. Mais, you think you gone sell for a brood cow, one with the womb, it, hanging out? Ainh? What you think, you? Ainh? What, you think they got blind men, them, at the sale at Carencro?"

Now Leland's father took on a sly, matter-of-fact look, leaning back as though he were going to take a deep breath and tucking his chin downward slightly. His gut stuck out.

"No, no. But, that was not my intention, to bring her as she is. It is very clear what we should do is remove this disgusting thing and when she does not reproduce in a year or two she'll be sold for hamburger then, and they will take the loss."

Now Antoine looked into his brother's face, a shadow of pain about his eyes. But he said nothing. He turned back to the cow and pried apart the hog clamps. The details of the uterus and the vulva were becoming obscured by the fading of the light, but he worked deftly. He dropped the hog clamps one by one at his feet.

"Save them in the box, ainh?" he said to Leland. "Maybe we use them again, us, ainh?" Then he turned back to the cow. But the father's anger interrupted him. The anger came swiftly, so swiftly it startled Leland and made him afraid. Emile leaned over the chute and jabbed his finger into the opaque tissue which connected the womb.

"Cut that off!" he said.

Leland's uncle lifted his arm quickly to block the jab, as a boxer will ward off blows to his own body. But he missed the block and brought his arm instead away from the chute. He had been lubricating the womb with olive oil, and as he swung his arm over, the oil spurted from the bottle and trailed an arc in the twilight. He dropped the bottle and it landed upright. The boy grabbed for it quickly, but it was not going to spill any more than it had. As Leland grabbed for it, his head bent to the level of his uncle's fist, white at the knuckles. But his uncle never raised it. He stood at the side of the chute, muscles in his jaw quivering, his fist still at his side. And with his left hand he never let go of the uterus he was supporting to take the strain off the connective tissue.

"Me, I'm tired of fooling with her, me?" the boy's father said.

"Yeah? And who's fooling?" the uncle said. The father turned and walked to the house. The uncle and the boy watched him go.

"Mais, you better go too, you, yeah you." Antoine said.

"Me, I'll stay," the boy said.

The uncle shrugged and went back to work. He reinserted the uterus, twisting slightly and feeling for its correct position. The boy was not sure, then, if the cow had groaned or if the swelling movement from deep inside her was such that he imagined her groaning. The uncle had sunk his arm up to the elbow. Once, he delicately began to withdraw, but quickly plunged again deep inside her. Again he twisted. And this time he came out. With the hog clamps, he sealed the slit, feeling to work in the darkness.

Leland helped him clean the tools. Antoine spoke from the darkness at the spigot as he washed his arm and hands. There seemed to be a great weariness in his voice.

"Me, I'm going to back her up the chute," he said. "Mais, pull the chocks, you, ainh?"

The boy went down the line of the chute. He pulled out the pipes and propped them ready for their next use. The uncle was seated on the walk when he returned, hunched wearily forward. He did not move or say anything as the boy gathered up the tools and the box of clamps and rinsed the syringe with water from the spigot. He put the tools and clamps and syringe in the room with the small refrigerator and returned. The uncle was still sitting silently on the walk. The boy rinsed the pail and was returning to the room when Antoine spoke.

"Mais, leave the bucket, you," he said. "I'm going to leave her in the chute at the back where it's wide so she can rest, her. Mais, get you some water in the bucket and put it for her back there, ainh?"

Leland filled the bucket and propped it against one of the posts where she would not be likely to knock it over. Together, they released her from the trap and edged her backward down the chute to the vee where there was room for her to move.

"Now you go get you your supper, you," his uncle said to him, his voice slow and deep with weariness like a phonograph record on the wrong speed. "And bring me my frog light, you, when you done eating. Me, I'm going to stay and watch."

Now it was almost full night. In the course of the long day the rouge line of morning beneath the retreating rain clouds in the east had been replaced with a diffused glow of crimson in the west, dying slowly upward into a clear, cold black night sky dotted with the silver tips of stars. The windows of the house were a bright yellow in the darkness.

He went around to the front of the house, though the cold was creeping through his clothes, and going through the house would have been faster. He picked up his books and entered through the living room. He dreaded facing his mother with the torn trousers, but he could put if off no longer. His father was speaking of Antoine's "waste," that he wasted everything, even himself. That he had no judgment. That he was stubborn and pig-headed.

"Mais, oh Leland, no!" his mother said when she saw him. "Oh, no, Leland. Mais, look at them clothes, them. Oh, Leland, no. Mais, what you do, you?"

"Mais, I was working, me," he said, looking toward his father. The portly man was seated at table, the food pushed away and the coffee cup ringed by a hand. He did not deny Leland had been working. And he did not support him.

"Waste," he said, instead. "Waste everywhere, yeah."

"Pa-Paw, he told me to hurry, him. Soon as I got home from school, me."

His grandfather had gone to bed, but even if he were still up he would not deny it. It was the truth.

"Pa-Paw told me to hurry, him. Mais as soon as Rabelais, him, he dropped me off from school, Pa-Paw said, him, he said to hurry. So me, I run, me. Mais I drop my books and I run, me. I work, too, yes."

"Mais, waste, yeah," his father said at the table. He was pouring whiskey into the coffee. "Mais, haste make waste, yeah."

"Yes, but Leland, cher," his mother said, dropping her hands to her sides then brushing her black hair from her face, "your clothes. Oh, Lord, your good clothes, them. Mais, what I'm going to do, ainh? Oh, Lord. Lord knows you waste what we give you."

And with that it trailed away. There was still the matter of the note. Perhaps in the end they would simply not connect the clothes with the fighting. Though his clothes were already soiled and torn, he changed into his jeans before he went out again to his uncle. He thought it better not to remind them of the torn trousers.

His mother piled a large plate high with food and wrapped it with aluminum foil and told him to take two cans of beer from the refrigerator. His father was saying that the uncle would rather dine with the cattle than his own family. The boy tucked the large square battery of the light into one of his jacket pockets. He held the lamp of the headlight in the hand with the two beers, the elastic headband wrapped around his fingers.

It lit the way to the pens. He shone the strong beam on the ground before him for obstacles and searched the pear tree for raccoons. He found nothing in the tree. The only eyes reflected back at him were those of the cattle, gathered near the pens and barn, watery points of reflected light, dull yet eerie at night, animals always chewing and waiting, subdued yet powerful.

The uncle was at the chute, frantically busy. The uterus had torn loose again.

"Put that stuff down, you," he said sharply. "Mais, hold that light where I can see what I'm doing, me."

Now in the light the ragged edges of the slit were as defined as etched in stone, sharp in red-flesh outline. Clearer, harsher. His uncle's face was pained as it had not been before. In the unrelenting beam of light the lines of his face, too, were etched with shadow. His lips were pulled back from his teeth as though he were straining with a heavy weight, or some intolerable smell. When they finished this time they left her standing in the trap. They loosened the squeeze and let her head out of the grip, and Leland lowered the water bucket through the head catcher.

"Me, I hope she don't go down in the trap, her," Antoine said as he wearily sat on the walk. "Mais, it gone take Benoit's winch to get her out, she go down, yeah."

The food, now, was nearly as cold as the beer. His uncle picked over it without appetite. The boy offered to bring it in to heat, but the uncle declined. Quickly, he drained one can of beer and opened the other, scooting back and leaning on the boards of the chute, his boots on the walk and knees jutting high. He thanked the boy, then, and they didn't speak again.

The boy went back into the house. His mother and father had gone to bed, also. The door to their bedroom was lined in yellow light. Other than that, the only lights were a small one over the stove and one in the bathroom. She had drawn his bath as a reminder but the water had cooled.

She insisted he bathe every night during school. In the trapping camp he only had to wash his face and hands before meals and take a sponge bath in the galvanized tub once a week. He added hot water and inside the bath he began to enjoy the heat. He even pulled the plug for a while to allow for more hot water. He did this at intervals until his father banged on the wall to signal he had used too much water. But by then his body was pink and tingling.

He soaped and rinsed and lay in the water until he no longer felt so hot. Then, before the mirror that reflected no lower than his nipples, he toweled dry his head, face, neck and shoulders, and back. Making sure the door was locked, he took out of the cabinet behind the mirror his uncle's razor. As he opened the mirror door, his reflection slipped away from him and then back again. His uncle and his father used straight razors, but the boy had no fear of them. He'd watched them used often enough and at boucheries he'd even used them to shave the bristles from the hogs after they'd been scalded.

Uncircumcised, his foreskin puckered at the end, giving the appearance of a snail or the bud of a flower. He gripped the foreskin and pulled outward, stretching taut the skin. The reddish hairs were not a quarter-inch long. They had just started coming and still lay flat against his skin so that he moved the edge of the blade against their grain, lifting them at the tips and sliding under to cut them at their bases, exactly as with the bristles of the cochon-de-lait.

When he was done the tender skin looked and felt raw, discolored from the shaving and pimply. It resembled a plucked duck to him. But he felt cleaner, had felt it during the shaving and felt it now. His fingers once again touched him there, baby smooth. He dressed in pajamas for bed.

He was not ready, he was not ready. But he now felt nervous, expectant, as though something were coming. As though something were happening to him without his knowledge that would have a profound effect on him. He could not sleep. He tossed wearily, acutely aware of his smooth but sensitive pubis pressed through the thin pajama fabric against the bed. He was not ready, he was not ready.

And then the words of the hymn came to him and frightened him so that he lay still in the darkness as they ran again and again through his mind. "Oh, Lord, I am not worthy that thou shouldst come to me. But speak the words of comfort, my spirit healed shall be. Then humbly I'll beseech thee, the bridegroom of my soul, no more by sin to grieve Thee or fly Thy sweet control. Oh, mighty eternal spirit. . . ."

In the morning, his uncle had not slept. His bed was undisturbed. The boy and his father saw him as they rounded the barn. He stood above the gray, brindled, and brown-black raised puddle that had been the cow. Now limp with legs folded under her. Neck extended, chin forward. He had bled her with his pocketknife after she fell. The blood was still fresh and unclotted from her shoulder where he'd hit the artery with one swift, small stroke, to the small pool at his feet. The uncle stood over her, looking down as they approached.

"You damn fool, you," the boy's father said as they reached him. "For why you no wait for Benoit, you?"

"Me, I couldn't wait no more," he said softly. His hands were empty. He turned and went into the house.

"He is wasteful and foolish," the boy's father said in French as they watched him go to the house. "He should have waited for Benoit. Well, at least he killed her outside the pens, where the truck would find no difficulty reaching her."

The father continued into the pasture. He did not ask the boy to go with him, and the boy did not even look at him as he went. He was fascinated with the carcass. The womb had torn loose again and again in the night, for the flesh bordering the slit was lacy with tears and the huge walnut of the uterus now bulged farther on the stem of its opaque connective tissue. Antoine had released her from the trap and let her walk clear of the pens when she still had lots of life left in her. And he had killed her standing so that she fell straight down, already dead before her knees finally bent and she went down with head forward.

The boy found the hole just behind the cross-ridge from which grew her horns. He had shot her where the brain extends from the skull to the spine, exactly. The hole was the size of the .41 caliber, and there were tiny black blotches from the powder on the skin. And it was fresh. It had been done while they were dressing or even on the walk from the house. But they hadn't heard the shot and they hadn't seen the deadly little derringer. It was almost as if the uncle had willed the death standing solid with his empty hands hanging at his sides.

II

The bateau was loaded and moored broadside to the heavy oak beams of the dock, secured close yet rocking slightly in the gentle tidal drift. He held the bowline and pulled it even tighter as the old people, first his grandmother and then his grandfather, were helped into the boat. Hands reaching up to them and hands gently helping them downward. Smiles of embarrassment in the cold, pre-dawn darkness. And smiles of eagerness. His own broad smile of eagerness.

The old people went forward into the cabin. The diesels rumbled instantly to deep-throated, growling power. And he tossed the line onto the deck of the hull at his uncle's nodded signal, pushed the nose slanting into the silky blackness of the canal, then ran to unravel the hitches on the huge, anvil-shaped tiedown at the stern. Holding the loose end of the sternline not to have it foul the propellers, he jumped lightly to the gunwale, stepped to the stern deck, and saw his uncle's face in the cabin glow watching to be certain he was securely aboard. Then Antoine turned, pushed the ball-topped throttle levers forward, and they were moving.

Moving forward. Moving into the lush marsh darkness. Cleaving the dark waters and the thick, cold marsh night. He climbed around the cabin to the bow, inching his shoes into the narrow space and holding to the rail on the cabin top. He was cold and he pulled his jacket about him against the biting wind, but he also felt wonderful to be alone in the pull of the wind rushing past his body and the exuberance of going into the marsh for the trapping season. Leaving school, leaving everything behind.

He leaned against the center support of the windshield, sitting with his legs stretched before him on the foredeck. The cabin glow was behind him. Above him were the millions of stars in the clear winter sky. The boat split the outline of the canal, marsh darker at the borders and scrub trees bushy-rounded and reflected in the water. He could not hear above the diesel sound, of course, the voices of the marsh, nor the splash of animals sliding, running to the water in fear or in play. But he knew they were there. Occasionally, his uncle shined the high overhead light from bank to bank, a powerful beam of almost purifying white light that showed every detail starkly.

In this way Antoine ascertained the distance of each bank, but Leland used these opportunities to search for animals, and he saw many of them, or at least what he thought were animals at times. Clearly he saw their eyes reflecting, or the gray-brown of their fur, or sometimes he saw them standing in clear view on the levee, looking curiously and directly into the light.

They took the inland route to the cheniere. The boat weaved through the bayous and canals almost magically, almost as if by feel in the shades of darkness. They passed many trappers' cabins, shacks of scrap lumber and tarpaper with the empty drying racks like tall hitching posts surrounding them on the levees.

But after they had entered the family's marsh, there were no more cabins. The Viators leased no trapping grounds or hunting rights outside the family. Anyone else on their ground was a trespasser. A local trapper could follow wounded game onto the land if he obeyed the marsh proprieties of cleanliness and respect for its owners. But strangers were strictly purged. So many had been sent on over the decades by Viators with shotguns close by if not in their hands, their faces stern enough to make their point without words, that the area around Cheniere au Tigre was the most destitute of human company in the parish. And all shooting, even by the family itself, was forbidden by tradition on the island.

Foxes, rare to the point of nonexistence in the rest of the parish, calmly trotted beside strollers on the island like household dogs. Deer and rabbits often came onto the porch of the house during the night, and the opening and slamming shut of doors in the morning did little more than ripple their coats with nervousness. Even the alligators, in the late spring after their long sleep and the first gorging to fill their skins, crossed the island slowly, with impunity, to bathe in the Gulf's salt water and rid themselves of fresh-water leeches. The squirrels in the huge old hurricane-twisted oaks thrived and chattered and were the island's clowns. One mile long and two-hundred yards wide, the island was one family's truce with nature, a sanctuary for men and beasts together.

When the boat thumped against the hard ground of the cheniere, the boy jumped quickly to the land and made the proper wraps of the bowline to the oak beam sunk into the rich ground. Then he secured the sternline tossed by his father. The diesels quieted. Except for the voices within the cabin of the bateau, the marsh sounds came to him purely, with a message of closeness.

The boy wished to run. He wanted to run straight across the island and see the vastness of the Gulf, hear close-hand the waves upon the silty beaches. He wanted to watch the starlight upon the pitted and sunbleached shells of the cemetery and run the line of oaks to where the ridge finally gave to the marsh and the sea and the hunting and trapping began. Or to climb inside the still-standing hollow giant oak up to the narrow opening at the branching of the limbs, finding the secret crevices of his boyhood. But he stayed and calmed his excitement and helped with the unloading.

The whole cheniere had once been cultivated in fruit trees and vegetable gardens and fields for farming. And among the fruitful plants roamed many beasts, peacefully, even large predators of Africa and Asia imported at tremendous cost through New Orleans in the days of sailing vessels.

Nothing, then, went to waste. Everything was stored and canned and processed and preserved. Even now fruit trees blossomed and bore alone in the most primevally primitive parts of the island, the oranges or lemons or pears or peaches sometimes breaking the branches with their weight only to lie and rot and return to the soil.

Leland had been born on the island. He was the last of the Viators to be born there. Now, the hospital was necessary. The first sounds he had heard were the waves on the beach and wind in the trees and the hollow sounds of the family in the camp. His first smells that of blood and fluid and the kerosene lamp. First sight the unpainted cypress tinted yellow by the lamplight and the sunlight through the window and the limbs of trees.

At the last laden trip to the house from the boat dock, the sun was rising. In winter the sun rose and set exactly on the east-west, land-water line. It rose red, the bare oak branches filigreed against it. And the child quality rose in him too strongly, then, and he whooped and ran the line of trees that were like soldiers on review to the sun, yelling and hearing his voice echo like ghosts. Radiating outward from him the rabbits and squirrels and foxes and deer and muskrat, even otter and mink and nutria scampered, scratching and rattling the brush like accompanying giggles. And the branches of the oaks unlayered as he ran, like lacy veils removed one-by-one from some bright, glowing jewel at once huge and warm. Until he stood at the juncture of beach and marsh and land, and man and life and death. The sun had risen, born of both the grass and the sea, and hovered above him, lighting the waving greens and browns of the marsh and the heaving grays and greens and blues of the sea, and the panting, smiling boy with the rose of morning.

The family worked lightly, easily that morning and into the early afternoon making comfortable their living space. Dust swirled golden in the sunlight from the women's brooms, and the men scrubbed the windows so the sun and the sights around them would be clear. Beds were made, a cloth spread upon the old oak table. The stove and oven were cleaned and oiled and lit. The lamps were checked and cleaned where necessary. They ate a good, hearty meal, one of the last that would not have some game included, at the table with the door wide open to the

sunlight, warm even in the winter chill. The guns were
racked in their cases, oiled inside against the gulf's intruding salt. The boots and the duck and goose calls, the favored lucky hunting coats and hats hung near each indi-
vidual's bed, ready, at hand.

Only then, their living space readied, did the men bring
out from storage the traps and skin stretchers. They piled
them in the sun against the south wall and sat around
them. The boy sat on the floor of the porch with his back
against the overlapping edges of the boards. His uncle sat
at the edge of the porch, one leg extending to the ground
and a post at his back for support. The father was seated
on an upturned five-gallon oil can just barely ample for his
more than ample frame.

"She looks good this year, is this not so?" the boy's father asked the old man. The old man was sharpening
skinning knives. He had a knack for it, a practiced ability
to hold a blade at just the right angle against the whetstone, a perfect little circular stroke and infinite patience.
This produced a blade that seemed to sculpture the skins
away. The rest of them went over the traps, testing the
strength of the springs, then piling them for oiling.

"But, yes. Well, that is to say it should be a good year,"
the old man replied. He had a raspy voice and his teeth
were gone. In these inactive years he had gone slightly to
fat so that his red, shiny cheeks seemed as active in the
talking as his mouth. And he resembled more closely the
boy's father than the uncle, who was lean and somehow
always pale though his skin lined in deep, narrow creases,
was as toughened by the wind as the others. But all of
them had the same eyes, a striking blue, which identified
them, set them apart. Even the dark, common eyes of the
boy's mother and grandmother had not tainted the strain.
"There seems to be much water. The rats are plentiful this
year. And it is my cheerful belief Monsieur Le Cocodrille

has done his work on the nutria before going to bed, and so we may have more muskrat and mink this season."

Nothing pleased the boy's father more than a few words from the old man. Sometimes it seemed it meant little what the old man said. His father beamed brightly in his red face all the same. His uncle, by contrast, smiled little secret smiles only when the old man lied. The lies were easy to recognize. They were not deceptions but narrations hilariously exaggerated. Such as when he caught a crab too big for any pot so built a fence around him and charged admission. The old man told funny true stories, also, about the famous pranks of his youth and young manhood, some of the pranks involving his sons. But the uncle never laughed at these. He listened fondly, but never laughed.

"The pelts of the nutria will bring good money this year," his uncle said.

The old man spat. After a short time, the boy's father spat, also.

"Ah, after all," the old man said, "it is not only a matter of money. The nutria, he is a rogue. He is a spoiler and a waster. He does not belong here."

There was a small flock of sandcranes flying the beach line beyond the roseaux and scrub trees. They flew so effortlessly they seemed to have no weight at all. The boy estimated each almost casual wingbeat sent them into a soft, slow glide of ten, perhaps fifteen, yards.

"Yes," his father said. "He should never have been brought into this marsh. And the McIlhennys should be made to pay."

The flock, in concert, dipped below the scrub and the boy thought they had gone to feed, but they reappeared ten yards farther down and he lost sight of them in the line of oaks.

"The nutria, he will pay for us coming into the marsh,"

the uncle said quietly, his face down, intent upon the trap in his hands, turning its flat metal surfaces in his fingers as if he could feel its defects as well as see them. "More each year he will pay. We shall make our season in his hides this very year and every year to come. He is no longer an outlander."

The boy's father spat contemptuously, but said nothing. The old man sighed, shrugged his shoulders, and turned the blade of the knife against the stone. His tiny circles made little scraping sounds in rhythm.

"Money is in the harvest, the harvest is money," he said, then smiled, then laughed, and, with the thumb of his left hand against the flat of the blade immobilizing it against the stone, he freed his right hand to slap the boy's shoulder stoutly and said quite loudly:

"But I don't want you to stop your murdering of him in the ricefields. Kill him where you see him and leave him for Monsieur Le Cocodrille."

Antoine did not laugh.

"Leland did our rice levees a great service this summer," he said. "It cannot be denied. The nutria is a pest and a nuisance in the ricefields. The holes he makes in the levees cannot be tolerated. But his skins will make our season here."

"And he has made our young Leland a fine shot," the old man said.

"He's a fine shot," said the uncle.

"If the Doctor had told us where our gold was buried we'd have no need of nutrias nor ricefields neither," Leland's father said. Often, the talk of success in the trapping triggered talk of the gold in Emile.

"Pa-Paw," Leland said, "is it possible the Doctor buried gold even here on the cheniere?"

The old man shook his head and smiled. He did not take his eyes from the knife and whetstone, and his cheeks seemed to rise and redden when he smiled, then drop into paleness, slack, when he spoke.

"No, no, my boy," he said. "Not here. Only at Big Woods. Well, I mean that is to say there was a pot at Mont Blanc and an even larger one at Live Oak Plantation by Rose Hill where he lived many years as a boy, I believe. But both of these locations he left us in his will. And why he did not tell us where the Big Woods gold was buried I do not know. He left us all but that. I was just a boy, of course, but he could have told my father, or Uncle René."

"Hainh!" Leland's father said. "I know, me, why he no tell René, him. René, him, he was a waster, yeah. Look how he wasted the rest, ainh? Mais, we lucky, us, to have left the cheniere and don't forget before René, him, he come along the cheniere was a health resort, yeah. Not just a trapping camp. And of course, we still got, us, the vachery at Mont Blanc. But what is that, ainh? I mean, compared to Live Oak. Them that live at Live Oak, them, they rich. Maybe we be rich, too, us, we live us at Live Oak. Who knows?"

Now there was a long silence. Leland had not known his great-great uncle René, of course, but he knew his father hated him. And he knew that the end of the health resort came when the new section of the Intracoastal Canal was opened and the beach silted up. But finally, it was so clear to him that here in the marsh they were rich.

"Well, tomorrow begins the work," he said importantly. And then the others laughed, inexplicably. Even his uncle smiled and glanced at him with merry eyes. Truly, sometimes it was very difficult to understand grown men and women.

But the work did begin that next morning. Early in the first gust of light before sunrise, in the strength of the dependable morning gulf breeze, they set the burn. But they were in the marsh long before daylight, while night still held the marsh in its grip and its night creatures were bold, when sounds have a great significance and a thud against the pirogue or a splash a yard away in that almost complete blackness is like a cymbal or a gong.

They took three pirogues. Antoine first, then his father, then Leland, so that when they stopped to speak the boy went forward to the bow to hear them, the three of them standing with pushpoles anchored in the sunken loam of the narrow channel. But Antoine, in the stern of the pirogue spoke aft in whispers to Emile. The boy, one pirogue length behind, twelve feet too far, could not hear. Even though he was not hunting, Antoine kept a hunter's silence in the marsh. They all did. Especially at night did the marsh seem the place for quiet, but in daylight also. It was something the boy had noticed in all of them. It was the same at the spired church in Abbeville. Then a gusting swirl of wind eddied about them and brought to Leland a few whispered words of a muskrat town.

Antoine would be setting the burn well away from the muskrat town, of course. They wanted to burn only the dead grass tops, to uncover the trails. The water was high. It was nearly perfect for burning. The fire would not reach even the roots of the grass. Not even the chewy stems would be burned. Animals would run in terror, of course, but the actual danger would be little.

The men began nodding to each other, and his father came back to the stern. But he ignored the boy, planted the pole, and pushed immediately. Antoine was already three pirogue lengths ahead in the tiny channel. In all, they were two full hours in the marsh darkness planning the burn. They finished the planning in a shallow lake familiar to the boy. It was where they hunted duck when there was time and they needed meat. Though the darkness obscured them completely, the boy could accurately point to each of the three blind frames, now denuded of last year's camouflage. They pulled the pirogues stern-to-stern, forming a little star in the lake. And the two men and the boy stood close to one another, each leaning on his pushpole as they described the burn to the boy. Antoine had designed a sickle pattern, using the gulf breeze and Bayou Cocodrille to contain the fire. It would burn in upon itself at the mouth and leave them almost an exact disk in which to set their traps to begin the season. They leaned on their poles and discussed this in detail, but hurriedly and in hushed tones.

The boy would go to the mouth of Bayou Cocodrille, then make his way walking the marsh gulfward until he found a good place where he could see in a line both ways. There he would shoot meat. He suggested that he go across the marsh instead of taking the bayou, but the men insisted he go the longer but surer route. The boy knew he would never lose direction in the marsh. But sometimes the channels had a way of disappearing before one's eyes. They were talking time, and in the marsh time depended entirely on circumstance. Shorter was not faster. And certain was only certain for the short length of its changing existence.

"Rabbit, Leland," his uncle said. In French the words for rabbit and bread were so much alike Leland naturally thought of food. "Or a brace of duck if you jump them. But of deer only a small one, young and tender. Please shoot you no old men with rocking chairs on their heads."

"Let the boy shoot himself a prize," his father said.

"No. This is not sport. He can shoot his prize later. This is business and food. It is not cold enough to keep too much venison. A small one, Leland. Do you have fours or twos?"

"Shoot what you want," his father said. Leland said

nothing. He hoped by looking into both of their faces he could remain neutral.

"Twos and fours," he said, then, to his uncle. "And sixes for rabbit and seven-and-one-halfs for duck."

"Good. Good boy. Load only the sevens in the bayou. There should be canvasback sleeping. You will have to shoot for the sound, there is no moon. Lead them well. And on the line kill no more than three or four rabbits. Keep a number two second in the magazine, a six in the chamber. If you see a deer, eject and fire. Do not forget to reload each time you fire at a rabbit. The number two will cut even a marsh rabbit in half."

They laughed at the thought of the foulup. The men wished him luck, and he pointed his pirogue for the channel that led to Bayou Cocodrille. But he did not load the twenty-gauge for the trip down the bayou. He would not even try for duck. He wanted to enjoy his trip down the winding bayou at night alone. Also, shooting at the whistle of wings was tricky, and they would hear the shot and know later if he had missed. But finally he wanted to be exactly positioned when they started the burn. So he poled deliberately, not so much with haste as with determination. With him all the way to the mouth were the occasional sounds of fast-beat, whistling wings and the beauty of the winding old bayou, lighter than the marsh and with the shadows of small trees at its flanks, silky-still in its reflection of the sky broken in flowing ripple lines by the smoothness of his pirogue's path.

He was in a good spot when the first gray light penetrated behind him and, as if on cue, the gulf breeze blew lightly upon him as the first orange flames against the still black marsh leapt skyward. It seemed as though the cold sight of the distant fire made him shiver, but the morning breeze off the gulf was taking power. The fire and the wind grew in unison, seeming to feed one another. But the sun, also, rose swiftly, casting a mantel of light across the flat surface of the marsh and sapping some of the fierceness of the fire.

The fire's sound was a small, popping growl. And the boy could smell it. Not the odor of wood smoke but something less dense, less pleasant. Already there were stirrings in the grass around him.

Now the animals began to bound through the grass toward him and across his shooting line. And his sense of time was lost in a flurry of activity. It seemed minutes, but it could have been an hour before he stood, the fire raging swiftly toward him, the shooting done, and three rabbits and a spike buck deer dead in plain sight. He had missed only once.

Then he saw a mink running in that serpentine gait for the high grass, back curved and flexible and almost not a back of a mammal at all but some form of lizard or snake. It ran toward him for a few strides, shining bright red in the morning sunlight. Leland wondered if the sixes would ruin the coat. It was their best-priced pelt. One would bring enough to make a trapper's daily expenses alone. He did not risk it. A spoiled pelt is a sadness compared to the lovely, laughing gait of the mink through the grass.

Soon, the mink had come so close a shot was no longer even a matter for consideration. Then it stopped, as the first rabbit had done, a twitching of scent in its nostrils. Not the scent of fire, but of man.

Leland stood perfectly still and watched the mink. The fire scent was very strong, now, and he wondered that the mink could separate the odors, untangle, and identify them. Cold soot now drifted down upon them. Then beyond the mink, far down the trail, Leland saw a huge old gray-coated buck deer with a good sixteen points on his rack. He walked with his head arched back so that his neck bowed outward like the fur buyer's paunch. He

seemed indignant at the inconvenience of the fire and re-
fusing to rush out of stubbornness. He strode through the
heavy grass and stopped broadside in Leland's shooting
line.

Leland snicked the six from the shotgun and brought
the number two into the chamber. But he did not even
bring the shotgun to his shoulder. The buck paused. Then
a doe, dainty on slender limbs, skittered nervously across
and into the far grass cover. The buck rotated his deco-
rated head and looked toward Leland then back all the
way around as if he, too, were hunting on that line. Finally, he walked nobly into the far cover behind the doe,
the fire almost on his short, white tail.

The mink, of course, was gone. Leland found the number six in the grass and hurriedly put it into his pocket.
Animals, particularly rabbits, now were bolting, bursting
from the grass everywhere. But Leland had shot enough.
And he was beginning to be spooked by the furiousness of
the fire, himself.

He went directly to the spike buck, small and on its side
as though sleeping. He prodded the animal with the gun-
barrel. They can get you with their feet. Now the roar of
the fire was full in his ears. The smell of smoke was all
around him. Soot flew skyward like bats from a cave or
birds in a frenzy over insects at twilight. Quickly, Leland
took his pocketknife out and bled the deer. He had to
search for the artery, probing with the blade. But the blood
finally came, and Leland elevated the hind quarters and
collected the rabbits.

He could not carry all at once, so he brought the rabbits
to the pirogue first, thudding them into a furry, limp pile
in the bow. Then he went back for the deer. The heat of the
fire was scorching, now. And the flames leapt twenty feet
higher than his head. He could look up and see them
bending to the gulf wind, towering over him. And he was

hurrying, he admitted, because he was afraid. He had even left the gun in the pirogue so that he might return faster.

There were already flies at the bright, red pool of blood against the yellow-white grass at the deer's shoulder. Leland guessed the fire had awakened them, warmed them into an early spring. They buzzed into a cloud as he grabbed the horns and began dragging the deer toward the pirogue. It seemed so far, and the fire so loud and threatening. And once he thought of leaving the deer and going alone to the pirogue to sit in the middle of Bayou Cocodrille until the fire had died. But he dragged on. And the gulf wind did, indeed, blow the fire from him.

In fact, as planned, it blew the fire back upon itself and upon Bayou Cocodrille so that even as Leland loaded the deer and pushpoled out into the bayou the fierce towers of flames had dwindled to a flicker among the blackened and scorched grass stems. As he poled, he could clearly see the trails. And though the air was still thick and gray from the burning, the smell was not so overpowering, and the heat was gone so that he buttoned his hunting jacket against that same gulf wind. He had done well, and before the skinning and dressing had been completed, the smell of the fire on his clothes had a pleasant, familiar odor he was glad to carry with him that whole day.

They had time before the noon meal to work. With a small file, the old man sharpened the cane knives. The flat, broad thin blades shone with sharpness a quarter-inch at the edges. Especially when they first began to cut the bamboo from the grove planted in the west point of the island, the blades sank deep and easily into the cane. Each cane they cut had to be at least nine feet long and pointed sharply on the sturdy ground end. But with the sharp cane knives this was easy to do. One downward slanting stroke severed the bamboo from its roots and gave the cane its point. A baton twirler's twist to bring the top down and one soft swing of the knife trimmed it.

At first Leland's uncle and father went much faster, but Leland eventually got the rhythm of the work, and there was less discrepancy in their efforts. It was work for the entire body. Each part of him had a synchronized duty. Hands for holding and cutting, torso to bob close then straighten for the trim, feet for position in safely cutting, and so on. Once he discovered the rhythm of the work he began to experiment with it. He knew there was much waste in his efforts, for though the two men did the same thing their movements were fluid and calm and they still went much faster, but Leland was probing for that system. Much is lost in learning.

It was Leland's father who stopped work first. Until Emile's cane knife ceased falling, Leland had become unaware of the sounds of the knives against the cane. Then he became acutely aware of his and his uncle's knives, the quick, rhythmical chop, chop, chop.

"We have enough cane for the first line," Emile said. "Let's set the line and have furs to dry by nightfall."

"This idea is very good," his uncle agreed. "Two of us together should set each line so we will have two who know where each trap is waiting."

The men wiped sweat from their foreheads with their coat sleeves. Though it was cold and the gulf breeze was brisk, the work had heated them. Leland said nothing. He bent again to the cutting. They'd need at least twice the amount to be certain. The men left their knives in full view, so that the blades would be exposed to easy sight and not hazards. Leland continued cutting into the grove. He enjoyed the sappy, sweet smell of the new-cut cane.

The grove had been planted by an ancestor. Perhaps the

Doctor. No one, not even Leland's grandfather was certain who had sunk the first bamboo into the soil of the island. But it was a long time ago, and Viators had been cutting cane from the grove ever since. The bamboo was perfect for marking the traps. Standing singly among the native roseaux and grass, it was easily seen by any practiced eye.

Leland had noticed where men trapped on the edges of the marsh, near the ricefields, where one could go to town each night if one cared, they sometimes tied little ribbons, bright ribbons of red and orange, to the poles. He considered this more a mark of incompetence in the trapper than anything else. Anyone who could not separate at a glance a cane native to Japan and one that grows naturally in the marsh of Louisiana had no business trapping at all, he believed. Indeed, everyone in the family was amused at the sight of the little ribbons in the marsh of other trappers.

He was tiring, now, and he pushed his body on into the fatigue. This was his season for work. The sooner he pushed his body into the fatigue and emerged through the soreness on the other side, the sooner he could settle to his destiny in comfort. The first pile of cane grew high enough and he started another. Now the movements were smoother. He took pride in the economical swing of the cane knife. The muscles between his thumb and forefinger on his right hand, a webbing of muscles, tired greatly and began to cramp. He paused briefly to knead away the cramp, then continued.

Suddenly, fear coursing through him, his body involuntarily and uncontrollably reeled and ran two steps before he fully realized he had just cut into the nest of snakes. Cottonmouths, young and old. Coiled tightly about one another. They writhed in the broken stupor of hibernation and fear and the electric pain of their marvelous nervous systems against the unconscious stroke of the knife that had discovered them, severed one thick dark body at the mid-point, and cut into several others, leaving wide, pink, and meaty gashes in the scale-patterned flesh.

Slowly, or at least more slowly than in summer hunting swiftness, two or three were attempting to wind back among the cane stalks. So Leland forced himself immediately back and swung, now, in quick staccato strokes against the snakes. White mouths barbed with long, venomous, quite dangerous fangs opened wide in real threat. But Leland severed heads from bodies when he got the chance and chopped anywhere he could when he did not. He killed them all. Seven of them. Their bodies writhed long after they were dead, and he scooped them up with the flat of his knife blade and tossed them high upon the solid ground behind him so that they, too, like the other cane knives, would not be nuisances to his work, frightening him anew each time he happened to turn and see them.

So the blade was smeared with blood as it bit back into the grove of bamboo. Leland was at first fascinated with the blood rubbing onto the stems as the blade cut tightly into the stalks, white-green thinly smeared with red. But then the work cleaned the blade, and he was again mesmerized by the rhythm of the work itself. He was absorbed by the building fatigue and the sounds of the cane-knife chopping and the slightly mewing sound of the gulf breeze in the tops of the uncut bamboo, fluttering the long, pointed leaves.

"I'm glad I came." The words startled Leland almost as much as the snakes had frightened him. His grandfather was seated on the rise above him. Leland looked back at him across a wide expanse of severed, pointed bamboo roots. "I think if it were not for dinner you might cut your way through the bamboo and into the marsh grass and by supper have cut a swath all the way to Forked Island."

The old man seemed pleased and happy.

"You found some playmates in the cane, I see."

"Yes," Leland said, "they frightened me and I killed them."

His grandfather felt it a waste of time to kill snakes, there were so many of them. And because of the tradition of no shooting on the island, Leland felt self-conscious about killing even deadly cottonmouths with his caneknife.

"It is a pity we cannot kill them all," his grandfather said, surprisingly. "Come, let's eat. The boys are late. No need for all of us to eat cold food."

Then the old man swung awkwardly to his feet and walked to the large old house without looking back. But Leland bundled the two piles and shoved the blades safely deep between the stalks of one of the piles before he followed. He carried the bundle with the knives with him. He could smell the aromas of rabbit and venison, but he went back for the second bundle before he washed for the noon meal. His mother and grandmother could cook the same rabbit a dozen different ways and each morsel would taste delicious and different from the others. But Leland would not feel right sitting to the meal without first completing the work. And he wanted the two men to see the large amount of cane he'd cut when they returned. He had cut enough for the entire season, enough even for another line of traps.

The family had just seated themselves when the men emerged from the marsh. They were exuberant about the burn. Already, green chutes were appearing in the grass. And they'd seen many rats, muskrat as well as nutria. And signs of otter and more mink than in recent years. It would be a good season. They'd seen lots of raccoons and signs of more, but they would be no nuisance. The Viators had never trapped raccoons. And since the raccoon is very intelligent, he rarely fouled up their traps with his flesh.

That afternoon the brothers brought in many skins. Leland set himself immediately to scraping. He took his father's scraping bench, stretching the sleevelike hides down the contoured board that rose between his knees and drawing the scraping tool down the white undersurface. Most trappers used knife blades, but Leland's ancestor the Doctor had invented a tool much like a rasp, which took the flesh effectively from the skins and did not cut into and ruin the pelts. Indeed, they still used tools he made at the old brick forge now crumbling near the graveyard.

Leland worked as swiftly as he could without sacrificing efficiency. With the nutria pelts, especially, it was necessary to take care. The nutria flesh will cling to the hide, little bits to blacken and stink and rot the pelt. The muskrat, though, leaves a clean pelt. It is necessary only to remove that thin layer, almost a membrane, from the skin. The otter and mink are so special and valuable that Leland considered each pelt unique. Often, he would run his tired hand inside the sleeve to feel the softness of the coat. Otters were such lovely animals, pleasure-giving to watch in play. And, of course, they were great killers of snakes. So even with the high price paid for their pelts, it was not joyous to take them lifeless from the trap. Leland worked almost lovingly with the skins, it was so necessary not to waste.

The two scraping benches faced one another. At first Leland was aware of his uncle's progress at the other bench and gauged himself against it. But then he lost himself in his own work and forgot his uncle's swiftness and economy of movement. His uncle finished long before Leland, the unscraped pile having flowed smoothly and completely into the scraped one. Then, still at the scraping bench, he stretched the hides on the oval wire stretchers.

When the time came for Leland's chores, his father took

over the scraping, and it felt good to unkink his muscles and move around a bit. But he returned immediately after his chores were done and noted his father had not made much progress. In the west, across the gulf, the sky was a pale golden with the last of day. His uncle brough the gasoline lantern and set it on the highest outside step. It was as bright as an electric light, and Leland continued. He had only a dozen or so pelts to go. The crash of the wire stretchers startled him. His uncle smiled down at him.

"Do you want me to start stretching them?" Antoine asked.

"No," Leland said and did not look at his uncle again. He heard him enter the house and shut the door. Now he was alone outside with the hiss of the gasoline lantern and the marsh sounds and the shush of the scraper against the hides.

When he had finally finished scraping and stretching the hides he was very tired. The drying shed already smelled rank when he entered. Not even the smell of kerosene in the heater could cover this day-one smell of the hides. But he was pleased he did not have to stand on tiptoes this year to hang the rings of the stretchers on the nails of the highest cross pieces. Last season he could barely reach them. This year it was quite easy.

Inside the big house they had waited supper for him. The men were drinking coffee, and the food was still steaming on the table. But his appetite was not adequate for the meal. His arms were numb, and it seemed an effort to raise the fork to his mouth. The muscles around his shoulders and upper arms felt swollen, as though wasps had stung them. After the meal the men and women talked happily. It had been a good day, a good start. They talked of other good starts, and poor ones. But Leland did not care for the conversation. He went to his bed, left his clothes where they fell in a kind of pool around his feet, and fell into bed in long underwear and socks, folding himself into the covers even as he went to sleep. He did not dream and he slept through breakfast.

The sun was full bright, and his uncle and father had left for the traplines before he awoke. He awoke swiftly, but groggily, and his mother and grandmother thought it great sport he did not remember how they all tried to wake him earlier with the men. He was angry as he dressed. His grandfather was even doing Leland's chores. Leland took them over immediately, without eating, and the old man left him for coffee with the women. The muscles of his stomach and back were sore, and his calves ached when he bent his feet upward, stretching the large muscles behind. His arms felt more tight than sore, but there were small blisters on his hands where the Doctor's scraper had rubbed.

When the skins came in that mid-morning, though, he devised a way of holding the scraper that did not irritate the blisters. Leland and Antoine worked silently, the piles on one side of their benches diminishing into piles on the other side freshly scraped. Each skin dropped soundlessly. The sound of the scraper against the flesh side of the pelts was almost hypnotic. Shush, shush, shush. And the easy flow of the tool in a path that left pure skin. One could lose sense of time, keeping only mindful of the skins flowing from one side of the bench to another.

That afternoon, while the men were running the lines, he set a trotline in the canal landward of the island. He took the rolled line, already set with hooks and spaced properly, from the kit stowed forward in the cabin of the bateau and baited it with bits of the entrails from the rabbits and deer. The entrails had been tossed into the marsh in the sun where decomposition would be swifter and the return to marsh would be that much sooner. Maggots were already thriving. He also used several of the large, white ones to bait the line.

He took a pirogue and several of the bamboo poles he'd cut the day before and set the line not across the canal where it would be a hazard, but parallel to the east levee a few feet out and at the correct depth. Then he rested in the pirogue, lying flat on the bottom as it drifted free, enjoying the feeling of buoyancy, the slight rocking of the water, the sounds of the marsh around him and the warmth of the sun through his jacket and hunting pants and long underwear. With the chill wind broken by the marsh grass, the sun was quite warm and pleasant. He could easily have slept, but he did not allow it. Instead he identified the sounds of the marsh with the animal that made it, lazily picturing each animal in his mind. He roused himself when it was time for the men to return with the furs.

And so it went. The pattern established itself. The trotline yielded catfish, some perch, and now and then a buffalofish or two. He added the cleaning and scaling to his other chores and sat at the scraping bench, now, twice a day without interruption.

The furs in the drying shed amassed, the layered racks hanging thick and brown as a forest. Each day they circulated the older, better-cured hides to the outside racks to dry in the sun, piling them at night on the floor of the tarpaper shed. Soon, the buyer would come to empty their store and they would gather it full again. It was a fine season, many rats. His hands callused over the blisters and no longer bothered him. The soreness yielded to hardness, and he no longer fell so exhaustedly asleep or needed to be awakened in the morning. He and his father and his uncle rose silently in the darkness and dressed—dipping, rounded shapes and shadows in the winter-closed house, silently in unison to pull on pants and boots, to stretch into shirts and coats. And it was Leland who lit the lamps and the stove and oven while the men outside readied themselves for the first trap run each day. Then the time to go into town for mass had come, and he knew he would have to confront his mother because he did not want to leave the marsh.

"I want to run the traps . . . I need to run the traps to-day . . . we need for me to run the traps today," he stammered finally at breakfast.

"And why?" his father calmly, almost trivially, asked. *Et pourquoi?* Without so much as looking up from his biscuit with butter and pear preserves.

"Because I want to work instead of going to town tomorrow," he said, knowing that "ville" would not be heard but "eglise" heard instead, and appropriately so.

To his astonishment, his grandmother said nothing. His uncle, he had known, would say nothing, but that his grandmother would remain silent on the subject of religion was unthinkable. Yet, his mother did not disappoint him. Shock, open-mouthed. Drop the cleaning cloth. Then the onslaught of words.

"No, no, Leland. Oh, no," she said. "Not Godless. I will not have you lose your God. No, no. A boy needs mass, to keep him close to the Holy Spirit. To hold Him in his heart. Close to the Good Lord, to Jesus."

His grandmother continued to the table with the platter of marinated venison fried crisp, brown, and sizzling. But she deposited it on the bare wood of the table and went back to the stove, and took a rag in makework, rubbing the polished and unsoiled handles. Leland took heart.

"I will say my prayers, night and morning as always and a special prayer at the time of the mass," he said. "I shall pause while I am working like the picture of *The Angelus,* which Sister shows us at school. She says it tells perfectly the example God expects from those who toil. 'They pause in their work but do not falter,' she says."

Antoine poured another cup of coffee and lit a cigarette from Emile's pack on the table. It was rare for him to smoke. But he said nothing. Now he puffed nervously. The smoke from the cigarette curled upward in blue, flowing lines and tight little swirls. When he puffed he blew the smoke out hurriedly, as though he did not really take it into his body, and he looked through the glassed upper half of the door as though he were transporting himself outside.

"The good nuns . . . it is true . . ." his mother said falteringly. "We send you to them for guidance . . . It is true. But you must attend mass."

His grandfather, though, was cheerful. He smiled toothless and red-cheeked.

"A man must work," he said. And Leland knew he had won.

"We will ask the priest tomorrow, after mass," his father said. "We will ask Monseigneur Fuselier. He is a hunter. We shall ask him. Perhaps we will have him here to hunt. What is the name of that picture?"

His grandmother came to him and ladled venison and hotcakes into his plate. Leland was suddenly quite hungry. His uncle went to the door and looked through the glass at the coming morning. The smoke seemed to drift from his head.

"*The Angelus*," Leland said. "A man and some women working in a field. It looks like sugarcane, but they carry no cane knives. The man holds his hat and they kneel. There is a church in the background. They pray amid their work."

"To cut the cane is bad work," the old man said. "Sugar is sweet, but the work is sour. Thank God we have the

Negroes." He was still quite cheerful. Perhaps it was because they were going into town.

"Then we will ask the priest," his mother said with determination.

"For tomorrow, though, until we hear from the priest, he stays here," his father said. "Antoine will need help with the work. The boy is big enough to help him."

Now Antoine turned swiftly from the door and crushed out his cigarette among the eggs still untouched on his plate. Leland had never seen him, or anyone else in their family do that. It was like a desecration.

"If he works like a man, he is a man," his uncle said simply, with a touch of the tone of warning and even of bitterness. "There is no other way. This afternoon I will show you the lines."

Now when Leland's father spoke it was with the brutal self-assuredness of a businessman making the only deal possible, everything totally in his favor, and with the calmly insulting tone of a man who is throwing something useless away.

"Show him this morning," he said. "Why not? I will load the bateau."

Emile did not look up from yet another biscuit and more pear preserves, so he did not see the harshness of his brother's eyes.

Leland and his uncle were in the marsh, halfway through the first line, when they saw the cabin roof of the bateau across the tops of the grass. From where they picked their way from pole to pole across the floating marsh, the cabin roof seemed to slide on its own, disconnected and floating on the grass, itself. Leland paused to watch it out of sight at the edge of the roseaux, and so he had to hurry after his uncle who had continued in his swift, sure dance across the trembling terrain.

He had reached the next nutria and killed him with that short, swift, deadly blow of his forked walking stick and had made the deft stroke with his narrow, sharp skinning blade before Leland reached him. His boot on the nutria's two black webbed hind feet, holding them fast to the soft loam, he pulled upward with a fluid motion and the inside-out fur peeled from the nude pink flesh with the hollow sound of adhesive tape being stripped from a roll. The body seemed to reach upward through the skin until it fell released to the mud. Grasping the foot-long, hairless tail, his uncle spun the carcass and sent it sailing into the grass, and in the same motion he was already walking so that Leland had to hurry again to keep up.

"Come on," Antoine said. "It's double work this morning. I'll show you both lines. Unless I miss my guess you'll need to know Emile's line, also. Hurry! In the traps they are suffering. To let them suffer is the only sin."

Leland followed him through both lines, but through his father's line he was able to keep up. The traps were poorly placed and Antoine repositioned them. They had been set almost surgically precise on line, without much regard for the trails the animals had made. Only where walking in the marsh was difficult were the traps out of line, skirting the bad places. Sometimes in repositioning a trap his uncle angrily jammed the anchor-marker pole deep into the marsh. But the killing and skinning was as swift. One-by-one the pink, denuded carcasses flew tossed to either side of the line, far into the marsh. Except for the last animal. It was a nutria, caught by its left hind leg.

His uncle was ahead of him two paces but stopped so that Leland came up to his side, and the two of them looked down on the nutria hissing in anger, pain, and fear. The trap had cut through the skin, and the meat around the smooth black clamps was red and swollen.

"Kill him," his uncle said.

Leland raised his stick and struck. But the blow glanced off the head and the nutria merely folded himself down against the marsh, accentuating the natural hunch of his spine, hissing low in pain.

"Kill him!" his uncle said again. "You're not playing games here. For games you stay at the camp with the old man and the women, or at the school with the nuns. This is not a playground! This is work, serious work. Kill him quickly. He is suffering."

This time when Leland brought down the stick he thought it was one of the forks of the seasoned oak that cracked, but it was the animal's skull. There was a shiver, flexed, of the rat's long, thick body and he was dead. Leland skinned him out, not making the proper cuts at first, but compensating with another slash so that the long sliver of white, fibrous flesh ceased flowing with the hide. Then the skin came smoothly free, all the way to the cuts at the nose and four orange protruding teeth.

"It has been a good morning," his uncle said happily as they walked in with the furs. "Long, though, but good. But good. And that line, now, will yield better, placed now as it is. And the work this afternoon, it will go much faster with both of us working each a line. But in the matter of dinner, who shall cook, you or I? Ainh? I'll cook. This day you have learned enough. And the food one must not take chances with, food for strength."

There had been just enough humor in his voice to negate tactlessness, and Leland was looking forward to efficiency at the stove, for he had never seen or heard of his uncle cooking, and he thought this could be considered a test whether efficiency was instinctive. But the others had left a full meal on the kerosene stove. Until they returned the next evening, however, Leland was not disappointed.

They ate well, Antoine cooking calmly and Leland washing afterward. And the work went smoothly. He ran his father's line that afternoon and in the morning.

Returning, his father seemed very pleased. When he cleared his throat and began to talk of the priest, Leland's uncle for the second time of the season lit a cigarette with one of the large matches from the holder on the wall by the stove, but walked out into the cold without his coat. Leland's father sipped his coffee as the door creaked and squealed on its spring and hinges then banged shut.

"I did not speak to the monseigneur. He was hunting as I expected. Perhaps at some place like the Florence Club below Gueydan," he said chuckling. "But I spoke to that young priest Father Fontenot. A very bright young man. And pious, too, very holy." Leland's mother was taking something from the stove and his father now glanced quickly at her. "Anyway, he said you have learned your lessons from the good sisters very well, particularly that of the beauty and sanctity of work. He says, of course, that during the nontrapping months you should make every effort not to interrupt your nine First Fridays . . ."

Now his mother came quickly to the table and sat. Absently, she pulled at the cleaning rag in her hands.

"And your daily prayers," she said, looking worriedly into Leland's face. "And night prayers, too. And the rosary. He said you must say the rosary."

"Yes, yes. The rosary," Leland's father said, irritated. "All of that, all of that. We do not . . . we will not have you lose touch with your religion, of course. But of course if it were not for this desire to insure your soul . . . to insure that your soul would have . . . would have nourishment, then we would not go to the expense of sending you to the Catholic school."

Now Leland's grandfather cut in very joyful.

"Hainh! Fifteen minutes with a priest and he talks as

though he were in the priesthood, himself, is this not so?"

"And why not?" Leland's grandmother said. "He bears the word of God from one of the priests He sent to us. I would that God would give us a priest for our family, out of our very blood."

"Our blood, a priest? Hainh!" the old man said. "Priests think too much. It is a disease. Caused by lack of richness to the blood. No women, I believe."

"Hush, you!" the old woman said, gesturing slightly with a hand of thick, scarred fingers toward Leland, turning the attention again to Leland so that his father cleared his throat regally in preparation for speaking with authority. The old man poured whiskey into his coffee. He was the only one allowed to drink during the season. Drunken trappers are an abomination.

"The priest said that especially with a person of your youthful purity . . . that was how he said it, 'youthful purity.' . . . This young priest speaks the other French, but he speaks it well and is easily understood."

"Hainh!" the old man said, but said no more, because Leland's mother slapped the table in his direction. Leland could not tell if the "hainh" was for the priest's French or for Leland's purity.

"Nonetheless," his father continued, "the priest said that your understanding of the holy picture is wise beyond your years and that you do not have to go to mass as long as you remain in the marsh to work."

"As a man is excused from mass in order to work," Leland said.

"Well, yes, for work," Leland's father said after a pause.

"Hainh! I would like to know what a priest thinks he knows of work," the old man said, then. "With him sitting in his big free house in town."

"And what do you know of the priest's work?" the grandmother argued. "A priest works hard, works sad work. He visits the sick and the dying. The imprisoned. Sad work."

"Of course sad work," the old man said. "The sick and imprisoned and the dead put no money in the collection basket. Sad work indeed."

It was a good place to end a tense conversation, and Leland let it end there. After a while his uncle came in and took his coffee. No one ever mentioned the prayers again. Almost immediately, he began running his father's trapline more often than did his father, who proved adept at designing work on the island, sometimes running the trotline though Leland still did the cleaning and scaling. Between runs one day his uncle built from cypress boards torn from the ruined walls of the old hotel a new scraping bench, fitting the height and the contour of the bench to Leland's body like a good saddle so that sometimes during the long hours scraping hides he remembered the free, flowing feel of a horse beneath him.

By the time the fur buyer came, the drying shed was packed and the racks outside hung heavy, and even the bent nails in the ceiling of the porch hung with hides like short, furry sleeves thicker than Christmas tree ornaments. The fur buyer was a large fat man with a moustache who carried a large pistol on his hip and large amounts of cash in his pockets. And he carried whiskey and traded jokes, both designed to lubricate the dealing. He poured the whiskey into his coffee and offered it to the men whenever they discussed price. If the price proved difficult, he told a joke or asked that a joke be told.

Jokes and whiskey in the marsh were the province of the old man. This was understood. What the buyer did not understand was that according to family tradition, as opposed to the traditions of other families of the marsh, the old man had long ago given up responsibility in business matters. He was free to drink and tell jokes without worry. The fat man kept shifting his bulk in the chair and drinking whiskey-laced coffee and trading jokes with the grandfather, each time shifting his gun around the poles of the chairback and growing more weary as the old man glowed brighter and brighter with the humor and the free strong drink. Finally the advantage the buyer had hoped for had turned.

The buyer made an offer that the old man pretended to consider out of politeness but refused out of established form. The first offer is always refused. After more whiskey and another joke came a second offer, this one much more liberal. Antoine and Leland were seated on the floor, leaning against the wall. From his chair at the table with the buyer and the old man, Leland's father looked at Antoine, who slowly and insignificantly raised his hands and placed them on his knees. The old man paused, now not out of politeness but to allow time for the unspoken considerations, then refused.

The buyer had offered round figures. Now Leland's father suggested they consider each fur separately. There were a mink and an otter fur on the the table, gleaming in different shades of brown-red in the sun through the window, the otter pelt also glistening from the isolated black-tipped hairs. The buyer had been stroking the pelts absently, but now he refused to deal with each pelt exclusively, a time-consuming ordeal, and took his fingers from the hides. At this, Antoine rose, stripped the furs to the floor, went to the stove and poured another cup of strong black coffee, then returned to his seat beside Leland, the furs between them.

The buyer poured whiskey into the old man's cup but did not offer it to the others. The next offer must be a good one. The old man now began telling another joke. He was anxious that the deal not be terminated yet. It was one of the old man's flexible stories, like an accordion, and he played it and drew it out through yet another drink before the buyer made another offer.

This time Antoine rubbed the bridge of his long, thin nose all the way from the eyes to the tip, lightly and slowly. Emile knocked on the table as though he were summoning coffee from a slave, and the old man accepted the deal after a pause during which Leland's mother brought Emile coffee to complete the deception. By now the old man was obviously drunk. His face was red with a sheen. His eyes were curved with mirth, and it was clear the world was revolving around him for his pleasure, alone, a panorama of color and sound. He was famous among families of the marsh for his ability to make deals through whiskey fogs. He came with them to load the furs and had to be helped down the stairs and to the edge of the canal where he teetered slightly but did not fall in.

In the stern of the buyer's boat was a sack of number two steel traps. Antoine moved them aside to stack the furs and hefted the sack as he did, counting the traps by weight.

"Mais, for who them traps?" he asked when they were through with loading the furs.

"I brought them for François DesHotels," the buyer said. "But his season is so bad he doesn't want them. Not many trappers are having a season like yours."

"Mais, for them how much you want, you?" Antoine asked.

The buyer set a price and Antoine did not quibble.

"His money give the man," Antoine said to the old man. The buyer had given the thick roll of bills to Leland's grandfather and he had put it into the pocket of his shirt. Now the old man handed the money to Antoine who counted out the correct amount and gave the balance back to him. He paid the buyer who counted the money tactlessly and got into the boat.

"Let me ask you this," he said from the boat. "Are you sure ya'll can use all those traps?"

"The rats, we got plenty," Antoine said. "And we got another trapper, us, in the marsh this year."

He did not look at Leland when he said it, but Leland knew what he meant, and he did not have to look at his father to know something was wrong, something was jolted in him. Leland could feel the tension exuding from the man like heat.

"Well, look here," the buyer said, oblivious of the subtle but powerful feelings between the brothers, "I'm buying meat this year. I got a solid price I offer everybody and I don't dicker. A nickel a pound, dressed, no heads, no feet, no tail. Nickel a pound. You can pick up some change. Not many in the marsh this year are having the season ya'll are having. Think about it. Fresh, though. Fresh, not spoiled stuff. See you."

And he started the motors without a reply. They stood on the bank and watched with amusement and waved goodbye when he had finally gotten the boat around, stirring mud at the stern and jamming the bank with the bow. When the buyer's boat was around the first bend, the old man removed the money from his shirt pocket and gave it to Emile. He shook his head and smiled.

"Po, yi. That was hard work for an old man," he said, and Leland knew, then, that he had not sensed what must be between the two brothers and Leland only.

The old man walked ahead of them toward the house and Leland carried the traps. His father had his head down and his hands jammed in his pockets. The three of them walked slowly, more slowly than the old man who swayed around the corner of the house and out of sight. Immediately the words came as whispered shouts, breath held too long suddenly expired with a hiss.

"Mais, how come you do that, you? Ainh? And the stranger, in front of him, too, you, ainh? What with Pa-Paw half-drunk. Ainh? Why? Ainh?"

"The traps were there. Leland traps like a man. There are many rats."

Speaking, his uncle seemed calm, almost amused. Leland was afraid, but his uncle stood relaxed, quiet, hands hanging easy at his sides. Nothing was directed toward Leland. It was as if Leland did not exist, or existed simply as a symbol. And the most frightening thing for him was that he was content that the action revolve without him. The silent fury put a laxness in him, a weakness that actually made the traps sag lower. He could not act. He did not understand. But what he felt was not confusion.

"It is *my* decision," Emile said, resorting to French.

"Non," his brother said so quiet and forceful, almost with pity.

Now Emile paused and the tension built like the clarity of air in an electrical storm.

"Is he not my son?!" he said, challenging.

Now it was Antoine who hesitated. "He belongs to the family," he finally said, first dropping his eyes to the soil of the cheniere then shifting them to the marsh.

Now Emile had his hands out of his pockets and quickly he grabbed Antoine's shirt, leaning his bulk into the slender man and shoving him against the house.

"You *know* you are to say nothing. Nothing!"

Antoine had not resisted. This had encouraged Emile, and so he jerked back his right fist to strike his brother. Leland dropped the sack of traps, grappled with the arm, and was flung to the ground. But as Leland was shoved, Antoine, with a great burst of strength, freed himself and caught the fist before the punch got moving, holding, stifling the blow. Now he shoved his brother backward, staggering him and breaking contact. Emile stood before him, his fist still jerking up and settling down as though he were building energy for some great motion, one leg forward, threatening to run toward his brother with fury. But Antoine did not move. He did not assume a fighting stance.

"That part is over," Antoine said. "The hitting is done with. He's no more baby to beat down."

"*You* tell *me*?" his father said.

"He'll tell you himself soon enough," Antoine said. "That part is over."

But Leland knew of nothing to say, felt like saying nothing. His father scarcely glanced at him as he moved skittering around the house, arms outward and crooked, a bit like a sand crab. Antoine came to him and helped him up.

"Come on," he said. "Don't worry."

But Leland was afraid as they entered the house. He expected some sort of argument as they entered, but Emile sat at the table, silently looking into his coffee cup. Antoine went to the stove and poured his cup full. Then he stood near the table, took one sip and seemed very pleased as he glanced at Leland's mother and then spoke.

"Well," he said, "the family of Viator has yet another trapper, full-fledged and competent. Now our profits go up and are divided by yet another share. Is this not the way?"

"Yes, yes," the old man said, "this is the way."

His mother's eyes were sad, but she nodded her approval and glanced furtively at Antoine. His grandmother's voice was soft as she agreed. Emile said nothing. Antoine sat at the table across from him and, as Emile looked up, two sets of eyes ice-blue and veiled of emotion locked upon one another viciously for an instant.

"And what say you?" Antoine asked.

"He's just a boy," Emile said, then dropped his gaze, looked at nothing. "I want him a little longer."

"He works," Antoine said. "He does the same work. We were no older than he is now."

"That is correct. That is correct," the old man said. "Nor older than was I. And we had no motors for our boats. In the winter . . ."

"A full worker's share," Antoine said.

"He is too young for such money," Emile said. "Things are not as they were for us."

"Then we shall put it in the bank for him," his mother said, almost rushing to the table. She was crying. "He'll need it someday. To build a house. To . . . to . . ."

"He will always have a house," the old man said.

"Our house," Antoine said. Now Emile looked at him more harshly and more bitterly than he had looked at his brother in the yard when he had tried to strike him.

"Then perhaps the university," his mother said. "Must Viators forever live in the marsh and trap rats?"

"Yes, well, he is free, of course, as are all Viators," the old man said. "But from this day forward all of his expenses must come out of his share. That is the way."

"Good," Emile said.

"And I think it is proper to save the money for him," the old man continued, quite rational despite the drinking bout which still colored his face red. "But no man works so hard for very long without some reward. We must triple his allowance, though now it is of course a share to an equal and not a gift."

"Is everyone agreed?" Antoine asked quickly. Only Leland and Emile remained silent.

"Are you agreed?" Antoine asked his brother softly. "Or is all of that . . ." He gestured with a sweep of his hand toward the old man ". . . for nothing?"

"Agreed," Emile said with thickness.

"Agreed?" Antoine asked Leland happily.

"Ainh?" Leland said startled. "Mais, but of course," he said. The tension in the house broke with laughter and Emile walking out. His uncle and his grandfather now shook his hand in turn.

"Come," Antoine said. "Let us now ready the traps. You haven't enough new ones for a full line. We'll have to select from the best which are left from the old ones."

Antoine led him from the house to the ruins of the old hotel where traps and tools were stored in the two or three remaining rooms. The yellow afternoon sunlight streamed through paneless windows, and the musty odor of days dead and gone came to them as they entered. A rotted mattress of Spanish moss half-pulled from a rusted iron bed was a home for field mice. Together they squatted on the floor and went through the traps, trying the spring-arms for strength, examining the central trigger-plate and checking generally for rust on each trap, its chain and ring.

"Those weaker ones you must place on the muskrat trails," his uncle said. "You know the difference, how to recognize it?"

"Yes."

"The muskrat, he is not so stupid as the nutria, who sometimes seems to want to step into a trap just because it is there. For the muskrat, concealment is sometimes necessary. After a while, you will begin to see things as he sees them and to know what he does not see. Think always that he is so much smaller than you. And he cannot think, not in the ways we do, but he has gifts we have lost with all our comforts. Do not forget this. But the ability to understand and see the way he does, it will come. This comes with experience, unexplained. But always be careful that there is nothing in your method that will foul your own snare. Do you understand?"

"Yes."

"Good. Well, you have run our lines. Do you now want me to help you set yours?"

"No," he said. "I want to set my own. I have chosen a wide circle off the hunting lake by Cocodrille."

Antoine nodded approval.

"That is good muskrat country," he said. "But the marsh is floating. The walking there is difficult. And it is very far. You will have to pole there, to Cocodrille."

"This is nothing," Leland said. "Some mornings I will leave early and shoot ducks in the hunting pond before I run the traps. And I shall use only the first fifteen minutes of daylight so that the rats do not suffer."

Now lines Leland had never seen before in his uncle's face appeared in the diffused light, the half-darkness of the old hotel. Now his uncle reached out his hand and clutched Leland's shoulder very hard. He smiled, then, and looked about them.

"Do you know whose room this was?" Antoine asked. Leland did not answer. "It was the bedroom of the Doctor, first." Now Antoine took his hand away. A silence gathered with the failing light.

Late in the evening Leland saw his father walking down the long line of oaks toward the old graveyard. He did not return until very late. The next morning Leland set his traps. He set them in a broad half-circle around the lake beginning and ending on Bayou Cocodrille. As his uncle had said, the walking was very difficult, especially in the first part of the line where the entire marsh was floating and where each step sent the marsh trembling yards away like sluggish water. Once his foot broke through and he went up over the tops of his boot through the turf and into the water below. The water invaded his hip boot, and he suffered and shivered until he had warmed the water inside and then it was merely uncomfortable and a little shameful as when one in sickness soils oneself.

But there was much three-cornered grass and many signs of muskrat and few of nutria. He set the weaker traps here and did not compromise in their placing. There would be adjustments to make, but he set them the best he knew how the first time, so it took much longer than he had thought it would. He was relieved when he reached the more solid part of the marsh. His legs were aching in the thighs and calves, his back was very sore where he had carried the sack of traps, and his hand hurt from the tight-wrapped line dragging the pile of bamboo behind him. The weight of the traps, though, and the poles he dragged diminished with each snare he set, so his load lightened exactly as he wearied. And from then on he would have only the skins to carry or whatever other bounty he took from the marsh, the ratio of weight and weariness reversing.

"But I will be growing stronger," he said aloud, "and that will make all the difference."

His own words, said aloud, startled him just as the old man's words had startled him that day he cut the cane and killed the nest of cottonmouths. There was something about this work that freed a part of him. He had just set a trap in a nutria trail, standing on the spring-powered wing-arms, flipping the catch over the clamp and wedging the tip of it in the groove of the central trigger plate. It was then, just as he had stepped from the clamps of the trap slowly and allowed them to poise themselves against the catch and the trigger, that the words had come from him, from a place inside him which was functioning on another level.

Leland paused and looked about him. He had been

seeing so many things. That kingfisher at Tiger Lagoon, plunging and rising and hovering, aiming his body like a spear. The volleys of small ricebirds. That dot of a falcon lazily riding the wind and searching for prey. The trails around him with all their signs. The grass, itself, each type an indicator of opportunity. That occasional tiny, tinkling splash beyond his vision that he knew to be a mink following him in curiosity. The smell of the marsh that had turned from the heavy sulphur of the gumbo floating marsh to that of the rich river smell of rotting loam, and the delicate odor of animals near him, not the polecat scent of the sleeping cottonmouths or the tepid quality of turtles, stronger from the alligators, all of them sleeping, dormant for the winter, but the slightly starch or scratch-paper smell of fur, raw fur, the way it smells when taken directly from the trap or, now he knew, directly before it is snared. And there had been the feeling of the marsh against his skin, the cold eddies of the wind and the water and soil against his boots and his hands when he bent to set the traps, and the squish of the water in his boot and the tickle of the tips of the grass against his hands and cheeks.

And the physical nature of the weariness, there had been that. The cutting rope about his hand, the banging rattle of the traps against his body. And the mental work, the constant judgment, the weighing, juggling of so many factors to choose the finest selection.

And something else, something a part of all of these yet separate. Another awareness made possible by all of these. He stood in the echo of his spoken words and knew that he had lost it and that it would come again. He made another wrap of the rope about his hand and jerked the pile of bamboo free of the place it had settled in inertia then walked on. The trail snaked forward and made a slight but abrupt turn. A good place, in the lee of that clump of jeansonne grass.

He did grow stronger. And once he had settled the line and running it had become not easy but at least swifter, he began hunting each day for duck. At first he tried to get up earlier each morning to be in the blind in that good shooting time of the graying before day. It gave him only a half-hour or so before he would have to be on line. The shooting was difficult in the poor light, but also fast and exciting, because one did not see the ducks until they were close up and so the shooting had to be by reflex and not design. But rising early proved too much. He was too tempted to lie in the soft, warm bed, too afraid to wake the others early and too sluggish from sleep to enjoy poling Bayou Cocodrille to the hunting pond. So he began sleeping in the marsh.

When the others made ready for bed, he left the house and took the pirogue across the marsh down channels he knew well. Then he took Cocodrille to the pond, the best part of the trip because Cocodrille was wide and lovely, silky-smooth, and gentle-twisting, filled with life and subtle little surprises like otter bumping his boat.

He had closed the dam to the pond to keep the water level high and so had to drag the pirogue across the levee into the pond. But then it was a short trip to the blind across the still water of the pond, and ducks always got up from the pond before him because it was a fine feeding pond growing wild rice and duckweed. Even in the darkness he could see their gray shapes, so close he was to them, and on moonlit nights he could judge their size and see their markings, but he did not shoot. He knew he could hit them, but he could lose them in the marsh, also, and he did not want to expend shotgun shells to feed raccoons and foxes who were well enough adept at feeding themselves.

Once he had hidden himself in the pirogue among the roseaux of the blind and stripped his clothes to the foot of the twelve-foot featherbed—six feet of it beneath him against the dry bottom of the pirogue and six feet of it covering him with warmth—ducks began to drop again into the pond. He let the sounds of their quiet chatter and the whistling of their cupped, descending wings lull him to sleep, and it was the same whistling sounds that awoke him in the morning. Many mornings when the sun had not even begun to peek redly over the flat rim of the marsh, his ducks lay gutted and the featherbed rolled in the prow of the pirogue, the shotgun unloaded and cased across the bundles and Leland on line at the first trap.

He worked his way in the circle around the lake and walked the edge of Cocodrille, back to the pirogue, then poled home. Each morning the sun was lower on the horizon as he started poling. As the soreness in his body disappeared the routine took so little time that he had finished scraping the skins and doing his chores with time to waste before the meal was ready.

One morning he took an old icebox, unused for many years, from the ruins of the old hotel and anchored it in the canal in a frame of oak boards he'd salvaged from the scrap pile. He designed it to float with its double doors out of water, cooled by the canal. Once it had been cooled by ice shipped in sailboats through Southwest Pass. The nutria carcasses would not spoil between visits of the fur buyer.

"It is a good idea," his uncle said. "I mean about the icebox. I think that part will work. But have you considered how difficult it will be to bring that meat from the marsh?"

"But, yes," Leland said. "The fur buyer, he comes every two weeks and I estimate the box, it will be filled in one week. So this effort is only meant for alternate weeks, you understand."

"Yes, yes. This I understand well, this is very simple. It is the work that will be very difficult, in a very simple way."

Unless you have trained those nutria to follow behind your pirogue out of the marsh, the way sheep follow a Judas goat."

His uncle showed nothing to indicate he was joking, but it was something Leland understood to be funny. So he responded quickly, practically before he knew it, and so he certainly hadn't planned it, but it was humor of his uncle's odd sort and very comfortable.

"No, no, I haven't time for that," he said, "I'll have to butcher them in the marsh."

"Then perhaps you can train them to help you with the butchering. Or breed for a strain with zippers."

"I have been training them with my skinning knife. This training, it is very effective."

"Ah," his uncle said, and looked out over the marsh. Leland knew he was no longer in jest. "I think the cadavers should return to the marsh."

"If skins are taken, why not meat?"

"It is only this feeling I have, this feeling that we should take out as little as possible. That meat was built on the marsh and the marsh renourishes itself. Also, a nickel a pound is very little money. And it goes into the shares."

"That doesn't matter," Leland said.

"No, that doesn't matter," his uncle agreed.

So in the morning Leland dumped the first of the nutria carcasses into the floating cooler. He still skinned the muskrat on the line, tossing their bodies into the grass, but he carried the nutrias whole on the line and butchered them all on Cocodrille. Inside the cooler, the carcasses on top turned red and dry, stretched hard across the surfaces of the meat. But none spoiled and those on the bottom remained white and tender. He estimated the box held almost a thousand pounds floating deep in the canal and he easily filled it in one week.

But at first it was very difficult to carry the carcasses. In the beginning he just grasped as many hard, hairless tails as he could and staggered like a man carrying two heavy buckets across a loose trampoline. Then he brought cord into the marsh and hung their bodies across him, swinging and jarring against him, their sloping heads bouncing along his thighs and knees, small dead myopic eyes and orange-tooth grins fixed permanent. Then he devised a kind of pack from a feed sack, tying string to tufted corners until his grandmother sewed straps for his shoulders and—at his direction—one that fit across his upper forehead and allowed him to use properly the muscles of his back and neck and still retain balance.

Now the walking was much improved, and, leaning forward, he could almost equalize the weight with leverage. He cut another forked walking stick and walked with four points to the marsh. His back humped with the bulging sack, a rolling gait across the flat, soft, quiet earth; he resembled less a man than some hybrid of a marsh creature and a hominid. Often different birds and furbearers came close to watch as he traversed the marsh from bamboo cane to bamboo cane. He devised an ability to toss the whole carcasses of nutria over his shoulder into the open lip of the sack. Once a raccoon burst through the heavy grass and stood in the trail, looking at him. The raccoon then backed into the fighting position and opened his mouth in his hissing growl. But he stood fast, transfixed by the sight of Leland, then rocked backward on his wide, black, smooth hind feet until he could pivot safely around and he fled. And the raccoons and foxes and other predators or scavengers soon found where Leland skinned and cleaned the nutria at the end of the run. It became a feasting place for all of them.

He could have set traps around the pile of entrails and heads; feet and tails, but he felt the scavengers were doing him a service. This piece of marsh he now considered in his keeping, and it gave him pleasure to see it cleaned from week to week. The debris diminished regularly and the skulls were cleaned of meat so that they gleamed whitely, scattered along the edge of the bayou, the orange teeth sharp against the light bone and winter dun of the grass.

He skinned and dressed the freshest first. Especially on the colder days of the winter was it more pleasant to push his fingers into the warm bodies. Sometimes the offal steamed in the cold winter air. But the blood dried cold on his hands and he did not like pushing his fingers into the cold, tight-wound entrails of the earliest of the day's catch. So it was always with relief that he washed his hands in the clear, stagnant pond water, which was often warmer than the air.

One morning as he skinned and dressed the nutria, listening to bird calls, he heard his name. His uncle was on the other side of the bayou. Once Leland had seen him he did not call again. They expressed themselves in gestures. Antoine's arm waved over his head for Leland to come get him in the pirogue. Leland gestured with both hands open, palms upward and the knife held with the thumb against the palm of his right hand, hands moving in circles above the pile of carcasses. The uncle nodded and squatted in the grass so that only his hat and eyes were visible.

The marsh sounds resumed quickly because the men had not interrupted them unnecessarily. Leland continued to listen as he made the cuts and pulled the skins and emptied the cavities of their bowels. And each time he straightened with another skin he scanned the marsh, taking in as much as he could in one sweep, even his uncle's solitary and unblinking eyes beneath the hat.

It was late in the morning for ducks to fly, but he saw several dots far away on the horizon, rising and falling. The day was bright, with high, misty clouds that would not rain and did nothing to stop the glare of the sun, so it was possible to see far distances over the marsh. Far to the east, near White Lake, he saw what resembled a cloud of insects rise and move and settle. He knew the cloud was geese and the movement was a feeding swarm in an area of little food. In the west a duck hawk circled high and went into a fast, deep dive but pulled out before he broke the height of the marsh grass. It was a curious maneuver; one might suspect he had dived on a wooden decoy and discovered his mistake, but there would be no decoys on Viator marshland.

Now the hawk made a half-hearted swoop, curious also in the lack of determination and passion. Beneath him a brace of large duck, probably a male and female grayduck or mallard, rose and with heads held well forward on long necks they flapped wildly. Unaccountably, the duck hawk did not give chase. The brace made a wide circle and came in an arc toward them.

His uncle was well hidden, as well as if he had been hunting them. Leland stooped to make the cuts but watched them come in, glide down, paddle back with curved wings, and settle to a pothole on his side of the bayou a few dozen yards in the direction of the island. Straightening with the pelt, he marked bearings to find them. Then he bent resignedly to work, and when he had finished the skinning and dressing of the meat he loaded the pirogue and pushed across to his uncle.

"It is a long way you've walked," Leland said to him.

"This day, it is good for walking," he said. "And I wanted to ride in with you. Cocodrille from a pirogue is something I enjoy."

He put his walking stick across the gunwales in exactly the correct spot for balance near the bow and sat on it with his back to Leland. It was a marsh pirogue, points down flush not to rise on mudbanks and no seats, made for pushpoling from a standing position and for work. The

weight distribution to the keel was perfect, but Leland had
to adjust for the higher center of gravity as he poled. His
uncle's narrow frame was silhouetted against the gutted
but unfeathered teal and blackjack, the sack of skinned
nutria and the cased shotgun. Leland was aware of the
hundreds, perhaps thousands of hours he had sat the bow
of a pirogue with his uncle poling. He wondered that the
hard, narrow oak stick was not an uncomfortable seat. In
fact, he worried that it was.

Hunched over, head slightly bowed, arms resting on his
raised knees, the man seemed not a man at all, but a child
and Leland the man, instead. Leland felt a vague responsibility toward him. But this dissipated when Antoine spoke.

"It is very hard that you work," he said softly, as hunters
speak in pirogues in the marsh, and he did not move nor
turn nor give any physical indication he had spoken. The
voice seemed not a part of him. And that feeling of responsibility, which had seemed to dissolve as a morning mist
before a hot, noon sun, now in the interval before Leland's
reply seemed to move back in around them as fanned by
the most delicate of marsh breezes.

"It is why we have come," he said.

"This is true," his uncle said, nodding and so rocking
the pirogue lightly giving a physical nature to his words.
"But should you not be playing, also?"

"Playing?" Leland replied absently. He had just found
the proper spot to enter the marsh after the brace of
mallard.

"Yes," Antoine said. "As you used to do. Do you remember how hard it was to get you out of the hollow oak for
supper? And how you used to spend hours jumping from
the roof of the old hotel to that oak limb that tossed you
like a young colt? That was only last year."

Leland pushed the trailing, guiding foot to the left
against the set of the pole and the bow pivoted nicely to

the right and nestled solidly in the natural cleft of the bayou bank.

"What are you doing?" Antoine asked.

"I'm going in after that brace," Leland answered.

"Leave them. We've enough to eat."

"But few mallard this year," he said.

While Leland was anchoring the pirogue against the bank with his pushpole, Antoine uncased the shotgun and handed it to Leland. Leland stepped to the bank before he loaded the shotgun. He took a bearing on a high, solitary stand of roseaux and walked directly toward it. The marsh turned soft as soon as he had left the bayou bank. It was not the floating kind, but the grass had grown very thick since the burn. It was like a gigantic carpet spotted with potholes, which he circumnavigated with his head low, swinging his legs outwardly like a hurdler but with great slowness and deliberation. He had confidence in his direction, but it seemed he had gone a long way before he heard them talking.

It was the little satisfied murmur of the feed call. Now Leland rested because the walking had been difficult, and his breath, coming in audible pants, echoed off the marsh floor. He listened to the trill and flutter of the ducks. Nothing was flying that late in the morning so there would be no loud flocking call. It was midday, nearly, that long period for eating and relaxing between dawn and dusk, the time when all nature seems high-charged with urges beneath the sea, in the air, on the land, and here, which is neither sea nor land nor air.

Now he moved on, even more cautiously, not working toward the distant roseaux any more, but advancing on the more accurate beam of the sounds of the ducks, themselves. He had gone not three wide, side-swinging paces when the drake got up. A magnificent mallard drake, green head almost black with color in the bright light, white-ringed neck sharp against the shades of brown and black and green. Head well forward with greenish beak cutting sharply into the wind across his perfect, streamlined body. The rhythmical, wild, pushing flap of his wings.

Leland was not within range. The drake did not rise in high panic from the pothole. He came up just high enough to clear the tops of the grasses and start a shallow slant upward and away. Leland watched him with admiration until he was well in the distance before he started again toward the other.

The art of hunting ducks is to decoy them. One might shoot from a boat at night in a full moon, poling across the marsh and surprising them in the ponds. Or one might walk the levee, taking long shots to test skill. This is sport but it is not art. But creeping ducks is neither sport nor art and not as practical as a duck trap would be. Still, Leland went on but stopped cautiously when the drake returned.

He returned making the flocking call to the hen on the water. Calling from far off, more desperately as he approached. She answered him immediately, once, but did not take to the air. This was something very new to Leland. Ducks called one another to water, not to air.

"Who knows what sounds they make high above and out of human earshot," he whispered, the words in the distorted hiss of whisper echoing from the marsh back to him.

The drake flew tiny tight circles around the pond. His plaintive alarm played against the soft trill of her feed call. His deep-throated, loud blasts could not shake her from the water. As Leland moved just into range for a double shot, the drake moved off. He moved off with swift deliberation, straight in an unwavering line into the west. No circles, no swift pivots on wings in search for vacant water or a flock with which to feed. He was far away, an almost unnoticeable dot above the horizon, before she rose.

Leland was very close, not two paces from the edge of

the tiny pond, so he followed her exactly and unhurriedly with the bead of the sight on her breast until she was the correct distance to shoot. She rose straight up, not slanting as the drake had done. Straight up, her body almost perpendicular to the marsh, wings beating swiftly backward and long neck held forward and parallel to Leland for balance so that her panicked left eye was trained directly on him. Leland followed her until she leveled off. And in that instant when she hung motionless in the sky above him, in that still point of time and space when everything seemed to cease suspended, he squeezed the trigger.

She fell, a spin and whirl of lifeless feathers, no longer a grand design of movement and poise. She fell transformed, straight down, from such a height that her weight slapped the water of the pond flatly and sent a splash outward, almost to the edge where Leland now stood.

The pond was shallow and mud beneath it firm enough so that Leland had no trouble crossing to her. She was young, heavy, and tender. And she had fallen from such a height that her breast had split against the pond. Beneath the skin and brown-black feathers, the meat was white and soft.

As he looked back, Leland was surprised at how close the pirogue and his uncle were. His uncle sat in the bow, facing down the bayou, still hunched forward. But the fingers of his right hand pinched the bridge of his nose against his eyes. When Leland reached him and tossed the hen against the teal and blackjack in the bow, his uncle turned his head away, so that the brim of his hat obscured his face.

"Have you ever seen anything like that?" Leland asked. If his uncle replied, Leland did not hear him. But when Antoine did speak, his voice was so soft and thick that Leland thought perhaps he had replied.

"It is bad enough we must kill them to eat and live,"

Antoine said, "but worse that they should show us who they are."

Now Leland was certain his uncle had been weeping. He had never seen any full-grown man cry, and so he did not know what, if anything, to do. One comforted a woman or a child. Or perhaps if the child were a boy and needed spurring to grow up one ridiculed him. But for this Leland knew nothing to do and so he did nothing except pretend he did not know and pole quietly toward the island. There were no signs of weeping, and his uncle did not change position or speak the rest of the trip. Leland felt confusion and concern for his uncle, but no sadness over the death of the hen, and by supper he was quite glad he had shot her. For they had a special guest for supper, and his mother cut up the hen and baked her dry in a pot and they all had a piece of her and Leland was certain it was the best duck he had ever tasted.

"That's old Desormeaux," Leland's grandfather said happily when the men first heard the laughter across the marsh. Leland and Antoine got up from their scraping benches, and the four of them walked to the back of the house and saw him turn the bend. His white hair contrasted sharply with the dark water behind him. He did not stand with feet apart and one foot advanced in the pirogue as did the Viators and everybody else Leland knew. He stood with both feet together, facing forward as one would stand on solid ground.

And he poled with his left arm wrapping around his body with every push of the pole, but both his arms operated almost as though they were not parts of him, as though they were part of a mechanical method he had set in motion and now enjoyed without participation. Leland would have thought it impossible to pole a pirogue in this way, but there it was in front of him; delicacy, exactness, balance.

As the prow reached the bank Desormeaux made a slight jar with both feet and the pirogue rode halfway up the solid shore and settled rooted there. It was one of the old one-piece cypress dugout pirogues with carved prows fore and aft. First there had been the astonishing whiteness of the old man's thick hair, then the straightness and rigidness of his body, then his clothes.

He wore thick-soled leather workshoes with rawhide strings. Brown, patched hunting trousers, old and worn but clean and even creased, clamped at a narrow waist a red flannel shirt that stretched a little taut about a bulging chest and upper arms. Across his shoulders was a hide Leland could not identify. He guessed it was a goatskin, though it had no odor and was darker and not quite shaggy enough for a goat.

As he came up the bank, he extended his hand first to Leland's grandfather who quickly pulled his fingers from the grip and shook his hand with a comic expression indicating the hand had been broken in Desormeaux' grip. All the while, Desormeaux laughed. It was said Desormeaux' laugh was an indication of insanity, but the laugh was not obtrusive. Rather, it was infective. Leland had the feeling it was used sometimes instead of words. Then Desormeaux shook hands all around. As he shook Leland's hand he bent his shoulders close so that Leland had a good look at the hide. It had been trimmed, shaped. So it must have been a huge beast, much larger than a billygoat. It was tied with a leather thong about his neck.

"So this is the one I have been hearing so much about," he said holding Leland's hand in his longer than the others. The hands that held his were calloused and hard with muscle, but they held his hand gently. The grip was not firm at all, merely insistent. "This is the one."

"That's the one," his grandfather said.

"Yes, this one," Desormeaux said, breaking from laughter but not quite from a smile as he looked quite deeply into Leland's eyes. His face, despite its deep creases, seemed quite young, not lax or flabby, and square as if it had been blocked in wood with large features. "Yes, this one," he said again and now he was quite serious. "And this one, too," he said, dropping Leland's hand and looking at Antoine, "and are you armed, Antoine, have you a weapon?"

Now with a flourish and with a laughing face fixed on Antoine he untied the thong and sailed-flung the hide cape to the ground. Leland until then had never seen his uncle embarrassed, but now the man blushed red, stifled a smile with flexed mouth, and looked down to where he actually shuffled his feet against the borders of the hide. Now Desormeaux looked each one of them squarely in the eye in turn and laughed loudly. Already it had been more laughter than they had heard on that island in several days, and he laughed on, ringing it among the high oak branches. But when it ceased it ended abruptly.

"Come," Desormeaux said to the grandfather, "leave these young men to their work. I wish to walk with you and hear your idle stories and laugh with you. We will eat tonight, is this not so? Should you not tell your women to prepare?"

He laughed again, and with only a wink from the old man for a reply, they walked off together, down the long line of trees, his arm around the old man's shoulders, very erect, with the old man's arm around his waist.

"It is difficult to believe he is so much older than Pa-Paw," Leland said.

"There is much that is difficult to believe about old Desormeaux," his uncle replied. They went back to work. They did not touch the hide Desormeaux had dropped to the ground as they would not have fondled someone's overcoat hanging on a nail inside the house. And they had other hides to handle. It had been a good afternoon's catch for all of them, and Leland pulled the stern of his scraping bench into the red-golden sunset so that he could face eastward and look up from time to time into the branches of the oaks and see how they caught the light.

The two aged men paused for a long time at the rickety wire fence around the graveyard. He saw his grandfather pointing to graves then telling stories. And Desormeaux laughed at the edge of the cemetery as loudly as he laughed in the marsh, often throwing his head far back and laughing straight up into the sky. Then they walked off together slowly and for a time Leland could only see glimpses of Desormeaux' high white head between the oaks and among the brush. Then he could see nothing of them. He could only hear the laughter. Then there was not even the laughter. There was only the lovely way the sun colored the oaks.

The old man and Desormeaux took a long walk. They must have gone as far as the end of the island. When they returned there was only a shimmer of daylight in the west, and all the skins had been scraped and stretched and stored in the drying shed. It had grown colder, but Desormeaux did not reach for the hide, which lay where he had tossed it sailing. The smells from the kitchen had been making Leland's stomach growl for some time when the two old men came up the line of trees, and the five of them entered together.

They had fried some of the perch, crisp in cornmeal so that the fins crunched with flavor. With the catfish they had cooked a court-bouillon, fileting the large channel catfish, cooking a stock with the heads and skeletons and tails, then, after the stock had been drained from the waste, baking it all with pickled tomatoes, tomato paste, seasoning, lemon, and the "holy trinity" of bell pepper, garlic, and onion. Then jambalaya with bits of duck, rabbit, and muskrat cooked darkly in the rice. There was a baked teal for each of them and a platter of spare teal on the table, tiny succulent birds baked until the meat swelled and peeled back from the bones. And the pieces of the mallard hen baked dry in the old iron pot that carried the seasoned flavors of many other meals. For dessert a peach pie, bottom crust brown and liberal with salt and sugar, the top criss-crossed with strips of dough that merged at the joints and turned brown and crispy to the fork.

"This one," his grandfather said proudly over biscuit and preserves, "has fed us well this year." Both old men had left the pie to the others and were eating the pear preserves and doughy biscuit. "What you have eaten here, Desormeaux, he has provided. Well, I mean, not the pie and these preserves, of course, but the meat. Fish, duck, geese, venison, rabbit. I have never eaten better."

"This I know," Desormeaux said with a wry smile for Leland.

"Except for the time of the hotel," his grandfather said, then, slowly and low, his eyes rising. Then he paused, staring into the darkness of the dormitory. It was so much as though he were seeing something that Leland followed his gaze. But there was nothing beyond his father that Leland could see, except the darkness of the unlit room. His father was scraping the gelatin and crumbs with the side of his fork against his plate. Leland looked again at his grandfather, and the eyes were still fixed, his face serious, and again Leland followed the gaze. The eyes had not been vacant, they had the look of seeing. But again there was nothing there except the darkness. All around them the sounds of dining rattled, but the conversation had lulled. Then Leland looked back at his grandfather in time to see the eyes suddenly break away from what they had been seeing almost as a duck breaks his descent quickly, with a rapid, almost wrenching movement when death has been sighted lurking with shotgun in a blind.

"Except for the hotel," Antoine said.

"Ainh?" the old man asked, almost puzzled.

"You were speaking of the hotel. The food at the hotel," Antoine reminded.

"Oh, yes, but of course. The hotel. Fine feasts. A normal meal was a feast, there, each day a celebration . . ."

And the others joined Leland's grandfather in this celebration of the past. Retelling stories of the good life that came before. But Leland was disturbed. And when he looked at Desormeaux he saw that Desormeaux was not participating. Desormeaux was studying Leland. He had stopped his fork midway to his mouth, and he continued to scrutinize Leland even after their eyes met. Desormeaux had very clear light-brown eyes, shiny as a child's but surrounded by lines that creased like channels of the marsh. Slowly, he put the food into his mouth and chewed without savoring but looked continually at Leland. Finally, Leland broke the gaze.

"I wish to hear the stories of the tricks," Desormeaux said over coffee.

"Of me and Brother?" the old man asked, though he knew perfectly well. His brother had been called Henri, but in the family only Frère. He had been a very creative jokester and Leland's grandfather had basked in his glow of fame until Brother had died. Now he told the stories.

"At Grosse Isle, you know? Where they had the big dances. People came from miles and miles. Wagons, you know. We would dance and dance and drink and drink. And you never got drunk, in those days, for all the dancing I suppose. We worked then, work these boys will never learn. Hot sun, cold water, calves as big as elephants to throw, and wild. And we were hard, young and hard, men as well as women."

His wife nodded broadly.

"Well, one time before I was married, Brother and I . . ."

you know we never missed a dance, us. Never. No matter how far. We'd dance and drink. Well, one night he decided to take all the wheels off the wagons, so nobody could go home, I believe. I seem to remember he wanted to hide the wheels. But when we got started he had a better idea, him. He decided to take all the wheels off the fronts of the wagons and put them on the back, and take the back wheels off and put them on the fronts. Well you know they had big wheels on the back and little wheels on the front, for turning. We missed some good music, yes, doing that.

"But it was worth it. Oh, there were some who noticed the difference right away. But, you know, they didn't say it. Oh, people could take a joke and go along with a joke in those days, yes. And those who noticed . . . it was full daylight before some of them left, and they said nothing to the others. So the others, they got into their wagons and went home. You know, the horses and the mules, them, they knew the way better than the people.

"So of course you didn't have to be sober to get home. Nobody was hurrying. Not like today. There was time enough for everything. Broussard from Mouton Cove, and Babineaux from Indian Bayou, even Segura from Rose Hill . . . and that wasn't too far away and without a rise in the land at all . . . they said they couldn't figure why they were going uphill all the time on the way home."

Now, strangely, Desormeaux did not laugh. He smiled almost politely and urged him on to another story.

"Well, oh yes, well the best one is . . . well, people in those days, at those dances they would dance . . . usually it was a dance at somebody's house, you know. Maybe a boucherie or maybe everybody would bring something for the gumbo, you see. But they would dance, them, and when the little children would get sleepy they'd put them to bed in the wagon. So they'd put the children to sleep and go back inside and dance. Nobody ever bothered them in those days. Certainly today you could not leave your children outside at night at a dance. Oh, perhaps the way we do it . . . the way we did it, I mean. But not like dances today. In the dark, my God! As though dancing were shameful! And very violent. With the cars crowding the highways, jammed. And not an accordion or a triangle and big radioes to make it loud. I . . . I . . ."

"The trick, good friend, the trick," Desormeaux said to the old man, reaching toward him and touching his forearm.

"Ah, yes, yes, the trick," the old man said, sipped whiskey-laced coffee, spoke again. "So, anyway, Brother, him, he got this idea in his head to switch the children in the wagons. It wasn't the same time as the wheels. I seem to remember it was before that. Or maybe it was later. Anyway, we tried to exchange a little girl for a little girl and a little boy for a little boy, but toward the end we got tired and we just worked by weight.

"And in the morning they got in the wagons, them, and they went on home, the Mama and the Papa on the seat and all the little children they thought were theirs asleep in the back. Man, they lived a long way apart, yes. And you couldn't travel like today. It was months before they got them changed back family-to-family. And like Brother used to say, on account of that, 'In Vermilion Parish, even today you don't know but what you might be marrying your first cousin.'"

Now there was nothing in the old man but mirth. Instead of staring wide into darkness, his eyes were again wood-carved curved slits.

"That was Brother's favorite joke. Of course, I prefer the one about the fur buyer and the alligator. But Brother, him, he always insisted that one was not a joke. That was education, he said.

"Problem was we had this fur buyer, a Johnson out of Gueydan. He came on the same day of the week. And the same time each trip. You could set your watch by it. And Brother, him, he was kind of strange, you know, about some things. He did not like something to be too regular. He wouldn't own a watch, him. Wouldn't have a clock around him. And sometimes it looked like he'd be late for something just for the hell of it, even if he knew the time. I think, myself, that he hated time. Well, anyway, this fur buyer coming at the same time and on the same day and all, rain or shine, it began to get to Brother. And as if that wasn't bad enough, the man drove his boat into the bank in the same place and stepped out with his right foot in the same spot every time he came to the island.

"Well, that was too much for Brother, let me tell you. If the water didn't rise from week to week, there would still be the same cut in the mud from that fur buyer's last visit. And when he came again he'd put that bow right into that cut. And if his boot print was still there, be damn if he didn't put his boot into it again.

"Brother, he started studying that cut in the bank and that boot print, and as the season got longer and longer it bothered him more and more. So one day I get back from my line before him, and I start scraping. I was half-way through my pile when I look up and I see him coming. He was staggering. He could hardly walk. On his back . . ." here the old man's right arm curved upward from his shoulder as though he were carrying something heavy there. "On his back he had about a nine-foot alligator. When I saw that I almost died. He had tied that alligator's mouth shut and strapped those short little mean legs to his sides. But he couldn't do anything with the tail. And you know the tail is the worst weapon an alligator has. He was swinging that tail right and left and every time he swung it Brother almost fell. And I guess he must have fallen plenty before the alligator got tired, too, because he was all muddy from his shoulders on down. You know, Brother was a strong man, but I still couldn't believe he carried that alligator all the way from Horse Lagoon. That's where he said he caught him, Horse Lagoon. That's a long way to go, even with a dead alligator. And he had his furs, too. And he just dumped that alligator down and wiped off his face on his sleeve and he sat down right at his scraping bench and started working. He didn't say a thing to me.

"I couldn't move. I just sat there. I couldn't even scrape my skins. Finally, I said to him, I said, 'Brother, for what you got an alligator?' And he said, 'For to cure me a fur buyer. He won't be here until two thirty-two. I got plenty time.' And that was all. He finished scraping his skins and no more as looked at the alligator until he was finished scraping and had eaten.

"Well, by then the alligator was tired, you know, laying in the sun all that time. And Brother, he got a pretty big chain and he tied that alligator around the chest behind his arms, you know . . ." The old man drew an imaginary line across his chest with his thumb, the thumbnail long and yellow and hard as a horn. "And we had a piece of pipe with a ring on it, I don't remember quite why, and he drove it into the mud and tied that alligator to it just exactly where that buyer's foot hit the bank. Then, and I couldn't believe this, he took out his pocketknife and he cut the ties on the alligator's mouth and legs. That gave him life right now, I want to tell you, and he thrashed around a while and then he got quiet.

"I told Brother he went too far, but Brother said he had to make sure, that he wouldn't have but one shot at curing a fur buyer. So he got some roseaux and covered the alligator good, and he hadn't laid the last roseau on when here comes Johnson's boat.

"And sure enough he put that bow just where he always

did, and when he got out he stepped right on that alligator. Man, you should have seen that fur buyer dance. That
alligator was all over him."

They were all laughing, now, Leland's grandmother slapping the table. The old man was trying to laugh and talk at
the same time, tears of joy at the corners of his eyes.

"But he . . . that fur buyer . . . he didn't get hurt. He
. . . he just . . . he just turned white, white, white. And
he could hardly deal, him. We . . . we got the best . . . the
best deal of the season that day. And whenever he came
back . . . he . . . he would just get close to the bank and
slow down and sometimes he'd stop and look before he
came in. And he never again stepped on even one roseau.
Sometimes Brother would lay one or two roseaux down
and bet me if the fur buyer would step on it, and he never
did. And he never hit the same place in the bank two
times in a row again."

"He put an alligator in my bed one night," Antoine said.

"Yes, but you were a little boy," the old man said. "So it
was a little alligator and he left the mouth and feet tied.
This was a jest, entirely, there was no education involved."

"Well, I checked my bed every night for a month before I
went to sleep," Antoine said seriously, and it was all very
funny.

Then there was a pause at the table while the laughter
died, and for a time everyone was staring at coffee cups
and the tabletop quietly and somberly. Then the women
began clearing the dishes, and Desormeaux stood above
them.

"Now I must go," he said.

They protested it was too far, invited him to spend the
night and insisted breakfast on the cheniere was better
than supper.

"No, I tell you the truth," he said, "and I mean no dis-
respect to those here who have fed me well and welcomed

me as a part of their family. It makes me sad but happy, too, to be here on this island. I have had the happiness and now I mean to cheat the sadness. Also, it is a fine night and I sleep very little anyway, and I am looking forward to my trip home."

"Well, that's you," the old man said. "Will you at least take some food with you? We are well provided here."

"No, no," Desormeaux said, slapping his stomach and laughing as he did when he arrived. "I eat little and sleep little these days, and you have fed me enough for a week."

They all went round again the cordialities, and Desormeaux asked Leland to light his way to the pirogue. Leland took the headlight from the hook near the door and followed him out into a bright, mildly cold, starlit and moonlit night. He flicked the light on but Desormeaux told him to turn it off.

"I don't need the light," he said. "And I want my eyes accustomed to the night. I merely wanted to speak to you alone." Then he turned and walked exactly to the pirogue floating lightly in the water at the stern and resting bow upon the bank.

Leland followed him. Desormeaux stood at the bow, then stretched his great arms wide and yawned. Then he reached into the boat and pulled up a patched, worn hunting jacket that matched the rest of his clothes in age.

"You know . . . many do not know this, but the night is the most beautiful time of the day," he said. Then he laughed the same insane laugh but controlled, hushed. "We are stewards, you know, Leland. Now you are among us. Our house is immense. And our children, they are plentiful. Some we nourish, Leland. And many, they nourish us, you know as well as any man. Well, I have been thinking of how I should tell you this and can find no words. It is something too simple for words, Leland. Words are designed for complex matters, to convey thoughts.

Words and thoughts are forever mixed. I wish I could open my head and let you see inside, for it is there inside in pictures."

Leland said nothing. It was well known that the wind had driven Desormeaux crazy. He listened to Desormeaux, but not attentively. There was a prattle of water in the marsh near them. Not ten yards distant. To the northeast. And Leland's mind was associating animals to it for a match. He had tried a raccoon dipping and so moistening his hand and that was almost it. The otter, sleek and light in the shine of the stars on his wet coat, had movement that did not match the sound. Perhaps a poule d'eau, but Leland couldn't find the movement. There were others, but none matched. The raccoon was the closest.

"So I say watch the birds, Leland," Desormeaux said. "The birds say it best. Lighting on a small tree limb, or perching on the edge of a nest woven of reed leaves like spider webs. They will tell you. And others will tell you, too, but the birds say it best. Do not be too busy or too fast to listen. Then they will tell you, plainly, without words remember. There were others before us here who listened, you know, but we may be the last to hear. It is true, what I say."

And with this he stepped into the pirogue and walked to the stern, and already the bow lifted and he drifted backward, he and the white of the cypress suspended in the darkness of the still water. Desormeaux picked up the pole.

"Good-bye, young Viator," he said.

"Wait," Leland called. "Your skin. You forgot the hide for your shoulders."

Then Desormeaux laughed again and made a throwaway motion with his hand toward Leland. In the deep night darkness it seemed his hands and face crowned by the shining white hair were existing apart from any body, floating above the dark canal.

"No. It is not mine. It belongs to you," Desormeaux said, using the French word for *you* which means more than one, many. "I was merely returning it." Now the loud laughter that sent a splashing scurry through the marsh. "Look to Outside Island for your children," he said, backing the boat around and now facing away from Leland. "They've reached full growth like you, Leland, almost like you."

And then he laughed again and the laughter died around the bend, and he was not with Leland anymore. Leland and no one else had touched the skin since Desormeaux had cast it to the ground. He went to it. It was like a pool against the darker ground. He found it easily. His eyes had grown accustomed to the darkness. He was surprised at the coarseness of the fur. The hide was very soft and pliable, but the fur was very coarse. Not silky like a goat, but more like that of a horse or beef except for the length. He rolled it and brought it into the house. They were talking of Desormeaux.

"I still think he should have stayed," Leland's mother said.

"He would not stay," said the old man. "He never stays anywhere but on his own. It is rare that he should have come at all. He has not been on the Island since the season before Brother died."

Leland seated himself and idly put the skin on a vacant chair beside him.

"But he lives so far away," his mother said. "I worry he will die in the marsh."

"He *will* die in the marsh," Antoine said quickly.

"Don't speak that way, Antoine," she said, making the sign of the cross.

"This that Antoine says is true," the old man said.

"I don't mean now, Jeanette," his uncle corrected. "He is old, but very strong. Healthy. But where else should he die than where he has always lived? Ainh? He has no family. He has lived all of his life, all year each year, in the marsh. Here is where he should die."

"Yes," the old man said, "and become part of the marsh like the carcasses we throw away. But not tonight, at least. Don't worry, Jeanette. Not tonight."

The knuckles of her hands were white.

"I do not like such talk," she said, and wriggled into a better position on the chair, gathering her skirts about her as she did. "Every Catholic should be buried in consecrated soil."

"Soil is soil," the old man said, "and marsh is soil and water. The Viators have always been buried here, on the Island, until the law against it."

She shrugged. "What's this?" she asked, pulling the rolled hide from the chair and placing it on the table.

"His cape," Leland said, and laughed at the word. "He left it for us. He said it belonged to us and he was returning it. He did not explain."

The old woman came in from the bedroom, where she rested a few minutes after each meal. They were all sitting at the table as Antoine unrolled the hide, fur upward. It was larger than the table. They lifted their coffee cups and the hide spilled over the edges of the table, smooth to the shape of the table, very soft except for the fur.

"What is it?" his mother asked. The old man lifted an edge quickly. He looked at the underside swiftly but with the precision of a jeweler.

"Beef," he said. The word *boeuf* meant beef or bull. "At least thirty years old. Older. Nicely cured."

"Beef?" Leland's father said. "Look at the thickness of that fur."

Leland had never heard even so much as this slight contradiction of the old man from his father, for even the old man's obvious lies were valued as truth.

"Beef," the old man said again without even so much as

looking at the hide. He was amused. The old woman was running tufts of the fur between her fingers as though her fingers were scissors and she were cutting it. His mother was now running her palms over it. Antoine had placed his coffee cup on the floor beside his chair and now held a corner in both his hands. One hand behind, on the leather side, held it and the fingers of his right hand plucked at the fur. Then one finger traced a line.

"Beef," he said suddenly. "Lift your cups." They lifted their cups, and very quickly Antoine spun the hide beneath the hands of the women, shoving the corner of the hide before the old man. "Beef, all right," he said. "Viator beef. Look here, Pa-Paw."

The old man took the hide again in his hand and examined it, the lids of his eyes very heavy as he looked down. He traced the line Antoine had traced. Then he leaned forward, folding the hide under his elbows as he leaned on the table, holding the corner in both hands and looking at it with great amusement as though he were examining a tiny and interesting work of art.

"Yes," he said. "It is our brand. And the Doctor's iron. The one he forged not twenty yards over there." He flicked his fingers in the direction of the old hotel. "See how the left prong slants inward." He pointed out the left prong of the Y-C brand as Leland and the women went behind the old man's chair to see. Leland watched the old man part the thick fur to show the outlines of the brand that the Viators had always used and the origins of which were obscure. This brand was boldly blocked and had been burned in by that branding iron that had hung all of Leland's life above the mantle of their living room at home on the mainland.

Now the old man tossed the hide folded upon the tabletop and took up his coffee. Leland reached across his shoulder and touched the brand. Often, he had examined the iron on the wall above the mantle, but never before had he seen it upon leather. They had three others in the little room beside the chute and trap, all made at the machine shop in Abbeville by welders, and one designed so that one had only to plug it into an electrical outlet to heat it burning hot. Only the Doctor's had been hand forged and bore that slanting prong.

"Well, he did not steal it, that is certain," Pa-Paw said. "Desormeaux does not steal."

"Then how did he come by it? And when? We have not used that brand in thirty years," Leland's father said. He seemed very irritated, almost angry. The old man opened his arms, gesturing that he did not know.

"Well, we used it then," he said, tapping the brand with a horny fingernail. "And on a calf at the full moon. See how the brand has grown. It takes branding in the full moon to do this, to make it grow with the beef."

"Pa-Paw," Antoine said, a softness of respect and curiosity unusual in his voice, "the thickness of the coat. A winter coat?"

"No, no, boy. What are you thinking? This is no winter coat. At least none such as I have ever seen. You've seen many winter coats. Is this like those?"

"No," Antoine said frankly. "Then what?"

"A winter coat, no more nor less," Leland's father said, then, and the contradiction was again startling to Leland.

"No no," the old man said, calmly, amused, his eyes heavy lidded with Gallic confidence. "This creature was given a very thick coat for some purpose other than cold. Someone clothes them in the winter and allows them to shed warmth before the heat of summer. Take an animal that has been bred for a thousand years in the South and bring him North and that first winter he will grow a coat thicker than any of his ancestors have had. Take him South again and the coat will not be so thick. Someone clothes them and all the animals we trap. This we all know. And we know why. For warmth and coolness. Simple, is it not. But answer me how. How? How this creature came to wear this fur is the great mystery, but one we live with so closely we no longer are amazed by it. Like the Trinity, perhaps it cannot be understood. But why he came to wear it, that is a mystery with an answer, though I do not know it."

They silently regarded the hide for a time.

"Did Desormeaux say anything else?" Antoine finally asked.

"About the hide, no," Leland answered. "He merely said it was ours and he was returning it. And he spoke about the marsh and the islands."

"What did he say, exactly?"

"Well, but . . . exactly, I do not remember. He said the animals were our children."

"Hainh!" Leland's father snorted. "Living so long without women in this marsh, there are probably many nutria who are *his* children, but none of mine."

"Oh, hush, you," his mother said.

"Well, I don't know," the old man said, puzzled. "It means something, though. Something. It will make a fine rug, though. Let us put it by the fire, on the floor before the mantel at home. A thirty-year-old hide, perhaps even sixty years old, thick and warm for our feet in winter, with the Doctor's brand. Old Desormeaux has given us a fine gift, no matter how he came upon it. Perhaps that is all it means. A fine gift. I wonder."

And so they rolled it and stored it in a canvas bag. And if they thought of it again, they did not discuss it. Spring came swiftly, then, and Leland felt the days warming but did not ask the date. One morning on the line he noticed the snakes were crawling. The next afternoon he saw a fourteen-foot alligator in plain sight on the island, away from water and cover, almost casually crossing to the gulf to bathe away the fresh-water leeches. The alligator was old, and thin, and still drowsy from his long sleep. And he went slowly and deliberately across the island toward the sleepy sound of the small waves on the mud-sand beach.

The next day they took in their traps with their final take of skins. They waited on the island for a few days, tending to the drying of the freshest skins and doing the work of storing and of sealing the camp. The old man weeded the cemetery and straightened the piles of bleached, pitted conch shells there. He worked one whole day alone, pausing only for meals taken somberly, reflectively.

There was a reluctance to leave. But finally everything was done, the gear all stored upon the bateau, including the canvas bag with the beef hide. With Antoine at the wheel again and Leland on the bow, braced against the mid support of the windshield, they made their way toward the mainland. Leland was amazed at how green the marsh grass had become.

III

Leland had forgotten the pleasant smell of horses. And he had forgotten the creak of saddle leather and the metallic sounds of the tack. Willy and Prince loaded willingly, stomping irregular drumbeats on the wood-metal ramp that was also the horse-trailer gate. But Beau champed the bit and balked at first, and when he finally went in he deliberately hung a stirrup on the frame and so backed out again quickly and tossed his head and showed every sign of being an embarrassment that day.

"Me, I thought he'd do something like that, him," Antoine said. The day was bright, one of those early days of spring when winter had definitely surrendered and the heat of summer had not yet made its first assault. In the brightness Antoine looked trim and healthy. He even looked young. He crossed quickly to the trailer, thudded the heel of his hand dully and forcefully into the horse's rump.

"Hunh! Hunh! You, Beau!"

Now the horse went in easily. Antoine and Leland lifted the gate and put in the pins.

"Mais, he young, him, yes," Antoine said. "A child, him. But he going to be good, him, yes. Soon as we get to Pine Island, you ride him out, you. And if he want for to jump, him, mais, let him jump. Mais, you keep you your spurs, them, out of him, yes, you. And don't you be ashamed for to hold on with your hands, you, no. You hold on your hands, you. He can't throw you, no, but what you let him, you. Beau, for to just feel good, him, and he don't know no other way for to show it, him."

When Leland's father came out of the house they got wordlessly into the truck and turned wordlessly from the yard onto the gravel-and-shell road away from the bend with the old dead tree and toward Pine Island. His father's mood had been morose and sullen since the trapping season. Almost always, he snapped at whatever Leland said.

Most of the pickups had arrived by the time they crossed the Warren Ditch on the wooden bridge to Pine Island. The trucks with trailers behind were parked in line to lengthen the wing of the pens. Whitney Broussard's black crew had unloaded the big tubs of ice and beer and had placed them in the shade and covered them with thick canvas. Antoine, at the wheel, made a half-circle then straightened to come in bumper to the back of the last trailer. They unloaded the horses and tied Prince and Willy in the shade.

Tied farther than kicking distances apart in the thick shade of the forest were approximately a dozen horses of every sort of description and shape. Short, thick, quick and cattle-wise quarter horses the Viators and Broussards rode. Long-legged, thoroughbred mixes favored at the Cajun tracks on Sundays and wonderful when a swift-wild cow broke from a herd into a long pasture. Pintos, Appaloosas, mongrels of every color and shape of head. And one small squat horse almost a Shetland pony, bushy with untrimmed mane, his eye open but his demeanor down to his lax left rear hoof that of a horse asleep.

In a soft lot between the ditch and the road, Leland let Beau buck himself out. It was just a few jumps to get the kinks out. Like a man stretches his muscles before work. Going back toward the others, Leland noticed again what a fine day it was to ride.

Those too young to ride, or those not to be trusted to ride because they had no horse, horsemanship, or sense of responsibility on the sometimes delicate roundup through the woods would remain behind to help with the repairing of the pens. The others had either already saddled their horses or were in the last stages of saddling. Loveless, Leland's second cousin, had a new light red horse Leland had not seen before. The horse was rather small, green broke, seeming tall because of slimness. As Loveless saddled him he held his head high with ears perked tightly up, his eyes rolling whitely. He trembled all over like a rabbit in a trap and held his thin neck so high he resembled the photographs of llamas Leland had seen in his geography book. The horse had been chained to a tree and the neck was worn raw with scabs and broken skin of many other chainings, so it was no secret the horse was not only a bolter but a rein-breaker as well.

Loveless unloosened the chain nervously, threatening the horse in French with a voice low, not for the animal but to hide the horse's embarrassing traits from the men. The threats did little good. As soon as he had swung into the

saddle the horse whirled two or three times, and when
Loveless tried desperately to pull his head around nose-to-
boot to force him to a halt, they went crashing to the ground
on the horse's right side. Loveless took the ground on his
feet, apparently practiced in the maneuver, and held on
to the chain as he might the bowline of a boat drifting
unmanned out to sea in a brisk current. The horse, for
his part, got swiftly up and backed wide-legged away as
though he were a fine roping horse and Loveless a snared
calf. But he ceased pulling after ten or fifteen yards and
allowed Loveless to walk to him.

Whitney Broussard gave Loveless a strong, disapprov-
ing look, but he said nothing. He did not have to say anything. As soon as Loveless had gotten the horse under
control, or at least what passed between them as control,
Loveless reassured Whitney.

"That's all right, that's all right," he said breathlessly.
"He always do that, yeah, the first time, him. He going
calm down, yeah. Give me good work, him."

Whitney was mounted, and without speaking he turned
his horse to the road. From the shade of the trees on the
other side rode Mon Negre. Mon Negre had a marvelous
horse and an aged, high-cantled saddle. He had a dramatic
gray drooping moustache and rather fierce dark eyes with
yellowed whites and a blue-jean jacket he wore buttoned
to the collar in whatever weather. And he was the most
noble Negro and possibly the most noble man of any race
that Leland had ever seen. Certainly he carried himself
well, head high, calm manner. And he looked where and
how he pleased. Into white men's eyes if he pleased. But
he spoke only to Whitney.

Mon Negre sat his horse in the road and Whitney came
up beside him. Most of them were mounted, now, and
they clustered unevenly around the two riders conferring
on the shell-gravel-dirt road baked hard by the sun. Whit-

ney and Mon Negre spoke for two or three minutes only.
Then Whitney turned and spoke to all of them in English.
"Mais, we go, us, down the canal road and to the woods,
us. Don't make you no noise, no. They wild, yes, them.
And they hear us, they go to the bad places, them. Comprend?"

But before anyone could answer, Whitney's brother,
Nose, burst into them on the shaggy little pony. The pony
was perfectly calm, it was Nose in this case who enjoyed
bursting into crowds and scattering dust. The horse,
mounted by Nose with his long, thin legs, seemed even
more ridiculous.

Nose laughed with them. "Mais, you like my horse, ainh,
ya'll? Gonna run Evangeline Downs, us, yeah. Sat'day,"
he said.

"Mais, laugh now, ya'll, but not in the woods," Whitney
said. "But I gone tell you something, yes. Ya'll ain't gone
laugh at all, you see what that horse do, yeah. Mais, that
horse, that our secret weapon, yes, him. Mais, that the
atom bomb of the drive, yes. Ya'll see, yeah."

And he turned and followed Mon Negre on the smaller
wagon track where Leland had calmed Beau. Then they
turned again and went down the hot twin rows of truck
ruts into woods thick as a dusty green wall. But the dust
penetrated only the outer layer of trees and brush. Inside,
things were green and still, and the only dust raised was
by their horses' hooves. Already the insects attacked them.
Many of the horses had broken into a thin lather already, a
sure sign of winter inactivity, and this lather attracted the
horseflies and deerflies. Leland broke a small branch and
scraped the gray-black mottled deerflies and larger, black
horseflies from Beau's neck. The horses only skin-fluttered
at the bites, or tossed their heads and swished tails, but
each bite left a six-inch stream of blood against the dark-
lathered hide once the insect had been killed or pried

loose. If it weren't for the insects, the horses might have fixed themselves in a trance following the horse in front, a situation almost like sleep in which their eyes are open and the horses moving but not really alert, not completely awake.

Loveless' horse, though, skittered and jerked. Now and then Loveless hit him between the ears with his doubled fist. Leland even envied him, because the mosquitoes had begun to weave their suckers between the fabric of his shirt and were torturing Leland's back. At least the craziness of Loveless' horse kept some mosquitoes from him. Leland leaned forward, got Beau into a trot and passed several riders to come abreast of his uncle. He spoke to him in very low whispers in French, aware he had to have some reason for breaking line.

"The horse which Monsieur Nose rides," he whispered, "he is a Shetland mix?"

"No, no, a Creole. You will see what work he does. They are very rare these days. Now get back in line and break a stick with spanish moss for the mosquitoes. Be very quiet. We are close, now."

Leland immediately reined Beau and waited in the enveloping mosquitoes for his place in line. His father glared at him as he went by. Many riders had clumps of spanish moss in their hands. Leland was ashamed it had been so obvious why he had broken the line. Neither Whitney nor Nose nor Antoine bothered with the insects. And he was disappointed with the Creole pony. He had heard of them all his life, of the work they did on the Louisiana prairies before the coming of the quarterhorse and the thoroughbred. He now convinced himself his uncle was wrong, that this was a mongrel. It had to be of Shetland mix.

Then the line stopped. Mon Negre and Whitney had pulled their horses head to rump and were conferring in whispers. Mon Negre had led them to exactly where the herd had spent the night. Like quail, cattle empty their bowels first thing in the morning. Also like quail, in the woods they sleep close-bunched. One can find where quail or cattle sleep by the tight clusters of waste on the ground. In the case of quail it is a dinner-plate size series of small gray dots. But before them in the woods now were hundreds of plots of manure buzzing with flies, scattered among the trees in an area dozens of yards in diameter.

The horses were stomping with the flies, now, trying to jar the deerflies and horseflies from their shoulders and legs. The men were all aflutter with spanish moss and switches as they formed a skirmish line on either side of Mon Negre and Whitney. Mon Negre nodded to Whitney, and Whitney waved them forward with his hand. They were able to advance well on line because the cattle had browsed the brush well here. Then they hit the Hills and as Leland looked left and right he saw riders and horses rising and falling exactly as boats upon a choppy sea.

The Hills area occupied the exact highest point of Pine Island. There were hundreds of little mounds scattered among the trees. No one knew what had caused them. Speculation ran from soil erosion to an extinct species of ants. But Leland was relieved the action would not start there. He had ridden hard among the mounds before, and it was dangerous enough to chase fast cattle in the woods with brush and vines without having the earth rise up and drop from under you.

Then they hit the vines. The blackjack vines dropped unevenly from the highest points of the narrow, close-trunked water oaks and whiteoaks, bending and sweeping to the ground in a criss-cross pattern which made the men weave their mounts around them. From jointlike formations, the vines dangled dark, amber strings, air roots that sometimes brushed their hats and shoulders as they went past. The Indians had learned a way to make bows from the vines, and dye, and even took from them moisture when the water had been spoiled. But now they had no use, and if the action started here they would be snares to riders of running horses. Still, the going was not bad and they had not seen a cow but the tracks told them the cattle were moving steadily forward in front of them somewhere beyond the constantly dissolving and reforming green curtain.

When they saw the first cow, the men immediately widened the line, those on the end swinging their horses outward and all those in between all the way to Whitney adjusting the distance to keep it as uniform as the woods would permit. It was not a question of the cattle breaking the line of riders. The cattle had lived all their lives in the fear of mounted men. They were only truly wild alone with the other animals. In the sight of men they were domesticated. They might break back around the flanks, however, and that was why Antoine took one point and Nose the other.

The cow they saw was a dark gray Brahma cross. She had no calf at her side so she had probably hidden it. She looked at them, snorted, and ran on, disappearing before them in the screen of tree trunks, vines, and leaves.

The line moved swifter, now, and the bugs made less difference. The sun and shadows fixed a bright mottled pattern to the greenness about them and sparkled the dust raised by the retreating feet of the cattle somewhere before them. Mon Negre rode before the line, his head bent forward and eyes turned upward beneath the brim of his hat as though with a special way he were seeing each cow hidden before them. The direction of his horse fixed the direction of the drive. The end horses, now, had snaked the line into a sickle, and they drove in a shallow crescent smoothly. There was time, now, to weave around the vines.

Only Nose did not have to weave his horse. The little

brushy gelding went straight on line, his back beneath the bend of the vines, and Nose with hands firmly on the saddle horn swiveled from the saddle to right and left, the vines scraping his shoulder as he dipped down parallel to the soil and level to the back of the horse, which never staggered or even braced himself against the swinging weight. Nose resembled one's wild dream of a drunken rider.

Then a crashing along the line sent everything into swift motion. The end riders rushed swiftly onward and outward, and the others moved their horses diagonally outward, without signal, needing no signal, not even looking toward the sound because the effect was all that mattered now, not the cause. They had to press them, now, to break them from the woods. Then Loveless crashed past them on the horse now bucking, now running, now tangled in the brush and vines. The horse thudded against the trunks of the trees.

A vine caught Leland at his left side and scraped all the way up his arm and left a blood-beaded trail across his neck and face. He lost his hat and heard a holler in French from far beyond Loveless. It was his uncle's voice and the cattle were breaking across that flank.

Now Leland saw the cows. The riders closed on the drag of the herd. The trees slid past and horses dodged them, and Leland took care he did not splatter against a tree. Then, quite suddenly, there was much light ahead and now there were no trees, and they had broken into the pasture, one-half of the line only.

To his right, cattle were still popping from the trees, but ahead and to the left the herd was bunched into two uneven strings, both heading for the drainage canal. Beyond that was a huge rice field, unplanted but flooded for water-leveling, the vital little rice levees still sodden and delicate. Leland raked his spurs and cut beside and behind the bunch before him, gaining the lead still far enough away that the others did not break back for the trees.

Beau broke into that swift, down-headed gallop full-flat and neck forward and pulling the ground away with great speed so that Leland felt he was sitting on a falling rail, swiftly falling straight down the steep side of something. Now he kept himself close to the side of the bunch of cattle, hoping to haze some of them away from the canal, though the first of the cattle to reach the water had entered it by the time Beau reached the never-mowed, thick stubble at the levee's border.

There was just that little jar as Beau changed leads with his front hooves to take the levee swifter, more certain, and they were sailing, now, not touching the ground, horse and man, a black running shadow on the bright surface of the silty water below them, which exploded when they crashed into it. The splash was all around him, swallowing and surging around him and cresting over the saddle and his thighs and hips even as Beau was already pulling from the canal, twice temporarily mired in mud as he lurched forward and freed them, and they were scrambling up the opposite levee.

Leland was still not through the shock of the cold water when Beau reached the top of the levee and stood trembling for just the second it took Leland to realize the horse, trembling and swallowing for air, did not know what to do. Still searching for the stirrups with his feet, Leland snapped the rein along Beau's neck and they crossed the ten or fifteen yards before the cows had a chance to climb the levee. Leland unsnared the whip and swung it over his head and popped it with great backward jerks as quickly as he could, the lash snapping dully at first then cracking loudly as the nylon freed itself of water. The cows made a quick turn and plunged without pausing back into the canal and swam to the other side. One of Leland's second

Les Perdues 195

cousins, Aubion Broussard, came up and stood a safe distance down the canal, rushing each cow as she came out of the water, hazing her on to the main bunch then retreating to the perfect position.

"Mais, you got you a horse there, you, ainh?" he said.

Leland and Beau stood higher on the far levee. Both of them still trembling and catching breath. The water still streaming from them to the dry gray soil below. Leland did not relish crossing the canal again because it was colder than the warm, bright sun indicated. But he also felt exhilarated. From the levee Leland had a good view of the entire pasture. He saw several cows and calves and the range bull pop out with Antoine and Nose behind them. Antoine's horse Prince was having a hard time keeping them from the woods, quartering swiftly side to side, but each yard from the trees took fight from them, and the little Creole pony was helping a lot just by keeping them bunched and sending the less aggressive on.

Aubion got the group from the canal started to the main bunch, which had merged in the pasture headed between riders for the corner and the long, safe way around to the pens. Leland's father had circled the herd to drive opposite the woods, where the action was less likely. Leland allowed Beau to pick his way slowly down the far levee to the canal but had to use his spurs to get him across this time.

On the other side, he sickled around and came up to Antoine from behind. The wind through his wet clothes was even colder, but the sun was warm on his back. Antoine sat low and hunched in the saddle, the reins slack along Prince's neck and the horse alert and intense because the cows tried every trick to turn back to the woods. Prince often jerked to left and right and advanced purely on his own. Antoine provided only the minimum of direction. Beau was not much farther along as a cutting horse than the little Creole, but they provided flank, and the bunch seemed to lose some resistance as soon as Beau reined in alongside. In contrast to the straining effort of the horse, Antoine was relaxed and happy.

"Yes, but Leland," his uncle said, "do you think it wise to swim before May? It is said one gets boils in this way, and we had other things in mind, this morning, when we came to Pine Island."

Antoine was known as a generally humorless man, but that winter in the marsh Leland had begun to understand him.

"It is not a matter of the time of the year, the getting of boils from water," Leland said with as much scholarliness as he could assume. "Rather it is the method of swimming. As you can clearly see I was not swimming at all but bathing my horse, which had not been washed since summer. Things, of course, were so boring at the time."

"Yes, yes. I agree and I apologize," Antoine said. Not a smile had passed between them. Leland left him for the flank of the bunch where a cow had broken and he hazed her back in.

The range bull was in the center of the cows and therefore quite calm, chewing his hairball, his great testicles slapping side to side outside and against each flank with his slow-trot gait. But Leland knew he could be vicious. Leland hated him and feared him because he had frightened him so greatly when Leland was very young. The bull was powerful and mean. Once he broke a steel cowtrap into pieces like a dog shaking water from his fur. He had lost his tail somehow, Leland believed in a fight, and he was now called the Bob-tailed Bull. They spared him from castration as a calf because of his black nose, said to be the sign of a hearty producer.

"How many did we drop?" Whitney called to Antoine as they turned into the last fenced lane to the pens.

"Beaucoup," Antoine said.

"Po, yi," Whitney replied.

There was one more tense moment as the cattle were penned behind the patched wooden barricades, but a visible relaxation came immediately when the gate was shut. The riders dismounted and breathed their horses then, clustering close and laughing about the drive. Many of them praised Leland for the action at the canal, but his father said nothing, glowering deeper and deeper as the compliments were passed around. Whitney's brother, Basile the cook, was barbecuing sausage for a snack, but the men did not have time to wait for it. Several riders downed a cold beer, then equipped themselves with extra ropes and went out after those cows and calves they'd left behind in the woods.

Mon Negre was the only rider who did not come this time. He loaded his horse, and he and the other blacks drove from the island. Mon Negre sat slightly slumped in the passenger seat of the pickup truck. The blacks never took part in this part of the work, nor in the cutting, nor in the pen work. Leland never knew if it was because it was too noble or too dirty to ask of them for the little money Whitney paid. Probably it was just because that was how it had always been.

On the road to the woods Leland was riding happily, joking with Loveless and Aubion when his father suddenly came up fast, grabbed the cheekstrap of Beau's bridle and dragged them off the road and out of earshot into the soft lot. Antoine halted his horse and watched from the road. Emile had both horses in a lope and Leland felt weak, afraid, ridiculous. Finally Emile dropped the bridle and whirled in front of Beau, halting both horses sharply.

"You little bastard, you!" he said to Leland and Leland could not face him. He dropped his eyes to the saddle horn. "And who you think's going to pay for your hospital, ainh? Who?! Them over there, them? Ainh? Running crazy and laughing all the time, you! You do that again, you, I'll get you, yeah!"

They sat their horses in the silence and the sunlight. The man was furious. Leland could not face him. Finally Emile said, "Hunh!" as one speaks to offending puppies, then kicked his horse toward the road. As Leland turned behind him he saw how heavily his father rode Willy, his hand braced on his left thigh and elbow outward. And he saw his uncle sitting Prince still at the edge of the road, though the others had ridden on. There was a shadow over his eyes from the brim of his oldtime hat, but his jaw in sunlight was set hard. Leland loped past him, afraid to look at him. Afraid he might weep like a girl if he did.

They found the cows and calves browsing but the animals quickly scattered. These were the wildest. They had to be roped and dragged in, cows as well as calves. Nose and Antoine, Whitney and Arsan Broussard did most of the roping. Leland and Loveless teamed with the dragging like the others, a cow between them on ropes and sometimes with each of them holding a small calf across the saddle. The trick, especially with cows that had not been dehorned, was for the rider in the rear to keep the cow from rushing the pulling horse and getting a horn in. Aside from that the only real danger was a cow inadvertently fouling the rope on a tree, strangling herself, or upsetting the rider or both. When he was not being used for roping, the Creole pony was wonderful in the dragging. It was much easier maneuvering him through the brush, and he was almost unbelievably powerful in pulling. And he seemed to have an instinct for knowing when the cow would snag the rope.

On the last run, Leland was dragging when Antoine came up free from behind. He had picked Leland's lost hat up in the woods, and as he put it on his head he shoved

Leland's skull over almost roughly so that he could see the abrasions better. Gently, he ran his thumb over the clotted blood, shook his head but said nothing.

Now they had time for sausage and beer. All except the cutting horses were unsaddled and the girths of the cutting horses loosened to give them room for wind. The sausage was pork and venison mixed, moist and tasty, but not greasy. They were sitting in the shade on saddles against the ground or on the roots of trees or fallen branches when a white van rattled across the rickety wooden bridge and halted in the dust and the sun outside the line of trucks and trailers still parked to extend the wing of the pens.

They watched the stranger emerge from the van. He was dressed in work clothes so new they shone, and he was wearing new tennis shoes. He had a little beard and moustache shaved at his cheeks like an island on his face. All the riders stopped talking as he walked up to them, but when he spoke they smiled, and some of them out of politeness turned their faces to laugh. He spoke the other French, the French which comes from schools.

Arsan turned his thin, dark face toward Leland and used a hand to shield his laughter from the stranger. His cheeks were thick with the dark whiskers of a days-old beard, and he smiled all the way to where greenish plaque lined his yellow teeth against his pale gums. They had already begun answering the stranger in English by the time Leland reached him.

"Mais, no. Mais, no. Mais, that what they got, them, on Pecan Island, you know. And on Grand Cheniere, too, yes. You ask the Marceaux on Grand Island, you. And you ask, you, the Veazeys on Pecan. Don't you take you the new road, no. The old road. When you get off the ferry. The old road. By the gulf, yeah. You stop any house. Them Veazeys, them, they good people, yeah. They treat you right, you bet."

The stranger seemed irritated. He seemed unable to wait for Whitney to stop talking, but no one ever interrupted Whitney. Still, as soon as Whitney had silenced he burst in.

"Yes, yes, I know. I did my doctoral dissertation on the chenieres. I know all about those mounds. Burial mounds. No, I'm interested only in mounds not yet excavated. You may have mounds here and do not know they are Indian mounds. All these salt dome outcroppings were inhabited at one time or another. Often for long periods. There must be some sign."

"You a doctor, you?" Leland asked.

"Of philosophy," the stranger said. "That is, not a regular doctor. Not an MD. I teach at the university in Lafayette."

"Mais, what about the Hills, them, in the blackjack?" Leland asked Whitney.

"Hainh? Well, I don't know, me," Whitney said. "Me, I think it was some old trees long ago, yes. Some trees long ago in a flood or something and the ground went away around the roots and the trees, them, they died and now they got just them little hills, yeah."

Basile came over with bottles of beer laced in his fingers and a paper plate of sausage. He passed both around and the stranger took both sausage and beer.

"Oh, yes, thank you very much," he said to Basile. Then to Leland, "Can you give me a description. Some kind of an idea. How big are they? How many? What shape?"

"Mais, about a hundred, I think, me," Leland said. "Maybe more, yes. Me, I never count them, no, me. In the woods, I too busy, yes, for to go counting hills in the ground, me."

They laughed and Basile offered Leland a beer and Leland waved his refusal.

"They about this high, yes," Leland said, drawing an

imaginary line across his chest with his thumb. "And about this big around, them." He took a stick and made a large circle in the dirt. The riders then gave a critique of his circle, not only arguing about the size but humorously complaining about the lack of artistry as well.

"Mais, yes, cher," Whitney said, "but some bigger, yes. And some littler, too, yes."

The stranger seemed excited.

"But that's perfect," he said. "A habitat. Could I see them? Which way? Who owns the property? Could I get permission?"

"Well, us, we all own the property, us," Whitney said laughing.

"Mais, but no," Arsan said. "Mais, the land, her, she owns us."

And they all laughed. Finally Whitney said in a large voice:

"Mais, it all right for this doctor, him, to dig in them mounds?"

Nobody said no. Some said, 'Of course, of course.' Only Nose spoke up.

"Sure, sure. Mais, you go dig, you, yeah. But some treasure, you give it us, yeah."

Some of the others laughed, but Nose did not laugh. The stranger was one who laughed.

"I don't expect to find anything of money value, and I don't want to take anything except something of significant anthropological value. I'm not interested in treasure. There was a man a few years ago in the Tunica Hills who got quite a lot of artifacts out of a Tunica burial ground, but he was hardly a scholar and what he did was a travesty."

"Mais, how you call that 'artificiacally'?" Nose asked, his eyes narrowing like a man reading fine print in a contract.

"Anthropological?" the stranger said. "Oh, something that tells us how man lived maybe thousands of years ago."

"Mais, you can you sell it, you?" Nose persisted.

"Sell it? Well, no, not really. That is, it isn't valued in dollars and cents . . ."

"Oh, well, keep it, then, you," Nose said with a slap of his hand in the air between them. They all laughed. "And to save you a little trouble, you, cher, I going to tell you something, yes." Now Nose lowered his voice to a whisper of confidence. "Thousands of years ago, yes, right here where you standing right now, yes? Mais, you listening close, you?" The stranger nodded. In fact they were all listening close. "Well, right here, where you standing right now, you, man used to live here with some sausage and some beer and a little pussy on the side, him! And damn good, too!"

Now they all roared, and when the laughter had subsided Leland's father said to him in a voice as loaded with deception as Nose's had been but serious, not in jest:

"Show him, Leland. Take him right now, you."

Leland reacted swiftly, before he could think. He spoke sharply, as fathers are not spoken to, and he saw the reaction in his father's face.

"Mais, no. I got work to do, me," Leland said.

He saw Emile's face redden, could feel the anger. But Whitney intervened and turned it.

"Mais, we all got work, yes, us. And we just talking here and not doing it, no, us. And Leland, him, he save me my rice field this morning, him. Who knows what he might save this afternoon. You wait, you," he said to the stranger. "We gone show you your hills, us. You wait. This my brother Basile, him. He cooks. He going to feed you good and get you drunk, him, you not careful. We got some work to do, us."

Basile was grinning at the prospect of getting the stranger drunk. Leland moved through the crowd away from Emile, but he could feel the man's eyes following him.

"I'd like to help, just show me what to do," the stranger said.

It was decided the stranger should do the vaccinating since he was a doctor. Leland wanted to work with the cutting, but he was anxious to avoid his father. So he helped Loveless with the spraying, instead, a job no one loves. As the cows were cut from the calves and brought through the pens, Leland and Loveless sprayed them until they were dripping with insecticide from a large vat equipped with a lawnmower motor and a hose with a tight nozzle. Then the animals went through the chute where they were vaccinated, dehorned when necessary, and wormed.

At the trap between vaccinations, the stranger told a joke about a black preacher who pretended he was Nat King Cole by singing "Rambling Rose" in order to seduce an attractive "high yellow" member of his flock. It was a great success, and thereafter he was referred to as Le Professeur Rose, or Professor Rose, or just plain Rose.

Leland was hiding behind the open gate to the spraying pen, and the cattle were nervously inching toward him when he realized it was his father who was pushing them. It was the last load of cows for spraying. They crowded through the gate, and Leland swung it shut and tried to get inside with them and busy before his father could speak to him. The gate was nearly shut when he felt it against his boot being pushed hard, knocking him to the insecticide-muddied earth of the pen. His father had dismounted rapidly, seeing Leland fleeing him, and like a rabbit snared him with the gate. Then he opened it quickly and dragged him outside with him, shutting the gate and latching the chain. He shoved Leland hard against the boards, shouting at him crazily so that Leland was afraid.

"To me for to talk like that, ainh?! For to talk like that! You! And my son no more you ain't, you think! Ainh! Mais, me, I'm for to give you a whip, you, yes. Like what you never did see, yes. Mais, you think I can't teach you who you is, you. Fils d' putain a la merde du cheu!" Son of a bitch out of the shit of the ass.

Leland managed a *yes sir* because he did not know what to do. It was as though he had gone limp. As though his father had sapped him of all the strength he had gathered in the long weeks of trapping. He felt weak, not only in his muscles but inside, also, and he could feel the baby's tears stinging in his nose and eyes and was very afraid he would weep.

"Me, I'm going to whip your ass for you, you!" his father shouted and then let him go, and Leland stood with his head down as Antoine on Prince came around the corner of the cutting pen and rode slowly toward them. Then his father shoved him again, not quite so hard. Antoine dismounted beside them and looked very hard at them. Then Emile looked at Antoine and back at Leland and shoved Leland hard against the boards of the gate and ordered him back to work, but did not look at Leland as he scrambled at the gate. He looked squarely at Antoine. The two men faced each other wordlessly, tightly, neither speaking until Emile smiled evilly and turned and walked to the pens. Antoine did not move. He stood watching his brother, the muscles of his jaw clenching. Then he, too, went to the chute, but he walked the long way around the pens.

After the cattle were sprayed, Leland kept busy packing the chute until all the cows were worked and released and standing and bawling for their calves. Then he went with the boys and Loveless and on foot herded the calves into the pens for the castrating.

Leland and Loveless teamed on the larger calves. Leland took the rear to throw them to the ground, and held the back legs apart with his hands and boots almost like rowing. There he could best observe and learn about the castrating. Whitney and Antoine were doing the castrating, the most sensitive process of the work because a calf could bleed to death if it were not done properly. The Professor Rose and two others were vaccinating. Nose was earmarking and Nelson Thibodeaux was smearing the pitch for protection against the larvae. Nelson also carried a paper bag into which he collected the testicles for frying. He would pick a testicle as small as his thumbnail from the dust and put it into the bag before swabbing the shining tar solution into the open, furry sack, now with the sliced edges white and the inside white and mottled red like the inside of any other skin. Some of those holding calves complained Nelson was wasting time over testicles too small to eat, but he argued none of them were too small.

Almost never did the calves seem in pain, though now and then one would suck a testicle up into his abdomen and the men would have to probe it down with their fingertips. The castrating did more than save the cattlemen from an overabundance of range bulls and assure the upgrading of stock. The expression was that it got the minds of the calves "off ass and on grass" and they gained weight rapidly toward slaughter.

When the calves were released to the cows the larger animals wandered frantically among the bunch of calves until they found their own. Some of the smallest calves seemed slightly stunned by the experience and trembled on thin legs. Others of the cows had hidden their calves in the woods and forgotten so their calves were not among those released, they were still hidden in the woods and would grow large and uncastrated to give the riders a rough time in the fall. These cows panicked and bawled and searched but did not find. A few dry cows and the bull were unconcerned.

The youngest boys stayed behind to clean up and the others went directly to the trees beside the barbecue pit, dug into the tubs of iced beer, and began drinking. They stood with beer in their hands and watched the newly de-horned cattle to assure themselves they did not bleed too much. Many of the other men, Leland's father among them, were already eating potato salad and jambalaya and red boudin and steak off paper plates.

The food was delicious, so the talking was scarce at first. But as the bellies filled and the beer began to lubricate the tongues, the conversation increased. The sun was weak-ening visibly and the younger boys were sent for firewood.

Then to Leland's intense embarrassment, his father be-gan to tell about the prophylactics and Leland's mother. He even described the sex he had shared with the barmaid so long ago. Those who had heard the story many times and were perhaps sensitive to Leland's feelings said, "Yes, Emile, we know, Emile." Antoine never spoke during these times. He grew sullen, instead, and angry in that dangerous, explosive way.

Leland suggested to Professor Rose they go to the Hills, and the professor eagerly accepted, gulping the rest of his food. Leland went to saddle the horses, glad to be out of earshot of his father. Years before, Leland's father had had an affair with a woman who ran a bar in Abbeville. She was rather a belle among washed-out barmaids, and so Emile took great pride in the event. Leland's mother one morning found the pack of rubbers in his jeans, emptying them for washing. It was at this point in the story that Le-land returned within earshot, leading the two horses.

"Mais, she didn't say nothing to me, no, when I walked in. But, I saw, me, them rubbers, them, on the counter, and I went for to check the pasture, me. And then it come on me fast, fast what to do, yeah. And when I got back, me, I say to her, 'Ho-boy, Jeanette, I made me some fun last night.' Po, yi, she look at me, right then, like she could kill me. Pretty good thing women not smart, no. She say, 'Oh, yeah, mais, and what you do, you?' I say, me, 'Oh, me and the boys we had some fun, yeah. You know what them crazy boys do, them? Me and Arsan Castinet and Babineaux and Peltier, we went, us, to Bonis' Cadillac Pool Hall in Abbeville, and you know what them boys do, them? You know how mean Peltier's wife is, her, ainh? Well, they put some rubbers in his pocket. Man, she find them rubbers, she going to give him hell, yes.'

"Man, she take them rubbers, them, and she throw them at me, her, and she say, 'Mais, look at what your good friends, them, did to you, you.' And I say, 'Well, my God damn son of my bitch, me.' And that's how I got out of that, yeah."

Professor Rose had listened to the story, then laughed. At last he came to Leland. He mounted and they turned into the woods. He rode like a sack of rice chaff, big belly hanging over the saddle horn, soft and lax so that Leland had the impression if the horse shifted Professor Rose would fall. The snakes were beginning to hunt. The woods were darkening, and Leland could see shadowy game around them, moving among the trees. And there was a constant attack of mosquitoes and jabber from the professor. It seemed as though something had been triggered or released in him. He never ceased talking, and Leland understood little from him, replying vaguely only when it seemed expected of him. Finally, they reached the Hills.

"This is it!" Rose said. "It! It! This was a town, Leland, a city. A city! Here they lived and gathered and sang and fought and stole and cheated and lied and sacrificed for one another and wondered about it all and died. Can you see it?"

"Mais, no," Leland said simply. "Just some bumps, them."

"Well, yes, I realize. I know. That's what's left. But from that, you see, we can tell it was a city. A city like all cities."

They dismounted. Leland took both horses' reins and followed Professor Rose around. The man was judging the size of the mounds and seemed to be looking for a pattern to them.

"Mais, you mean this was like Lafayette or New Orleans?" Leland asked.

"Yes, yes. Exactly. Oh, I don't mean buildings and paved roads and automobiles and skyscrapers and streetcars. None of that, of course, none of that. But you see in a sense that was farther away in time from those who lived here than this city is to you. You live not that differently. Off the land, close to it. Off nature. They were distant to us in a different direction. To them we were vastly in the future, in terms of human change existing in a fantasy. In fact they couldn't even fantasize about us. We can at least look down upon the remnants of their city. They could not predict the future. No one can predict the future. The one thing about life, which is merely a constant excursion into the future, is that it is unpredictable, one day to the next. Imagine predicting into the milleniums. What you call a city, New Orleans or Lafayette, had never been dreamed of, not even dreamed of. We can *see* this city, here, now, actually *see* it. Look. Each one of those 'bumps' as you call them was the site of a home. Think of it as a house, though it was not a house as you know it. Perhaps a hut of hide or sticks. We shall find out. But it was a home. A home, Leland. A home with everything every home has ever had since the beginning of mankind. Not dishwashers and television sets, but warmth and sharing and struggle, food and drink and sleep."

Rose was walking faster, now, from mound to mound.

The light was diminishing quickly. Often he bent to the mound and examined it closely. Now he reached and dug into the soil with his fingers. He brought up a shard of what looked like flat, heavy earth.

"Look, you see," he said, holding it out to Leland. "Pottery."

Leland took it and turned it over and examined the reddish surface with the gray soil still clinging to it. He handed it back to Rose, who placed it almost exactly where he had found it. Then he walked on.

"Mais, be careful of snakes, you, ainh?" Leland said. It had an electric effect on the professor. He looked immediately to his feet. "Mais, he's making night, him," Leland continued. "The snakes, them, they hunt at night, the bad ones."

"Well, perhaps we'd better go," Rose said, took the reins from Leland and struggled into the saddle. Leland swung up by the saddle horn then placed his boots into the stirrups. But Professor Rose sat his horse without moving in the slipping daylight. Now they could only see a few of the mounds.

"A city," he whispered with the first night hush. "A city, Leland, the feel of a city in this God-forsaken place. Let's go."

They turned the horses and walked them carefully from the Hills.

"Of course, it was not God-forsaken to them," he said suddenly loud and jolly. "Not to them, Leland. They were newly come to this land and left their mark, too. Just as the nineteen-forty-one flood released the Argentine coypu from their experimental compound and gave nutria to the marsh and changed that. And the oil companies, all that they've done and haven't even begun to do yet that will change this land forever. Them, too. And don't forget you, Leland, and your people. All of you and your ancestors or their brothers and cousins who brought horses here, Leland, and cattle. You changed the face of the land, civilized it as they say. You come by your abilities naturally, you see. You come by them as naturally as the abilities of the people who built that city back there. Lost civilizations are all around us, Leland, in every direction, inside us. They write books and make movies about lost civilizations, and they're always with towered halls and mysterious, decadent people and weird rites, et cetera. But the lost civilizations are with us always, always around us. We have only to look."

They rode, then, for a while in silence. Leland had nothing to guide him, but he was certain of the direction. There were only the black trunks of the trees to avoid. The horses were tired and docile.

"Mais, but, please tell me, you," Leland said. "It's true?"

"Is what true?" Rose asked as though he were coming out of a sleep. He was riding with both hands and the reins crossed over the saddle horn, a passenger and not a pilot of the horse.

"Mais, about the French, them, and the horses and the cattle?"

Professor Rose laughed, then deliberately reached a hand to place on Leland's shoulder in a gesture which meant the laugh carried no offense.

"Not the French, Leland. Your name is Viator, right? Well, originally it was Villatoro. Your ancestors are from Spain, the Province of Malaga in the Region of Andalusia. You're not French at all, but Spanish. It's all in the record, nothing mysterious about it."

"Now you tell me something," Rose said, taking his hand away.

"Mais, sure."

"How come you people won't let me speak French?"

Leland was embarrassed. He smiled down toward the

horse's withers then looked bravely into the professor's face.

"Mais, you speak, you, the other French, you," he said. "The one what comes from books, from school, him. We understand, us, your English better, yes. So we speak English so you have a hard time understand us, yes. But us, we understand you good. It's better for us than the other way, yes. Mais, don't forget, you, they got a lot of us and just one of you, yes. You see, you?"

Professor Rose laughed, then, and slapped Leland's shoulder, reaching far across in the darkness so that Leland was afraid his horse might sway outward and the Rose would fall. But he didn't. He had been holding to the saddle horn. As far as Leland could tell, he had not yet discovered the stirrups were for anything except holding boots, or in his case tennis shoes. Then Leland saw the fire ahead, flickering orange and yellow between the dark lines of trees and brush, perfectly on line.

Leland saw immediately on arriving that Antoine had the spur in him. Many of the riders, especially those with young sons, had left. Rose got down and Leland unsaddled and loaded both the horses. Then he came toward the fire. It was full dark, now, and the fire was leaping and crackling yellow-orange and blue-white dancing from the hardwood branches transforming into glowing coals.

Loveless gathered conspiratorially to Leland.

"Mais, you think the Professor Rose, him, he after Lafitte's treasure, or what?"

"Mais, what you think?" Leland said. "Lafitte, him, he going to come with his ships up the Warren Ditch? No, he just after for to learn, him. He say they used to be a city here, him."

"Mais, that crazy, yes," Loveless said. "They ain't even a store till Esther."

Maurice Fontenot had come over from Forked Island, as

usual too late for the work but in time for beer. He went into a long story about stealing a motorcycle but Whitney engineered the conversation to politics not to be a bad influence on the boys. And that was the beginning and the end of something with Antoine, as Leland could see. The skin was stretched tight across his uncle's forehead and the bones of his cheeks and eyes, tight and pale even in the flickering glow of the fire. Alcohol made him treacherous and mean instead of warm and friendly like the old man. He cared nothing for politics, had never even registered to vote, but the words he inserted into Maurice Fontenot's speech were barbed like fishhooks. Sooner or later, Antoine would snare him.

Emile seemed pleased. He encouraged the situation for a while, and he and Leland drove home. Both were glad to leave Antoine, Leland because there was nothing he could do and Emile because he didn't want to do anything, and as a brother he would be expected at least to prevent murder.

Leland unloaded the horses, put away the tack, and went to bed. Before he went to sleep he heard a couple of trucks pass in front of the house, but his uncle did not come home. In the morning before day, Antoine's bed had still not been slept in, and at breakfast Leland's mother's eyes were rimmed red beneath. She spent long moments at the stove, her back to them, doing nothing, just pausing with deep breaths before bringing them the dishes.

School was not so bad as Leland had remembered. He had more of his own money, now, and broke the rules by leaving the schoolground and taking his noon meals in town. Recesses he spent alone or talking to Essey. The others had new songs, new clothes, new things to think about. Marie had a new hair-do. The tight curls were now pulled back from her face and pinned behind to give the flavor of the mane of a horse, low to the ground and spread out in full gallop. It gave her face a new, fresh, clean, pure look and made things jump inside him. One day he tried to tell her.

"Your hairs, them, they look good, yes," he said, and she laughed. Her face was lovely, even laughing at him, the teeth the whitest he had ever seen, unreally white, and eyes brown and moist and bright, her skin perfect, and the dimple of her chin widening with the pulled-back, full lips so that her mouth was almost opening to him like a flower. She laughed and looked deeply at him, and at once Leland was bored. So he said nothing and left it alone from then on.

He took his meals at the restaurant beside the square in town. The restaurant had showcases built into the walls, and behind the glass were guns and Indian relics. The guns were mostly Colt pistols, and the arrowheads were placed in putty in designs of teepees and oak trees and an Indian's head. Leland usually ordered two hamburgers, french fries, and milk. He amused himself looking at the relics and wondering about the events that had surrounded them.

He walked back through Magdalene Square, past the rectory with its large, arched porticos, cut through the cemetery behind the church, weaving among the above-ground tombs of cement and crumbling brick to First Street and past Monsieur LeBlanc's yard, which in the spring was filled with flowers of hundreds of different colors so that on a bright day the flowers dazzled the eyes and tinted your clothes. Leland timed himself well and was never late. The afternoons were easier to endure because the end was closer.

The early evenings at home, with Emile at work in the fields and the grandfather overtaken with a curious almost childlike reverie, were to Leland the most pleasant he could remember. Even Antoine's absence did not quench the revelry Leland was experiencing just in the coming of spring and in his growing power and confidence. He yet missed Antoine, missed him as one misses a picture that hangs in a display and without which the arrangement is disquieting and incomplete. But he no longer required Antoine's presence to complete his own image of himself. Leland was content for a time in that which he saw, in that which he felt, and in that which he made of what he saw and what he felt for himself.

"The Professor Rose passed to see you today on his way to Pine Island," his mother told him after he had done his chores. The days were longer, now. "Why don't you saddle your horse and go to see him? That man, he seems so nice, educated. You, he likes, I believe. Perhaps he can help you someday to go to the university."

His father was in the field on the tractor, its wheels filled with water for traction, water leveling, as Leland rode past. Once inside the woods on Pine Island he heard Professor Rose's shovel, a ringing thud. He saw soon enough that the professor was tamping road shells into the mounds he had excavated. Leland could have ridden him down with the horse. There were spider lilies in the low spots, even in the shade among the trees, the long needles of their white petals extending curved and pointed from the rounded, swaying cup of the flower and the narrow delicate stem extended from the rich, dark earth. The professor squinted past his nose at Leland, less for vision than to keep his glasses on his sweating face.

"Ah, Leland," he said as though he were identifying *Lelandus Acadienae*, a rare example of fern, from among a forest of common types, "I'm glad you've come. I hoped you would. Did your mother tell you I asked about you?"

Leland dismounted and the professor followed him a few paces to the tree where he tethered Beau. "She is a beautiful woman, your mother. Did you know that? She has that Gallic quality about the eyes. Striking. I was surprised, taken aback, to find her. It is easier, now, to understand why Acadiens are so passionate. But you look nothing like her. You are like your uncle. Pale, with the long nose and those light blue eyes. Fish eyes, almost, which seem to look right through you . . ." His voice almost trailed off and he would have been staring if he had let the gaze linger an instant longer.

"But your mother's very beautiful," he said, snapping away the gaze. "I'm glad you've come. Come here, I want to show you. I've been very hard at work."

"Me, I can see that, yes," Leland said. The shells that had been tamped into the earth of the excavated and restored mounds had been carried to the site in a burlap sack. There was also on the ground a box made of one by sixes and bottomed with a screen for sifting. "And, mais, how many you dig, you, ainh?"

They had reached a larger mound, very near the center. It, too, had been excavated and re-covered with earth and road shells.

"I use the shells for holding in the earth after I've disturbed it. For erosion," Professor Rose said. "I don't want it to erode. I don't take anything, though truly here there are just trinkets. I want to save this as nearly as it was. Shed only a little of the mystery, as it were, though there's ample mystery remaining for all my work, I'll tell you. I suppose if there were going to be one of those damnable socially relevant things here, like a hospital or a school or a nuclear power plant or something, I might be persuaded to rifle these mounds, take the money, and run, as it were."

"Mais, treasure, you say, you?" Leland said suddenly. "They got treasure? They think, them, that you after Lafitte's treasure, you. It true, ainh? Or what?"

Professor Rose smiled, then, almost laughed. A healthy

slackness seemed to come to his shoulders. He dropped his arms in friendly exasperation so that they seemed longer against his swollen flanks and belly, comical, as though he were surrendering.

"No, no. Not the way they think," he said. "Is that what they think? It's positively amusing. Lafitte would have been a rich man, indeed, not only the heir to the throne of France but its purchaser as well if he could have afforded to sink that much money into Louisiana in every place he is rumored to have done so. No, the treasure here is in ideas. Look. This is where it started."

He knelt, began digging with his hands, as a dog digs with his forepaws. The earth was soft. It had been loosened. His hand blackened with it as he removed it from a ridge of other, older shells; oyster and clam and mussels. Some of the older shells had been blackened with fire. He lined them like pearls on the still earth-covered portions of what Leland could now see was a circular ridge. It circled one of the larger mounds. Then he quit, sat looking at them. That was it. That was all.

"Mais, what?" Leland asked.

"This is where it started. Right here. They found this place and sat down and had a big feast, first thing. The first thing they did was eat, around a fire, like we did that night. Maybe the men found this place on a hunting trip, then brought the rest here when the time came for a move. This is the exact highest point on the island, but of course you knew that. Did you know the island is sinking? All these salt domes are sinking. But, anyway, they came here and sat down and had a feast and threw the shells and the bones behind them, made a ring behind them. And they built right here, the first home right here, in the center of their first fire circle."

Professor Rose sat back against his heels and looked at

the shells and then put them back into the hole and covered them gently with the little levees of loose soil. Then he got up without a word and walked away. Leland followed him through the mounds to one that had a small tarpaulin staked over it. Pulling the stakes on two corners, Professor Rose flipped the tarp over and exposed a series of little red pieces of pottery stuck into the dirt beneath, forming a symmetrical pattern. The largest piece, in the center at the top of the mound, was also blackened from fire.

"Go ahead," Professor Rose said. "Take a piece out. Look at it. You can still see the straw design of the mold which probably burned away when it was fired. Look."

Leland took one of the larger pieces, turned it. The pattern was there, all right, exactly like the weave of a reed basket.

"I've photographed all of this well," the professor said. "But I really wish despite myself that I could slice the top of this off and take it back with me."

Leland tossed the piece back to its place. Professor Rose walked back to the box, sat on the loose mouth of the sack of shells, and picked up a canteen. He unscrewed the black top and tilted it back against his mouth but took only a swallow.

"Mais, what kind they were, them?" Leland asked. "Them Indians what lived here, them?"

"I don't know," Professor Rose said. "Perhaps Attakapas, but they lived slightly different. The Attakapas were very warlike, you know. Sometimes cannibals. And they had domesticated the whooping crane and lots of other animals, and I didn't find any evidence of this. I walked all over this island. It's a big island, you know. And no burials could I find. No burials and no dump. They were clean, for Indians, I'll say. I don't know where they could have buried. They were here for a long time. Where did they bury, Leland?"

At first Leland shrugged. He took the canteen and drank, squatting there among the mounds with Professor Rose. Then he handed the canteen back.

"Outside Island," he said.

"What?"

"Outside Island," Leland said again. "Mais, it the perfect place, it, for a graveyard, yes. Can't get to it. Mais, ain't nobody going to bother it, no."

"But where is it, Leland?"

Leland raised his arm straight out from his body and lowered his head as though he were sighting down a rifle barrel toward the gulf.

"There," he said. "Mais, it out there. In the marsh."

The professor followed his gaze and the point of his arm as though it would be possible to see the island, though it was far away and there were trees between them.

"But how did they get there, Leland?"

"Hainh! Mais, they get there, them, the same we get there, us. Pirogue."

"Can you take me?"

Leland answered immediately.

"Mais, oui, yes of course," he said. "And why not? But not with all this stuff, no. Just me and you, yes, and two of them little shovels what fold up and down. You know?"

"When?"

"Sat'day. Before day. Way before day. Two, three o'clock. And we back late, yes. After dark, us. You don't want, and me too, yes, to spend the night with them bugs, them, no."

Professor Rose smiled broadly, then, and brought his hand around wide, like a roundhouse punch, to shake Leland's hand and seal the bargain.

"Saturday, then," he said jubilantly. "Saturday."

That night Leland lay on the thick hide rug Desormeaux had brought them and was unable to study. He traced the Doctor's brand. Out of the marsh, his father had revived the habit of drinking each evening and now sat above Leland with the glass of whiskey and ice in his hand, his face blankly set, staring at the cold fireplace. His mother was reading. His grandfather was whittling shavings from a bare pine branch into an open section of newspaper at his feet. His grandmother was saying her rosary and reading her novena simultaneously, rocking back and forth quick and hypnotic.

"Pa-Paw," Leland said, "The Professor Rose, he says I inherited my skills with horse and cow from . . ."

His father's swift interruption was quiet but savage.

"Who cares what he says? What is it that he knows? He knows nothing. Nothing."

Emile was gripping the whiskey glass with fingers red at the centers, dark down the bone line and white at the edges, as though the glass might shatter in his hand. Leland looked to his mother, but she had turned her lips inward and was biting a white line against them. Leland felt the need to speak but could think of nothing to say since he did not know what he had said that had been so wrong.

"The Professor Rose, I think he is a very intelligent man," the old man said softly, lightly. He had lost weight since the winter and his color had faded. Now he resembled Antoine as much as Emile. "You know, he is a doctor of some sort." He was whittling exactly as before. He had not heard what Leland had heard in Emile's tone.

"He said, the Professor Rose, only that my ability with the horse . . ." Leland began, but his father stood, sloshed a heavy drop of whiskey to the hide and stalked from the room. As Leland spoke his mother's eyes clenched closed as though she had been struck and the white line of her lips spread. But as Emile left, her lips released, now, dark red, and she sighed long and whispering. Leland looked to her.

"He's tired, that's all, Leland," she said, and rose and followed him.

Leland's grandfather was still whittling. And from the bemused absorption Leland saw in his face, the lids far down on the down-looking eyes and the forehead lined with swaying rows like a cottonfield amid gentle hills meaning thought, Leland knew he had not witnessed what Leland had seen and heard. But his grandmother had. She was no longer looking into the novena. Her rocking had increased. Squeaking back and forth in rhythm. Back and forth rapidly, almost wild. And her eyes were wide and on the doorway almost fixed. Her mouth continued the words of the prayers rapidly, silently, the long, deep wrinkles opening and closing as the mouth moved without sound.

"Pa-paw," Leland said, "the Professor Rose, he says that we Viators are Spanish, not French, and first brought the cattle and horses here."

The old man smiled, then, but did not look up from the whittling. He shrugged his shoulders high in that supreme, even arrogant gesture of frankly admitted ignorance coupled with pure, mindless righteousness.

"Well," he said. "It is true that we brought the cattle here. This much is certain, and the horses, of course, with them. But we are as French as anyone, this much you can see. People who go to school do not learn everything."

The old woman had returned her gaze to her small prayerbook. She prayed almost constantly since the season in the marsh. Even while she worked, perhaps while she slept. She seemed to have many petitions before the good Lord, perhaps because it was Lent and she was preparing for Holy Week.

There were preparations at school, also, and this only served to make the time pass more slowly from Monday morning until Friday afternoon. Benediction in the afternoons, a cumbersome affair relieved only by the smell of incense and the golden sundisk showing of the host finally in the bright, dust-particled light of the high windows of the gymnasium, the only room large enough for the entire student body. And there were extra prayers all day; morning, after recess, before and after lunch, at the end of the day. It was a long week.

On Friday he went to bed early and slept soundly but awoke early Saturday morning in complete darkness. He fed and watered the stock and brushed down the horses by feel. Then he waited on the front steps. It was chilly and he was eager to get moving. He saw the lights of the van across the rice fields long before it reached the house.

"Stayed up all night," Professor Rose said. "Couldn't possibly have gotten up this early." The whole van smelled of beer. He had brought an impossible number of things. A lunch big enough for the two of them to live on for several days. Picks and shovels and sifting boxes. A cooler filled with beer and soft drinks. Two extra pairs of boots. Blankets. Rain gear complete with umbrella. And a liquid propane stove and lantern "for heating the food."

"Mais, we in a pirogue, yes, us, not a how-you-call . . . yacht, no," Leland said. He pulled a Coca-Cola from the cooler and a leg of chicken, a banana and a sandwich from the bag. He breakfasted on the way to Pine Island. He would rather the food be in his stomach than on the floor of the pirogue. For himself, Leland had brought only a bottle of water. He allowed only two small shovels, the smallest of the sifting boxes, and the food. Professor Rose brought two of the bottles of beer but didn't bring an opener and Leland did not show him how to open them on the gunwales. Later, when the professor had settled himself to sleep, Leland slipped them over the side into the water of the Warren Ditch.

He kept to the ditch until they were far into marsh on each side. The ditch angled away from Outside Island, but the ease of the poling made it worthwhile up to a point. And he was determined to find a good channel before he entered the marsh. It was still full dark when he heard the trickle of water and saw the mouth of the channel against the grass. He pivoted the bow around, leaned on the pole, and slid over the first mud buildup into the marsh. Now he anchored the pole and shook the professor awake by his foot.

"Ici," he said, handing him the little jar he had carried in his pocket. "Mais, you take and rub on your hands and face, yes. And you keep your hands in the boat, too, yes, 'less you want snakes hanging from your fingers, you. Mais, this time of year in the marsh they boss, yes, I want to tell you."

Professor Rose propped himself up and sniffed the ointment.

"Whew!"

"Oh, yes, it powerful, yes. But it better than the bugs, I want to tell you."

The professor rubbed it on and lay back to sleep. Leland was glad he had not asked what Granmere had boiled down to make it.

Now the work began. At first it was a good channel, with plenty of water and almost straight in the direction he hoped. But it soon ended. It ended in a small lake and Leland had to skirt the perimeter to try to pick it up again. He finally found the feed channel, but it was not a good direction. When he finally found one in a better direction it was very narrow, but with a good draft.

Dawn was coming grayly. The green of the marsh grass

was rich and thick. In the narrow channel it bent over the gunwales, brushing the coat of the sleeping Professor Rose, who began to whimper in his sleep, his feet making little jerky movements against the floor of the pirogue like a child. Leland knew the closeness of the grass made the presence of the snakes more dangerous, but there was nothing to do. The marsh was strangely devoid of animals. He wondered if it were just that he was experienced only in the winter marsh when the grass is dun-colored. The marsh was like a different world in this season, and he was aware that not all he knew applied. Then his mouth went dry and he paused to drink from the bottle. Now that the dawn had come and the sun was behind the clouds, he was lost.

It was irksome to him to be lost. He put the bottle back into the stern and continued poling. Thin buzzing clouds of mosquitoes clustered around them but could not alight to suck blood because of the ointment. For an instant he was aware how tantalized the bugs must be and actually felt sympathy for them. Now Leland could tell by the brightness of the clouds the general position of the sun, but it was exactness he craved. His choices were not mated to exactness; he had to bear in the direction of the island generally, at the whim of the channels. Still, it would be comforting to know his exact position.

There would be a drainage system from the island. There would have to be. And he would find it. But it was taking much longer than he had thought. Still, he would find it, this much he knew. He would have to find it. Professor Rose slept on, whimpering in his dreams now and then. Leland was grateful he was sleeping. He had time and the environment for thinking.

He found another channel, narrower still, but at a better slant, and followed it with the grass now crowding the pirogue, spilling over the sides from bow to stern complete so that it seemed they were sliding on a board and not a boat, and a narrow board, at that.

Then he saw it, a channel in the island's drainage system. It rushed with trickling whispers of brackish water at an opposite slant to the channel he was using, then eddied, and finally joined and flowed with that channel. Leland jerked and rocked around into it, and the professor jerked awake with a start and looked incredulously at Leland, then calmed saying, "Oh," and settled again to sleep. It was comical to Leland, and he was glad to have found the channel so he chuckled aloud.

The channel was wide enough at the first and grew wider with lots of draft and the poling was very easy, now, and he felt fine again. When he saw the island rise by the tops of its trees, it actually gave him strength. He pushed on harder, the island still rising before him, and knew he would rest soon.

But then, almost at once, the island seemed to rise above the marsh like a balloon or a mist or a cloud. It hovered there, suspended. It rose as the Fire Man is supposed to rise, which Leland had heard about but never seen. An island floating, floating not on water or even on marsh, but on the air itself.

The pirogue was in a glide, Leland trailing the pole motionlessly in the brackish water behind. The vision, itself, seemed to arrest the boat as the bow struck a small mud flat and came to rest. The cloud of mosquitoes engulfed his head and he swept them clear with his hand. He was aware his mouth was open only because he sucked some in and had to gag and sputter them out. Leland had no doubt what he beheld, though it was clearly impossible. Before him the island in its uninhabited, unused, and completely natural spring foliage floated above the marsh, not touching.

Leland pulled the pushpole beside him and leaned on it for balance. Tiny waves rocked and slapped at the sides of the pirogue, and he was grateful for the reality of the sounds. Professor Rose, too, shuddered and whimpered again. Leland did not wake him because he was afraid he would not see it. Or that the island would vanish before their eyes. So he swallowed hard, rocked back, and pushed on over the flat. A brown water snake took to the water before them for a turn and then was gone.

It was very difficult for Leland to avoid the flats, then, because he could not keep his eyes from the island, his goal, to watch each turn and twist in his path. He kept pushing the point of the pirogue into the grass and having to pull back to go ahead. But then he saw the rest of the island rise from the level of the grass and the trunks of the trees shaped to his vision, and he sighed and felt relieved and only a little foolish. The foliage low to the ground had been grazed away, simply. The brush and leaves and small limbs of the trees browsed bare, that was all. What he had seen from the distance had been only the lush tops of the trees. The ground beneath was gray and almost bare.

But when the professor awoke and sat up and saw the island and gasped, "My God!" with surprise and amazement and wonder, Leland thought he, too, had seen the island floating on the air and that the vision of a floating island was reserved for first sighting. In fact, he feared his own intelligence had tricked him, supplied a rational explanation for what would otherwise remain unexplained. Like a denial of the Trinity or Transubstantiation. But Professor Rose had not seen the phenomenon of the floating island.

"Jesus Christ, Leland, Goddamn it look at that!" he said. "The whole Goddamn place is one burial mound after another. Christ, man, look!" He was pointing as he shouted.

"There, near the marsh! And there by that tree, there! Goddamn, look at that one over there, it's huge! See the shapes of them, Leland? See the shapes? Goddamn!"

"Shhhh," Leland whispered softly. "Shhhhhhh." It did not seem right to talk so much or so loudly in boats or in the marsh. Professor Rose settled to his knees and Leland continued in the winding channel, the mounds becoming larger and more distinct. Just before the solid ground seemed to come forward to meet the prow of the pirogue, Leland saw the bleached bones of some large animal that had become mired in the marsh and had died there.

The illusion of the island rising in the air had inspired in Leland a passion for solid ground. He could feel himself trembling as he did when very tired or very hungry. And with the shaking came the unfamiliar notion of discovering buried treasure. The excitement of the prospect of hidden gold, even though he discounted all likelihood of it, seemed to spring from a tiny seed within him but spread rapidly, and he gave way to it as before a crest of seawater, let it course through him unimpeded. In haste and excitement, he did not give himself time to analyze the bones of the animal as he rocked back and pushed the pirogue onto the bank and scrambled to the shore.

It was a large island, quiet and bare. Leland pulled one of the shovels from the pirogue and started immediately up the slope. The professor took the other shovel and the sifter and started after him.

"Wait, wait," he called to Leland. "Take it easy. There's no rush. Let's select one to begin."

"Mais, what I think, me, is you select for you, you, and me, I select for me, me. Ainh?"

Professor Rose stopped, the sifter swinging at his side. He stared at Leland, studying him. Leland felt a sudden unexplained disgust for the professor, and mistrust.

"All right," Professor Rose said, finally. "Okay. But go careful. Start at the side. No use going in from the top. Like I showed you. Slow and careful. And if you find something, call me. Careful, Leland. This stuff's been here a long time and it's delicate. Okay?"

Leland said nothing. He turned and stalked up the slope and began digging in the first mound he reached. But he soon abandoned it and took another to the west, one larger and somehow more inviting. Professor Rose watched for a while and then selected one far to the east, out of sight.

Leland moved again and again, hardly digging enough to find anything, not breaking or sifting any of the clumps that cascaded down at each bite of the shovel. Finally, plunging the blade into the earth and slashing it away, the packed earth fell away like a slide and this gave him his first satisfaction. He found nothing, but he had liked the way the dirt fell away. He wiped his brow, and the dust on his hands mixed with sweat and created a muddy covering on his skin. Suddenly he hated Professor Rose, regretted the hospitality they had shown him, and the help he, himself, had given him. The man had done nothing for them, probably laughed at them and made fun of them and told all his rich, educated friends about how ignorant and naïve and easily manipulated they were. Leland the crudest, most stupid, most innocent, and malleable of the bunch.

It was then the spade bit that slashing sweep into the earth, and the cover fell away like a curtain, and the face with hollow sockets stared at him, yellowed and fleshless and profound. All the bones protruded from the earth. The hollowed sockets were dark and empty. The jaw was still intact and the teeth had been filed to points. The arms turned at the sides, the two bones of the lower arm and the many bones of the hands and fingers resting—at rest—

the entire body not merely at rest sitting against the earth but within the earth, itself. Uncovered and within the earth, itself.

The shovel dropped from his right hand as he reached his left hand to touch. The short time and short distance it took his fingers to traverse seemed immense, slowed, arrested. He had not reached all the way across when he heard the deep sound close to his right. So close he could feel the warmth and the familiar sweet breath and the tiny particles of dust that flew from the ground with the snort from the huge, black, rounded nostrils as Leland turned and looked into sensitive, seeing, intelligent eyes set in coarse, black, bristled features. Though Leland had seen very nearly the same thing countless times, he knew instantly in a place beyond intelligence that he had never really seen anything like this before in his life. As one knows from instinct the difference between a harmless green grass snake and one with venom and deadliness in that immeasurable instant it coils at your bare foot. And he saw beyond the horns to the huge not hump but gathered tossing muscle of the neck and then knew in the intelligence of his training that he had never seen this thing before. Now falling back, grasping for something, anything, no matter how puny and hopeless, to defend himself, he heard the shout, felt it, and heard it but did not identify it as part of himself as he fell backward against the earth.

"Aaayiiiiiiiii!!!"

And it was gone. A snort, a prance, and it was gone. Leland was sweating profusely, backing and clawing against the mound, his hand still holding some meager weapon randomly seized. Then Professor Rose came swiftly into his vision, knelt at the front of the skeleton.

"Marvelous, Leland," he said. "What a find. Nearly intact."

But Leland was shaking. Eyes wide, darting to whatever

he could see. But the professor did not notice. Until Leland ran; he ran toward the pirogue.

"Leland! Leland!" the professor shouted after him. "Wait! What the hell? What's the matter with you?"

Leland forced himself to stop and turn and face him, still trembling. His hands convulsing, still clutching what he had grabbed to help him fight. Still deathly afraid of a rush from the flank.

"Come on. Let's go, us," he said softly. "Mais, let us go."

"What?" Professor Rose said. "What are you talking about?"

"Let's go, us!" Leland shouted with all his might. And the professor stepped back a half-step. He paused just an instant.

"All right, Leland," he said. "All right. All right. We'll go. We'll go. But what's the matter, Leland? What's wrong?"

"Something, it is here," Leland whispered. "Something, him, it is here." Then he heard a snapping to his right and turned and ran. He ran all the way to the pirogue and stumbled at the bow and fell into it so hard he was afraid he had ruptured the seals of the hull to the gunwales. But the boat took no water pushpoling safely into the marsh. Only then did he notice the slightly curved, yellow bone in the bottom of the boat.

There was a long moment, then, when the dreadful silence of the island seemed to come toward him over the marsh and settle around him standing there in the pirogue with the pushpole grasped in both hands. Then he heard a kind of shuffling like the motion of a sandcrab across dry clay, magnified a thousand times. Finally, he saw Professor Rose come carrying all the tools and disgustedly disdaining to look Leland in the face. Leland hid the bone in his boot, the curve uncomfortable against his ankle, and poled in to pick up the professor.

During the long trip to the mainland they did not speak.

Professor Rose did not sleep, and out of sight of the island he only ate the rest of the food and looked bored about him. He sat with his back against the bow, his legs pulled up so that his paunch hung forward, watching the grass and an occasional snake or muskrat. The weight was poorly distributed but Leland was at first too shaken and then too ashamed to mention it.

It was full dark before they reached Pine Island. In the van the professor opened the ice chest and took out two beers. They were still cold, small lumps of ice still floating in the water around the bottles. They drank the beer, Rose practically absorbing his, and getting each another. Leland gulped the last swallow as the van pulled into the yard.

The house was dark and all were asleep. Some food had been left for him beneath the light of the stove. Though he was not hungry, he ate in the hopes it would calm him as the beer had done. He fell into bed unwashed and drifted into a troubled sleep.

Palm Sunday dawned bright, sunny, but with a chill wind from the north. It was the wind and not the sunlight that awakened him. It rattled the panes at his window. He dressed swiftly and hurried out to his chores. But he left the feeding when he saw his father walking in from checking the pasture. Leland walked out to meet him and told him what he had seen.

"Hainh! You'd do better not to fool around with that man, yes, you. What you going to do, you, with that kind, you, ainh? Nothing, no. For to be going off into the marsh for no reason, hainh! That crazy, yes."

It was exactly as if he had not heard. Even the old man did not reply at first as Leland finished the story over breakfast. ". . . and that is where the hide comes from, the one that bears the brand of the Doctor."

His mother held her nose as she served him breakfast.

"Po, yi, Leland," she said nasally. "Mais, you smell bad, yes. Mais, what that? That Granmere's mosquito stuff, ainh?"

"Non, non," the old woman protested. "That is not my medicine reeking so. That is like the smell of a male goat or of the long insects that swim in the water and stink when crushed."

"But they are our cattle, don't you see," Leland insisted. But his father was smiling broadly at the old woman's analysis of the smell.

"But you have to bathe, yes, Leland," his mother said. "Today is Palm Sunday, yes. And we all going to town, us, to get the palms blessed, yes. You too, and don't you know it, you. Mais, you going to stink the whole big church, you."

But now, finally, they noticed the old man. Since he had lost weight his eyes seemed to bulge slightly, pale and rheumy and imbedded in wrinkles. Often he seemed to stare into air, as now, when he swallowed hard and spoke hardly above a whisper but with great intensity.

"Yes, yes. It is as I said. When I was a boy. Oh, yes," he said, "I, too, was a boy whom no one would hear. We lost all our cattle, but I knew they were waiting for us. I said they could swim long distances by bloating themselves. And when I watched the marsh for the circling of the buzzards for two whole weeks and saw nothing but the expected carrion of the wild things, I knew it was so. Unless they had all been swept to sea, into the gulf. The boy is correct, even as I was when I was younger than he is now."

There was a silence, then, and the old man continued to stare into the air and did not resume eating.

"Finish your breakfast and do your chores," his father finally told Leland harshly. "Then bathe. You stink!"

Then the old man spoke again, still with gaze fixed on

the air, as if no one had spoken but himself and no time had elapsed since, and what he said transfixed Emile so that Emile forgot about Leland and Leland's odor.

"It is an omen," the old man said in a soft, amazed voice. "It is an omen, our cattle being returned to us. What can it mean? What can it mean?" Then something blazed in his eyes, a flicker of understanding. "The gold," he said. "The Doctor's gold. The gold will be found and the family's power restored."

Leland got up slowly from the table, then. His father leaned close to the old man.

"For true?" he said. "I mean, this you truly believe?"

But the old man did not seem to hear him.

"The gold," he said absently. "The Doctor's gold."

Leland went into his bedroom and took the bone from where he had hidden it between the mattresses. He brought it into the barnyard and shoved it deep into the mud, which was kept soft by the cattle entering and leaving the barn. Then he finished his work and bathed for church.

Abbeville was bright, and the chill of the wind seemed only to accentuate the springtime. The old man waited, smoking with other old men on the plaza outside the church, until the moment of consecration then entered. The blessing of the palms had lengthened the service. The parishioners lined the altar rails with bunches of bristling palm branches, and the holy water flew sparkling in the light colored from the lead-lined, stained-glass windows.

Monday at school began the retreat of Holy Week. All classes were suspended. The students saw their proper teachers only at first period when mimeographed prayers and hymns were handed out. From then on they were herded about by others in sequence and in silence. Participation in the retreat was not optional, neither was confession. Leland did not know whether to confess taking the bone. But once in that line to the confessional he had to confess something. The barriers that held them in line against that glazed brick wall were invisible but as rigid and as sturdy as oak boards. And the line advanced forward in increments of one toward that feared box where they would kneel, locked in by a curtain, waiting sometimes with held breath for that little door to slide back and leave open the yawning prospect of eternity. But in the end Leland withheld his secret even from God.

One afternoon the sisters took the boys and the girls in gender-segregated groups separately into the library and desexed them with the fear of unwanted pregnancies, treachery in prophylactic factories, and venereal disease.

But throughout it all, Leland continued taking his noon meal in town. It was very easy to just walk away from the crowd milling at the entrance to the cafeteria. But there was no one to talk to except for ordering his food, and he kept the rule of silence.

The rule continued at home. The others spoke among themselves, but not to him, and though his place was still set at table and he still did his chores, it was, in a sense, as though he were not there. It was as though a stranger slept in his bed. In the mornings he fed the stock and brushed the horses and had a mind always on what was buried in the soft black mud at the rear entrance of the barn where the cleft hooves kept the soil worked and broken and barren of grass.

His father no longer worked the fields each day. No one knew where he went, but he was making no more preparation for the planting. He left each morning in his pickup truck and returned each day at dusk. One evening, still during Holy Week, his father caught him in the hallway on the way to bed and whispered forcefully into his ear.

"Your precious Antoine is no longer here! Perhaps he

shall no longer return from New Orleans and the whores. A new time is coming! Pa-Paw has seen it! The deserving, the loyal shall inherit!"

Leland was grateful for the rule of silence the retreat imposed. He tried to edge by the man, but Emile now blocked him.

"And Pa-Paw has spoken to the Broussards," he continued. "Saturday we go to Outside Island if Antoine is here or not. And what we find shall *not* be shared as always. More to the deserving." Then he broke from the French, saying, "And what you think of that, you?!"

But Leland did not speak, and Emile let him pass. In his room before he slept he prayed for Antoine to come home. He held too many things within him. There was not enough strength. He was solaced only by the thought of returning what was buried in the barnyard.

Thursday morning at first period they chose hours for the vigil. Those of the country were exempt from this observance though they were supposed to spend one hour in meditation at home. This was the night Jesus sweated blood while the three apostles slept. He had asked them repeatedly would they not watch one hour with him, but each time they had slept. Then he was betrayed with a kiss. Peter cut away the soldier's ear and Jesus replaced it and still they crucified him. So the town students would watch the apostles' hour. They did not mind, most of them. For some it was an excuse to stay out late.

Leland left the lunch line as usual and walked to his dinner in the town. While he was admiring the artifacts behind the glass after eating, he heard them enter the restaurant with a blast of laughter as the door swung open. E. J. was with them and they were talking and laughing, and Butch was smoking a cigarette down to the filter and making a point of calling E. J. "CheeKat." E. J. reddened with suppressed anger each time. It was from a nonsense language song they'd made up that was supposed to mean E. J. was screwing Mable Mouton on the bayou every night. *CheeKat toe Melito on the bayou every night.* E. J. was CheeKat, *toe* was the verb for screwing, and *Melito* was code for Mable Mouton.

"Ah-hah! This is where he been hiding, eh?" Butch said when they saw him. What's the matter, Coffeepot? You don't like the food at school?"

Leland did not answer them, but gravitated to the pinball machine. They began taking turns in playing the Blackgold machine, and Butch lost the first nickel on the bells, bumpers, and bright lights. All the pinball machines had basically the same format—buxom blondes and redheads showing lots of bosom, rounded curves of breasts and buttocks. Blackgold had women in hard hats around a spouting Texas oilwell, tight bluejean shorts, mouths wet and open, and red-lipped around undivided white bars of teeth. When the specials were lit the score ran up the gusher and burst from the top in sparkling lights as the games knocked loudly and registered in a small box at the bottom right of the backboard. But Butch did not light the specials. He lost his nickel, then tilted the machine to retrieve some satisfaction.

There was a line of nickels on the glass against the wooden frame of the machine, which acted on the same principle as their books in line outside of class at school. Each nickel represented one of them in his turn at the machine. Leland put his own in the line. He watched the others lose games as his nickel advanced, learning as much as he could from observation. Flipper buttons. Flat jars with the heels of the hands to give more life to the bumpers. Shots from the flipper to the little buttons line the centers of flowers imbedded in the floor of the machine, which jiggled in little delicate circles noiselessly but ran up the score. Techniques of shooting the ball into play.

But when he got his turn he just pulled the plunger and let it go. The first ball would have gone all the way down without more than a tiny score if a small gate had not been closed at the end of a chute near the bottom, and so the ball ran over the flipper and he hit the button, and the ball went sliding up into a sort of wing and then into a pothole but flushed quickly, and without thinking he had flipped again and this the time the ball sailed all the way to the top of the machine and made a marvelous, glory-filled descent of bangs and bells and darts and stops and smatters of noise, and because he had noticed the spot on the flipper which aimed the ball he got it into the wedge-shaped wing and the pothole three more times, and each time it flushed he aimed it on the flipper and got it high on the machine. Then it went down with no hope of being flipped at all, and the score on the gusher of the backboard went up almost all the way to the elongated black drops of oil.

"That's what he's been doing," Butch said, then, as Leland pulled the plunger back again. "He's been playing pinball. He ain't been hiding."

"Huh! He's been playing pinball *and* hiding," E. J. said deep and threatening.

On the second ball the specials lit. Leland did not know how he had lit the specials, but they stood cherry-red against the sides, behind little square-shaped plastic doors with wrenches and wheels painted on them. He knew enough to try to hit them, but they were very difficult to hit and he did not know the spot on the flipper and the ball finally went down and the specials went out, and he forgot about the score because he had been so excited by the red little lights. His hands were sweating.

"He's lucky," Butch said. "If he'd just learn to flip."

"Yeah. But he's going to learn to flip," E. J. said ominously.

Leland let go the plunger, and this time, as mysteriously as the lighting of the specials, a game knocked loudly into place in the little box before the ball had crossed halfway down the course. This had a relaxing effect on Leland and he got lots of action around the flippers, rocked the little petal-buttons again and again, and then the specials came on again and he knocked the ball into them three times, and a game knocked in on the little square each time. On the next two balls he got three more games, and he felt wonderful.

He played four of the games and each time won at least two and at the most four more games so that he had amassed the figure of twelve in the little box by the time they had only ten minutes left of lunchtime and E. J. began tilting the machine. Leland did not want any trouble in the restaurant. And he had plenty of games. So he just punched another one off. But E. J. hit the machine immediately each time, scraping the metal tips across the concrete floor, glaring with challenge into Leland's face.

Leland knew it then, of course, that there would be no other way, that he was being left no other option. But he went through all twelve games as E. J. each time pushed harder and harder and glared each time more menacingly until the waitresses were looking toward them and Butch and the others had ceased giving attention to the machine at all and were giving all of it to E. J.

Leland said nothing. He considered his fear, savored it, it was there but there was something else there, too. There was something very good about what he felt. So he walked out of the restaurant, through the door, taking a deep breath, and across the street to the square as the others followed him. Before he had stepped onto the curb, E. J.

had shoved Leland's shoulder and darted in front of him and hit him on the forehead with the heel of his hand a blow of contempt, utterly fearless, which did not hurt but jarred Leland's head back.

"You not going to get away. You not going to run. You ain't got no old nun to save you now," E. J. said. Leland started to strike with his left fist but held it because E. J. brought his right arm up guarding well. "Oh-ho!" E. J. said almost jubilantly, as though the bait had been taken and the fish was hooked, and that was exactly the moment Leland got his right hand between E. J.'s arms and slapped him hard across the face. It left an immediate red mark in which one could distinguish the lines of Leland's fingers. But as E. J. stepped back in amazement, his entire face flushed redly so that the imprint disappeared.

"Oh, no, buddy," E. J. said. "That's one I'm going to give you back."

And he came on hard swinging his fists for Leland's face. Leland backed away and to the side and avoided the blows quite easily. They were in the shadows of the oaks, now, in the exact center of the town, and Leland hoped some responsible adult would come to stop the fight. But, though people walked the sidewalks and a couple of pickup trucks and a car slowed to watch as they rounded the corners, no one came near the fight except the crowd of boys eating potato chips from Butch's bag. E. J. recovered and came onto Leland again, and so Leland started with his left again, then dropped his right shoulder and went under and up through his guard and got him a second time in the same place.

E. J. dropped his guard to say, "That's two!" and Leland took the opportunity to slap him with a left this time. Now his face was white except for the two red slashes on each of his cheeks. And each time Leland went in, E. J. was so afraid of the blows that he brought his guard either very high or very low, and it was quite easy to get in and find his cheeks. Leland continued to slap, and E. J. counted each time, up to nine when in a rage he rushed to grab Leland and got him around the waist, and Leland was afraid he would go down so he hit him with the flat of his hand, and that was when E. J. bit him hard on the side. Then Leland panicked and hit him with his fist on the back of his head, feeling the knuckles solid against the bone, and E. J. released him and staggered back a step and brought his hand to the back of his head, and then Leland went in angry for the first time in the fight.

Leland went in with fists for the eyes. And he got two blows, right and left, one on an eye and the other to the side of the nose. E. J. started to go down but Leland did not want him to go down, wanted him to stand up for some more, so he caught him with upward blows. Then E. J. was going down, and there was no other way to hit except downward, so Leland went for any place on the head, first hitting near the ears, then the forehead, and finally the hair as E. J.'s face went forward out of sight and he was below Leland on his hands and knees.

Leland pulled back, breathing hard, now, his fists tingling, the burning of imminent weeping in his nose and eyes, watching the steady, not large but thick stream of blood from E. J.'s nose stain the pale green grass.

"Goddamn," someone whispered beside him. Leland found he had to almost force his fists down, then put them in his pockets. The others were helping E. J. to his feet, and he looked as though his knees and arms were difficult to straighten, as though he were a doll formed of wire and cloth. Leland did not want to see his face, so he turned and walked toward the river, crossing the street and taking the sidewalk in the shade of a liveoak tree, then the sunlight in front of the church.

"Leland!" someone called, he thought Butch, behind

him, "Come on! We're late!" But Leland did not look back. He quickened his pace and crossed in front of the church but did not make the sign of the cross because he still did not want to take his hands from his pockets. The knuckles were outlined, raised in little mounds, in the tight fabric of his trousers.

He walked on to the river but did not take the bridge. Instead, he went under the side and sat on the concrete slab there. Though the day was bright, beneath the bridge it was dark and very cool. He took his hands from his pockets, then, and rubbed the soreness of his knuckles. Then he wrapped his arms around his knees, pulled them to his chest and wept. He wept long and hard, and his sobs reverberated against the pilings and blended with the slapping of the ripples against the smooth, shiny mud bank. And he smelled the river and the creosote of the pilings and felt the deep coolness and tasted his salty tears.

He had wept in defeat and in victory. And now he knew there were tears in both paths.

Finally, he quit crying and breathed deeply of the sulphur smell and deep-channel odor of the river and rested until the church chimed the time for him to leave. He arrived at the school in the after-class flurry of children running and to the sounds of young voices shouting in the end-of-retreat release. Rabelais opened the bus door for Leland and said nothing.

There was a great silence as Leland entered. The bus was already moving as he made his way down the aisle, aware of the silence and the awed eyes of the other students on him and of the hard-ridged rubber mat beneath his feet. He sat in the rear, now, aware of the faces turned toward him. Finally, when they were nearly out of the town, Augustin Mestayer came toward him, sat beside him.

"Mais, didn't I tell you way back last fall, you, you were

going to get him? Ainh? Ainh? What I told you?" And he put his arm around Leland's neck and pulled him tightly in a headlock and rubbed him hard on the head and someone on the bus laughed. Leland had until Tuesday morning to deal with the nuns.

He opened the window and let the breeze flow over him, enjoying the curve around the last of the rice fields and over the last rice canal before Big Woods. Now they were on that stretch of road as wavy as water through the little cypress swamp, Leland gazing intently out of the window into the deep shade of cypress and oak, hickory and magnolia, when suddenly his hands flew to the windowsill and he stuck his head out of the window into the rushing wind to make sure. It was Emile's blue truck, all right, almost hidden behind a stand of willow. Truck tire ruts now marked the spot where the Doctor entered the woods so long ago on his returns from town, mudgrip tire ruts in the soft soil between the pavement and the stand of willow.

Leland got off at Esther, with the Mestayers.

"Mais, what you doing, you? You going look for your daddy, you, or what?" Augustin called to him as he started back down the road on foot.

"Mais, you know about it?"

"Mais, yes of course we know about it, us. What you think, you? You think somebody go crazy in the woods right here and we not find out? He don't hide too good no more, no. Early in the week, mais, that when he hide good, yes."

They all laughed, but it was somehow not the laughter of ridicule. None of them came with him. He turned at the little post office and walked down the lines of cypresses across the swamp in the cool, deep shade of the late afternoon as though he were walking into a tunnel to the past.

At the ruts, he crossed into the woods. The mud was dried hard on the wheels of the truck. Emile was easy to follow into the woods, for the soil was often flooded there, constantly moist between the trunks and the roots and the cypress knees. In fact, the lower bushes bore the coat of beige mud that testified to a recent flooding. The tracks were not the imprints of boots. Emile was too crafty for that. They were merely depressions a practiced eye could easily follow. He had walked in a straight line and had only used the roots when they were handy, and even then he carelessly left mud scraped from his soles, so it really was no deception at all.

There were dozens of holes. Shallow ones. Dug principally near trees or other permanent landmarks. Two hollow trees had been felled. Leland trailed between holes and left no tracks. When he saw Emile ahead, he bent low between the palmettoes and weaved silently among the vines and trees to a point where he could see clearly and not be seen. He watched and waited.

He dug each hole swiftly. It would not have been buried deep, after all. As soon as he reached a certain depth, he dropped the shovel and clawed the ground with his fingers. Then he would stand, lean lightly on the shovel, wipe his brow with his forearm, his hands caked with mud, then survey for the next likely spot.

Leland watched him for perhaps an hour. During that time he saw raccoon and opossum and squirrel come out onto the limbs of gum and oak trees and watch the man digging, also, not noticing Leland kneeling quietly among the palmettoes. And he heard the whistle-talk of wood-duck in the nearby swamp and saw woodcock and the usual jays and ricebirds and sparrows. But he also saw a canebreak rattlesnake perhaps seven feet long cross in front of him, coiling in a jagged line among the stalks of palmettoes and the clumps of brush.

The light had turned a greenish golden when Leland crept away and walked to the road and then to Esther where he got a ride on a pipeline truck as far as Forked Island. From Forked Island Marcel Leger of Pecan Island brought him all the way home, driving into Leland's front yard to let him out. Leland lied to him and explained he had missed his bus.

"That Rabelais, him," Leger had said, "he's mean as the devil himself, him."

That night Leland could not help but think of the hour's vigil. He thought about it before he went to sleep, lying awake in bed and rubbing his sore knuckles. His dreams were confused and troubled and highlighted with a vision of the bone shimmering with a white, bright light within the dark mud of the barnyard and throbbing as an abcessed tooth will sometimes throb. It was difficult for him to guess the time when he awoke in full darkness. And he did not know how long he had lain awake before he left his bed.

There was a dreamlike quality to his wandering through the house this time in darkness. He was not surprised, for instance, to see Antoine's truck parked in its place beneath the tree but at a hard angle to the whitewashed trunk, bumper touching bark. Leland let the curtain fall, silently crossed to the hall. The door, of course, was open.

He entered stealthily. He was aware of changes in the room, changes in the presence of the room. He knew, now, that the presence he felt in the entire house, but especially here in this room, was not Antoine. Antoine was there, in the bed, and Leland felt embarrassed and as though he were intruding for the first time in his life. A man, now, in another man's bedroom. An interloper. An odor in the room was familiar to him, but he did not identify it at first. It was a sweet smell, not like perfume but the antithesis of perfume. Not an artificial odor but something of the hard realities with which the family lived, something of thé source.

The presence was not Antoine, though Antoine was a part of it. Antoine was on the bed, a dark shadow in the blackness etched by the shimmer of the sheets. A garment or towel made a dark stain over the edge of the mattress, spilling from where Antoine's arm extended at an angle from his torso. The presence Leland felt was not Antoine, nor was it the shadows of ancestors or the auras of the others asleep in other rooms, though these were all part of it. The presence Leland had been feeling was himself, and now he knew it.

And he knew this was the last nocturnal visit to Antoine's room. He no longer needed the visits. Still, he took one final step toward that shiny object on the bedside table, reaching his fingers across that darkened distance and touching not the derringer but a pocketknife, the bone handle of a Case with a long skinning blade.

"C'est toi," Antoine said weakly from the bed, and instantly awarenesses exploded upon Leland. "That's yours," and the sweet, familiar smell was given picture and substance and meaning. He reached his fingers now toward the bed and deftly touched the damp, sticky sheet, knowing before he touched it what he would find. Blood.

Leland crossed quickly to the far wall and the light switch. The room was exposed in unrelenting light. The blood had soaked the sheet and mattress but was no longer even oozing from the holes in the forearm, one near the wrist and the other at the elbow, marking a tunnel through Antoine's flesh. Antoine half-rose in the bed, the sheet falling from a pale chest impossibly spare of muscle for his strength. His pale eyes did not blink in the harsh light but he seemed only vaguely conscious.

Leland ran from the room. He was barefoot and the floors were solid oak planks, thick, from another era, so he made little sound. But his own pulse and breath sounded heavily in his ears as the passages and objects of the house flew past him. He did not contain himself when he reached the room where his mother and Emile slept. Never in his memory had he entered here in their presence. Now he burst through, the door giving before him like a flimsy cloth curtain.

Even in darkness he had no trouble discerning his mother's sleeping figure. He knelt quickly and touched the softness of her upper arm. In French even before she was awake, he began to detail the situation. She rose from the bed and put on the light simultaneously. She did not speak to him and seemed to understand everything at once. She came from the bed already in action. Her breasts, unbound, swung heavily in her movements, and Leland could see the dark disks of her nipples through the soft, white fabric.

Beside her on the bed Emile grunted, protested, began to rise thickly. But as he turned and saw her running through the door he called softly but forcefully for her to stop.

"Jeanette! Mais, you bitch . . . you stop, you." Then he looked at Leland and began to come from the covers. He wore his white long underwear.

Leland followed his mother, running. Her hair, unbraided, hung below her waist in the downward, released cadence of the plaiting. It flowed in the darkened, shadowy house with each step. Leland thought it beautiful, as beautiful as anything he had ever seen.

Ahead of him she darted through Antoine's door. Leland reached the entrance to see her standing with hands on hips, a deep crease between her brows, unmindful of the dark disks of nipples and the shadow of dark triangle at her center showing through the thin cloth.

"My house is your house," Antoine said rather happily, and she sighed, said nothing, brushed her dark hair from her brow. She turned to Leland as though to speak but stopped. For an instant there was the look of recognition in her eyes. She glanced, once at Antoine then back to Leland and this time there was sadness, there, too. Then it was all gone, that fleeting look of understanding. Emile burst through the door and washed understanding away with a torrent of anger bellowed in whispers, the veins of his passion-pulsed purple face and neck bulging and his breath even in bellowing backed up, controlled and contracted and contorted.

"You son of my bitch," he said. "You kill somebody, now, or what, ainh? Mais, what more I got for to take from you, fils putin tu." Then he shifted his eyes to the woman.

"Quiet, Emile," she said softly but with authority in French. "There are the old ones. Should they know? Should they know everything?"

But Emile was in a rage. Words could not curb him. He went for Antoine with his fists, fists broad and hard and with the force of clubs. She tried to intercept him, but he put his left forearm across her chest like a great swinging boom and sent her sprawling to the wall. Now Leland had him around the neck, from behind, and was trying to choke him, but the big man pitched like a horse and almost dislodged Leland. Antoine came weakly to a sitting position and struck a blow which glanced impotently against his brother's jaw, and when the woman came up from the floor she went not for Emile but for Antoine. She put her body between them and buried her face for protection against Antoine's chest, pushing him against the bed.

Emile's rage, then, rose even higher and there was a tiny scream or wail from him as he swung a killing blow for Antoine's face, now contorted against the ridiculously inappropriate softness of her sleeping gown. The arch of the fist was partially contained by Leland's grip, and the forearm struck her back so that Antoine caught only a portion of the blow over one eye. But that was enough to send him full against the pillow.

Leland had a tight grip on Emile's throat. The muscles were so hard and flexed it was like strangling a knot of leather. But Leland finally drew him off balance and reeled him toward the door and put a blow to his mouth that stunned him and drew blood. And in the moment of advantage, Leland got a shoulder into him and drove him backward fast until he struck the jamb of the doorway, and his breath went out in a whoosh. Leland stood back, a guard between them, as Emile fought in gasps for his breath. When finally it came, it was rasping as before.

"The Holy Family," he said mocking in French. "The Trinity."

Then he spat blood and saliva toward the man and woman on the bed, and it struck the dark spot already saturated with the blood of his brother. He glared round a moment then left the room.

Leland was shaking from fear and exhilaration. His mother straightened at her position kneeling before the bed. Again she brushed the hair backward from her forehead. The whiteness of the room seemed to have taken the wrinkles from her face. She seemed young and quite beautiful. She seemed complete. The calm she assumed after Emile had left set Leland to wondering if it had really happened, the part with Emile, or if he had imagined the entire painful, thrilling episode. Only the tingling of his knuckles assured him.

"My sewing basket, Leland," she said. "And alcohol. And the bandages and cotton from the bathroom. And from the cabinet Pa-Paw's finest whiskey. Quickly."

"I do not need the whiskey," Antoine said.

"I need the whiskey," she answered.

It had happened, the confrontation with Emile. The big, heavy man paced the living room angrily. The blood was smeared about his mouth and jaw and spotted down his long underwear to his shanks. His bare feet gripped hard at the floor and at the shaggy hide before the fireplace. But he said nothing to Leland, and Leland gathered the things and brought them back into the room.

She cleaned the arm then sipped whiskey from the bottle before suturing the wounds with the same stitch she used to close circles of cloth for making rugs. She picked up the flesh with the point of the needle, pushed it through, made a rapid, skilled wrap with the thread, picked up the flesh, and began again swiftly, smoothly, without emotion. Antoine did not even grimace during the suturing. Only when she was finished and the arm sewed up and disinfected and bandaged, when her severe calm collapsed and emotion swept her and she wept and pressed her tear-bathed cheeks against his great-veined and callused and muscled hand, did his face show emotion. He smiled sweetly, almost serenely, and stretched his other hand to touch lightly the errant black strands of her hair. Stroking lightly, he said, "I shall be gunshot every night."

Leland stood for a moment at the doorway and watched them. She kissed the hand of the injured man. He stroked her hair and looked down into her face though she did not raise her eyes to meet his. Leland noticed for the first time the many scars Antoine carried. Then he reached his hand to turn out the light.

IV

There was no light, and Leland grappled with his fingers in the mud and cow dung for the bone. Several times, he thought he had it, but it turned out to be a stick or a piece of doubled wire. At first he squatted and probed for it between his knees. He had been certain at first that he could go to exactly where he had buried it in the mud by shoving it into the soil kept soft by the hooves of the cattle. But now he was on hands and knees, and the cold mud and dung had penetrated his trousers and chilled his knees. His hands were completely grimed to the cuffs of his shirt-sleeves and still he had not found it.

He tried to set bearings, crossing them from fenceposts to the corner of the barn, but that was backward thinking. He had set no bearings when he had buried the bone. When he had buried the bone he had had no intention of digging it up. He had only wanted to relieve himself of it, to put it quickly back into the earth, as one tries desperately to put a lie to rest when it begins to complicate and compound. The three horses in their stalls had crunched away all their corn, and in his search Leland had used up all the time it would have taken for him to load them into the trailer. Then he heard a door slam at the house, and he panicked and swept to another spot and probed.

His hands became claws in the mud and dung and his fingers at last touched it. Quickly, he pulled it out. There was a suction to it and a swish and a plop as it came sliding from the soil. He ran to the spigot and washed it and his hands, then lifted his trouser leg and shoved it into his boot, adjusting the curve around his ankle. It wedged painlessly against his skin.

When he came around the corner of the barn, it was Antoine's slim figure against the lights of the house. Prince had his long neck over the stall barrier so Antoine could adjust the halter about the horse's head. Even in this simple activity, Antoine favored the right arm.

"They just finished eating, them," Leland lied.

"Uhm," Antoine said. He had known of Leland's presence before Leland spoke, and he knew the horses had long since finished eating. So Leland decided not to lie to him again, and the best way to do this was to speak clearly what he was thinking. So he took a deep breath and stepped closer.

"I have much fear of him, now," he said.

Antoine glanced shortly at him. Leland's winter growth had put them almost eye level. When Antoine had finished buckling the halter, he faced Leland and leaned against the boards with his left arm. Prince nibbled playfully along his shirtsleeve, but Antoine showed no fear the horse would bite.

"So you know," he said.

"Yes."

"Did he tell you?"

"No."

"Did she?"

"No. No one told me. I just knew it suddenly, and then I knew I had known it for a long time."

Antoine did nothing. He did not even seem to breathe. Leland could not see his face in the dark silhouette against the houselight. The horse continued to mock-munch but got bored when there was no response and went back to the corn bin as though he might have left some feed by mistake. Then, because he had left nothing by mistake, he jerked his head importantly and ran the line along the wood. Antoine looked toward him, half away from Leland. His face was shiny in the light for an instant, no more. "You," he said threateningly to the horse, Tu.

"Well, it doesn't matter, now," he said, looking back at Leland. "You have nothing to fear from him. It's all over, now, anyway. You are a man. You will understand such things. It has been a long and bitter time, and you can be your own father, now. He would have killed me once, but for Pa-Paw and Ma-Mere and because he could *not* kill me, and knew this quite well. As well as I, he knew it. Perhaps better. Now none of us have anything to fear, not even knowledge. It is over, thank the good Lord."

Antoine's words were quite calm and assured, but Leland was not convinced.

"How goes the arm?" he said.

"It goes," Antoine answered and slid the bolt in the door of the stall and led Prince toward the trailer. Leland put the halters on Willy and Beau and led them from the barn. The horses loaded easily in the darkness, and Leland and Antoine climbed into the cab of the pickup truck as Emile came walking purposefully from the house.

Almost always Antoine drove. But this morning Emile took the driver's seat. Leland was nervous with Emile driving. And he was tense just sitting between the two men. Something almost tangible oozed from Emile. It heated Leland's left side. There was only a small blue line at the lip where Leland had struck him and drawn blood. Emile drove badly, as one always handles mechanical things when existing in emotion rather than logic. The wheels of the truck and of the trailer skittered alternately on the gravel buildup at the center of the road. Leland knew that loose gravel like deep pools of water can throw a trailer to the ditch, but Antoine seemed unmindful. He looked straight ahead, face relaxed, a tiny bump over the eye where Emile had hit him only hours before. He was pale but did not seem weak any longer. He exuded no heat. They rode silently and Leland was relieved to see Pine Island.

They unloaded the horses from the trailer beside the Warren Ditch. The bateau was hitched to the cattle barge and moored at the bridge. And Whitney was there with his brother Nose. And there were three of the Broussard distant cousins, and Maurice Fontenot with a claim that his family also had lost cattle in the flood. Maurice eyed Antoine with a curious mixture of wariness, anger, and sadness, but Antoine paid him no mind at all.

They loaded the horses onto the barge, and then Antoine went forward into the bateau and started the diesels. Nose had loaded some equipment onto the bateau, two heavy canvas bags with the clink of metal. Antoine moved them from the motorwell hatch to the afterdeck, opened the maw of the motorwell and made adjustments. Then he shut the bay, flipping the ring of the hatch into its groove, leveling it with the wood, and replaced the bags.

Leland, alone, stayed behind in the barge with the horses during the trip down the Warren Ditch. There were no bends in the ditch to hang the barge, but Leland had a pushpole in case they snagged some debris.

The horses at first stomped nervously or importantly, and Whitney's big bay bared teeth, extended his neck and nipped at Prince. Leland knew Antoine's horse would have none of that hierarchical meddling so while the barge moved steadily down the ditch he untied Prince and moved him to the side. The side of the barge is less pleasant for a horse. A horse wants his nose in the wind while moving. That's natural, as the pattern of hair in the front part of his body attests. When not moving, he turns his rump to the wind. This is why, for purposes of toughness, the leather from the rump is more satisfactory.

They had timed it to arrive at the marsh buggy and the sled just after daybreak. And the line of dawn spread horizontally under clouds to the east while they were still in the Warren Ditch. Leland watched the clouds closely, but as the light increased he saw the clouds were high and white and far away. In fact, as the sun rose to shine down through them, they disappeared. The light was no longer pink or with that amber quality of late sunrise or early sunset but had become a businesslike gray before they reached the marsh buggy and sled.

Whitney had borrowed them and the driver from a seismograph crew looking for natural gas on his land not far from there. The marsh buggy was the largest type, like a huge tractor on elephantine wheels of metal but hollow and buoyant and ridged with grips that slanted curved and pointed against the marsh. When they shut off the bateau motors the marsh buggy was already idling.

The sled was small for their purposes, not designed to haul cattle. For the day, they had built a corral on its perimeter. But it was much smaller than the barge, barely big enough for the horses and men. They'd have to make multiple trips to haul everything from the marsh.

Leland climbed with Whitney to the cab for a discussion with the driver. Over the rumble of the buggy, Leland could not hear the conversation, but he had really only wanted to look into the cab. There were many dials and levers Leland did not understand, somewhat like the cockpit of a cropduster, but there were also the elements of a boat, and it was clear the process of navigation was the same. Whitney had a chart with Outside Island and their starting position, each circled and a line drawn between them. The driver took the chart and stuffed it under his seat then shut tight the door as Leland and Whitney climbed down. He was no Frenchman, that driver.

They loaded the horses and climbed aboard the sled. Nose hoisted the two bags of equipment over the fence, Antoine helping him with both hands but still favoring the right arm. One bag had the twin handles of a posthole digger and two axe handles protruding from it. The other, an oversized open duffle, landed heavily on the deck of the sled. Inside Leland saw two butcherknives, cleavers, a hacksaw with extra blades, and several kinds of sharpeners. There was also a hand-hewn singletree, which had once yoked oxen around the horns and now was fitted to a block and tackle. Before they got moving all the men except Leland and Antoine slipped holstered small-caliber pistols onto their belts well back out of the way. Attached to Whitney's saddle was something Leland had never seen outside Western movies. It was a rifle boot, and from it extended the wooden stock of a twenty-two caliber Winchester slide-action rifle.

Antoine handed Leland and Emile each one of the heavy ponchos, reversible dark green on one side and bright yellow on the other, each tightly rolled and secured with fishing line. When Leland looked puzzled, Antoine nodded to a dark mass of clouds to the southwest. The clouds were more purple than blue or black and sat squarely against the marsh, directly in their path. Antoine bent close to Leland and spoke into his ear against the buggy noise.

"The marsh, she is after all as much sea as land, bearing both the curses and the qualities of each," he said.

Then as if to prove him right the squall swept upon them as quickly as on the gulf, directly from their path, into their faces. It reached them blue and blowing, surrounding them with gray sheets of rain. They could see no farther than the front of the marsh buggy pulling them. Only the driver was protected, enclosed. Whitney pulled his rifle from the saddle boot and put it beneath his poncho.

The buggy drove forward as a juggernaut, churning the surface of the marsh, tearing it and spinning it skyward on great, ridged wheels constantly washed clean by the driving rain. The water actually cascaded down the deep metal treads, pulling the rich, black mud and grass with it. The sled behind bolted against the marsh and rose and fell as a boat upon a stormy sea, but more violently, with less of the sliding, cushioning effect of the sea. And it left a wide, ugly swath, a gash dark behind it, an outrageous scar of shattered turf and writhing serpents and black, oozing, sulphurous, rotting loam where there had the instant before been grass.

And the scar, itself, was swallowed by the rain behind them. Against the wind, the men with hoods drawn up turned their backs and looked toward where they had been. The horses were much afraid, blinded by the rain and confused by the noise and the strange vehicle that was pulling them. The popping and fluttering of the ponchos in the wind frenzied them, and the men gathered the garments about their waists and held them tight and silent. Nose took off his belt and bound the poncho around his middle. Antoine gathered his about himself with his right arm from the inside, so that the rubberized fabric stretched tight across his shoulders and outlined his arm across his lower chest, horizontal, like a sling.

And perhaps because it was like a sling, he did not remove the poncho at first as the others did when the squall passed, the rain abated and the sun broke through the clouds at swift intervals, then constantly. He turned again toward the island, which was now forming ahead on the horizon, but did not strip the poncho from his shoulders. He continued to hold it against him, the right arm tightly gathered by the folds as they moved steadily and slowly toward where the tops of the trees seemed almost to grow upward from the marsh at the sound of their approach. Leland rolled his poncho and tied it on his saddle and climbed the fenced side of the sled where he saw animals radiating from them in the marsh like sparks of fear.

Panicked running. Deer bounding and flying across the marsh-grass tips. Marsh birds, the poule d'eaux and marsh hens, which almost never fly, now bursting from cover like quail and fast-beat winging away in curving, evasive flight. The snakes could not move quickly enough, and the great wheels crushed them in their path, snapped their thick, muscular bodies. The cottonmouths bared their white, needle-bristled mouths and struck in blind rage and pain at the huge metal monster crushing them and at the long metal tail the monster dragged.

It was an incredible sight. Leland alone had climbed the fence for a better, farther view. But all of them were watching it, pointing out particular scenes to one another in the broad collage around them. Only Antoine did not indulge in this. He alone, except for the driver possibly and who was not a part of them really, looked forward, his eyes fixed on the forming island. Poncho still pulled about him, feet spread for balance as though he were in a pirogue, the wounded arm still slung in the fabric from his shoulders. Pale, thin, serious, his long face set but lax still, the pale eyes like rifle sights intense and almost independent of each other on either side of his long, narrow nose. He was almost not a part of them, almost his own separate entity on some level impenetrable, benign but dangerous. He seemed to be waiting.

The buggy pulled them to the island, then made a half-circle and got the side of the sled with the gate in the corral almost against the solid earth where Leland had grounded his pirogue. To do this, the heavy wheels settled on the bleached skeleton of what Leland now recognized as a cow that had died after becoming mired in the marsh. He saw the skull, now, the horns denuded of the outer layer and pitted and bleached as the old conch shells of Cheniere au Tigre. The skull, with its inner horns intact, popped dryly and cracked under the crushing wheels.

The insects of the marsh overwhelmed them. Now, the moisture of the squall rose in evaporation. It soaked the dense air with a layer of concentrated heat. This brought out the insects, more horrible than usual. Throughout that day, no matter what the task, the men were waving, slapping hands and cursing.

First there was the unloading of the horses. There was a small gap between the sled and the solid ground. Some of the horses, already jittery from the long strange ride, refused to jump and had to be ridden ashore, balking, goaded with spurs until, with a great gathering of muscles, they vaulted the small gap easily and snorted and pranced on the island, fearful and offended.

There was a spirit of excitement and exuberance among the others, even Leland. But Antoine was in no hurry to set foot upon the island. As the others clambered their horses ashore, Antoine slowly removed the poncho, careful of the arm which now seemed more tender, rolled the garment, and tied it securely to the saddle using clove hitches with the trick for quick unfastening. Then he tightened the girth of the saddle moderately and stood watching with Prince from a far corner of the sled, the slack reins held loosely in his fingers, Prince with ears pricked forward, curious.

Finally, all the others were ashore. Antoine led Prince to the gate, speaking softly to him in French the nonsense phrases he always used with horses, sometimes words that would have been insults or curses but for the soft tones, sometimes loving tones. At the gate Prince paused, lowered his head, and sniffed the small border of marsh and the island beyond. In French, Antoine encouraged him to look well and satisfy himself as to the distance and the danger. Then, after the horse had raised his head and looked high onto the island, Antoine calmly but forcefully commanded him to jump, and Prince gathered his big-veined muscles quickly and sailed over the gap. Antoine held the end of the rein lightly, and the horse went no farther than its length, spinning around at the first tightening of the line and watching Antoine with that same curious ears-pricked stance, as Antoine also leapt the distance.

Nose's first act after directing the digging of the postholes was to cut logs and fill the space between the barge and the island. Antoine noted to him that this could have been done before they jumped the horses, and the animals could have walked across. Nose just smiled and shrugged his shoulders in that Frenchman's way of not speaking. They went to work building from the natural materials of the island two funneling wings of wood fencing to the gate of the barge. It was hot, miserable work, and they paused to drink ice water from the jugs when they were done, seated in what shade there was and constantly slapping at the insects. Nose had brought briar hooks and cane knives to clear the area through the funneling wings, but there was no brush on the island. The brush had been grazed away.

Then they cinched their saddles and rode away from the marsh buggy's idling engine. Leland could see enough of the driver to tell he was reading a magazine in the air-conditioned comfort of the cab and drinking a beer or a soft drink from a can in a styrofoam container. As they rode away and the sound died behind them, Leland realized that the sound reminded him of a street fair or of the heavy motors that ran the rides at the Dairy Festival or the Crawfish Fête or the Rice Festival or the Yambilee. As it died behind them the awesome silence of the island was broken only by the creak and clink of tack and the slaps of the riders against their own skin.

Nose led on the little Creole pony, winding amongst the burial mounds, keeping close at first to the perimeter of the island but eventually moving inward. The island had been grazed practically bare. Even the leaves and small branches of the trees had been cropped high. There was more cattle sign, and Leland marveled he had not seen it his first trip to the island. The soil was practically tilled with their cleft hooves.

Leland thought he would be able easily to tell to which mound to return the bone, but he had become bewildered. There were many, many mounds. It was far more extensive than either he or Professor Rose had anticipated. It seemed one mound rose upon another. The line of horses and riders rose before him and fell behind him in the cadence of the mounds. It was not that they all looked the same to him. Each was distinct, but none was the one he sought.

He had lost direction, now, and was as much dumbly following as Beau beneath him. The horse had become fixed, almost mesmerized, to the horse in front of him. So they were almost moving with no mind except that of Nose at the front, rising and falling like the body of a great snake following its head. Nose led them slowly and Leland had no need of thought. He had need only of action and reaction and following. He slumped in his saddle, hands against the saddle horn, reins lax and drooping. Horse and rider following the sway and step of horse and rider directly in front.

There were no birdsongs. Indeed, there was no scurrying or leaping or flying wildlife to break his trance. There was nothing. There was nothing except the plod of hoof upon sod.

Then Leland had a thought that excited him. It coursed through him so thrillingly that he sat upright in the saddle and felt the balls of his feet tight in the stirrups where they had been resting lightly, hardly touching a moment before. These were the first horses to set hoof on this island.

This soil, this land had never experienced the horse and the rider. They were almost like explorers.

And that was when the long snake of riders and horses contracted upon itself as a pit viper gathers uncoiled in a trail at contact with another dangerous living being. The horses, their attention set in following on line, tumbled one upon the other into the rumps of the horses in front of them as the men, equally entranced by the winding journey, now sat straight and hastily gathered reins.

Nose had stopped and Whitney's horse had pushed the Creole pony's rump around. Faces showed not confusion and awe but intense, curious interest. The Creole pony champed his bit lightly, the large, brown-black eyes accepting the scene nonchalantly, as though it was to be expected although all the other horses, when they caught sight or whiff of what was ahead, pranced and snorted, shied, and tossed their heads. The demeanor of the pony, Leland noted, was exactly that of Antoine.

Antoine alone had avoided the accordion effect of the other horses and riders by pulling Prince from the line. Now he and Prince stood slightly apart, elevated upon a low mound. Prince, too, shifted nervously. But Antoine sat him calmly, without tightening the reins, his pale eyes and face still set but lax, gazing straight ahead as though he had expected nothing other all along and accepted its inevitability as one would accept a rain one had seen building ten miles and sweeping onward.

Before them, gathered as tightly as they could have been packed into a pen under different circumstances, was the herd. Leland could not tell how many, but they seemed many indeed. And the most awesome nature of the picture, which was as still and colorful and dramatic as if it had been painted, an illusion on a screen or canvas, was the outer ring of animals. Surrounding the herd, pointed outward in each direction as precise as a ring of pikes, was a flank-to-flank unbroken line of range bulls. Leland could not guess how much one might weigh, though they all seemed very large. But what was striking about them were their horns, long and pointed and poised; the tremendous muscle, rippling erect, thick, tossing, from just behind the skull to just over the beginning of the wide, powerful shoulder and the long back; and their coats, shaggy and thick and of many colors, mottled, black, brown and white, peach in places, and sorrel, many like the skin that lay before the fireplace in the livingroom of the Viators.

The bulls slung their heads low, the points of their up-curving horns exactly outward, and watched the horsemen with the same calm and accepting demeanor as that of the Creole pony and of Antoine. None of the bulls moved. They did not paw the ground and they did not even chew their cuds. They watched as explosively as a pile of dynamite. And behind them in the herd they protected, there was only the movement of tufted tails after flies.

It was impossible to discern a leader, any bull that was stronger, bigger, more in command. It was more as though they were all in command, not only the outer ring of bulls, but the next ring of large cows and even the next ring of younger animals from yearlings to fall calves, heifers, and bulls alike, down to the center, where the smaller calves occasionally bawled. When men and horses finally began to move, it sent a sort of quiver like an electric current through the collective beast. It was akin in appearance to the rippling of a horse's hide when plagued with insects.

Nose led them in a wide arc, making of the riders a large U to drive the cattle straight across to the pen. Only Antoine did not move. The riders filed by him. He silently sat the horse, which stood with lowered head and curious ears pricked forward, horse and man in nearly the same attitude, a sameness surrounding them that set them apart from all the others, even Leland. Leland looked back as Beau followed on, carrying him on line, and was struck not only by the solitariness of Antoine and the horse he rode but by the bewildered faces of those who filed past them. Their faces were like question marks, pursed lips, raised eyebrows, and fear. Nose was the director, but no one had the answers to their unspoken questions.

Nose pulled his horse from the line at the bottom of the U and whispered something to each rider as he went by, beginning with Whitney who was to lead them to the tip of the far prong in the design. But Leland never heard what Nose had to whisper. Leland never reached him.

There was a slight shuffle in the outer ranks of the cattle when Whitney bent the line of horses and riders back toward them. They had not moved when the line went slowly past them, but the moment the forefeet of Whitney's big gelding turned to circle them, they shook their bodies violently, and from their backs rose dust in sunlit sparkling particles, and the herd seemed to turn and contract upon itself so that the lines of their backs made an almost swirling pattern, the noses bobbing and the eyes showing whites more fierce, the horns first hooking at the air, and then in an instant hooking at the horses as the bulls broke ranks and charged.

Whitney's gelding took a horn in the chest. Leland saw the horn go in and the horse go over backward onto his hind quarters and then completely over, the bull driving into the spurting blood and Whitney falling backward, trying to scramble from the back of the falling horse, arms and legs flailing like a rag doll, until he struck the ground and rolled; by then the bull was into the horse's belly with the same horn driven to the hilt. From that moment, Leland watched Whitney's actions in a sort of strobe-light sequence of separated movement, because there were bulls around him and other horses were being hit, and those that were not being hit were running well ahead of the onslaught. Beau had not been hit. They had run past him, one huge gray animal with a back wider than the horse and not much lower, shoved mightily against the horse's side with his own as he went by and Leland was driven with fear all through him that he would be unhorsed and find himself alone on foot in the melee.

He jammed spurs into Beau, and as the horse jerked forward with hardly enough room to move in the swirling, punching, pounding bovine bodies, Leland saw Whitney again, reaching for the rifle on the pitching, quivering horse. Then Beau crashed heavy on his forelegs, and Leland looked forward as his feet jammed in the stirrups, and he felt hard pain in his right ankle. The horse had hit the steep side of a high mound and had changed leads and was now pawing up the side of it, and Leland knew with relief that the pain had not been a horn in his leg but the bone in his boot crushed by the stirrup against his ankle.

Almost unconscious in the riding, he turned and looked over his left shoulder as Beau reached the crest of the mound and he saw Whitney fire one shot into the huge head pursuing him and even in the grunts and screams of the confusion Leland heard the bullet strike bone or horn and ricochet, whining off into the branches of the trees.

He heard more shots, but saw no animal fall; saw instead Whitney drop the rifle and run but saw no more of him, for Beau leapt outward from the mound, sailing until that great jar of his forelegs, which almost sent Leland over the horse's head. He was limp on the animal. It was as though all his strength had flowed out of him into the horse through his legs. Leland held to the saddle, and Beau pitched and leapt forward, pulled and scrambled and ran fiercely, with more fierceness than Leland had thought him capable of. The horse's grunts and swallowed gasps and the rattling of the tack and the bit loose against his teeth were fitting music to the wildness of the ride.

Now they were alone, Leland realizing that fear had made the horse wild, the sudden, unexpected fear. It was that quality of wildness that had allowed them to escape. Beau had no more mind for Leland on his back than for an irritating fly against his neck. They were alone, and Leland let him run out his fear. He did not try to stop or turn him. He rode, alert to low limbs. But there were no low limbs. So long had the tender twigs been eaten from the oaks as soon as they emerged that the trees grew straight up like pines, branchless ten to twelve feet from the ground. Leland held to the saddle, his feet wide, spurs far from the horse's hide. He breathed deeply and tried to calm his own fear, which seemed a lump somewhere deep inside him.

The fear, as it ebbed, was replaced by a deep anxiety. He knew he would have to return. He felt some duty to return, though he knew he could do nothing, was powerless against not only the horror of what they had found but its inevitability as well.

Then Beau slowed to a hard-bouncing trot, and Leland did nothing to inhibit this gait, either. It was the kind of trot ill-mannered and untrained horses take when they are avoiding capture in a pasture. And Beau did not cross the mounds in leaps and scrambles, now; instead he wove around them at their bases and finally came to a walk. Finally, at a place where the mounds made a ragged circle and the trees allowed sunlight to fall bare upon the damp ground, he stopped, heaving very hard in a heavy grass-scented breath and pawed the ground with a forefoot. The rain had merely wet the top layer of soil lightly. From beneath the dark, damp top layer the dust broke through dry and gray.

Leland, too, breathed deeply. He did not speak. He closed his eyes and let his head fall back and let the streaming sunlight make red orbs of his eyelids. Then he opened his eyes and gazed high into the sunlit branches of the white oaks and the water oaks around him and when he looked down again he realized with a start where the horse had brought him.

There was the tree with the diagonal root system. And the new-spaded ground. And the bits of hard clay that had ground at his knees when he knelt digging. Quickly, he dismounted and dropped the reins. The horse, fear run out of him, was tame again and would stand with the reins dropped and dangling from the bit to the ground. Leland felt the earth damp against his knee as he knelt and pulled the bone from his boot. The clay was thick and clinging against his fingers as he clawed at the mound, loosened the lumpy soil into a small hole, shoved the bone inside and covered it with his hands cupped, fingertips, thumbs together. When he took his hands away he saw the imprint of his palms against the clay of the mound.

When he heard the sound he knew this time before he turned what it would be. For he had seen it before, in exactly this same spot, from exactly this same vulnerability. But this time there was also the horse. And the bull turned his attention from Leland to Beau, and even as Leland was shouting for the horse to run and knowing that Beau, tame again and obedient to his training, would not move with the reins down, the bull in great-muscled swiftness charged into the side of the horse.

Beau went over with a grunt and a squealing scream. The bull, both horns into the horse's belly, seemed almost to lift him completely from the ground. He drove him sideward, the saddle and Beau's back striking the tree. Leland heard the rawhide-covered inner saddle tree crack and saw all four of Beau's steel-shod hooves pawing and scrambling in the air. And he saw the entrails follow the horns out of the barrel cavity and the horn go in once more, hooking. And then he knew that the high-pitched, terror-filled sound he heard was his own scream as the bull pulled back from the horse and turned snorting and pawing in Leland's direction.

The bull took two quick, pawing paces toward Leland, but then the horse struggled to his feet behind him, and the bull stopped, half-pivoted, and stood in profile. For the first time Leland could see the massive size of him. He was longer than the horse, hindquarters muscular and thick, balanced on splayed hooves that seemed small against the bulk above them. His tail swished constantly, almost casually, as a cat will dance his tail curling in swinging, slowly whipping rhythm. From there forward the animal was as solidly packed as a block of wood, obviously bred of beef cattle, but with something extra, now, something fundamentally violent. There was the shadow of the hump of the Brahma on his back, above the shoulders swollen with power, but what captured Leland's attention, fascinated him, mesmerized him with fear even more than did the large horns parallel to the ground, was the hunk of layered muscle between the withers and the head. Now hard and erect and alive, flexed in the manner of the biceps of a muscleman magnified hundredfolds.

The horse was obviously doomed, though still standing and quivering in shock, his eyes rolling the whites into view. He teetered, rather than stood. Once when he stumbled, almost fell so that the bull gave full attention to him, he caught himself by moving forward his left back leg and so stepped on a length of entrail. Thus he pulled from his own body a length of the white, blue-veined and lumpy line of tissue.

Then the bull's head swung on Leland again. Leland

knew he must not run. Running was hopeless. He must keep his front to the bull and rely on quickness and intelligence. He wanted the safety of a tree, but the branches were too high. The bull's face upon him was calm, one might think calculating. The eyes were amoral and innocent, round and beautiful, and perfectly vicious. Leland wished he could run up tree trunks like Essey, when the bull started his way first at a walk, then a slow trot, then loping, head lowered. Leland moved quickly behind a small water oak, took a step up the mound behind him and jumped for the nearest branch.

He missed, clawed at the bark, slid down the scraping surface, arms and hands bleeding, and saw the bull bearing down hard on him. There was a roaring of pulse in his ears that didn't allow him to hear the shouts until after the bull had turned and stopped, poised to take new direction as a duck will pause at the height of his climb to level for flight.

"Yi, yi, yi, yi, yi, yi!" Antoine came straight at the bull, as though Prince were to run the animal down, the horse's big-veined muscles straining. And the bull, accepting the charge, turned and went head on for the horse and rider. Antoine never took his eyes from the bull, but even as the bull lowered his head the final inches for the stroke of the horns, he yelled, "Ready yourself! Ready yourself!" Then with a whisper of the reins he got Prince to dance to the left, breaking the bull's charge just a shade enough for the horse and rider to suddenly reverse to the right and avoid the hit. They thundered by each other like opposing trains on different rails.

"Ready yourself! Away from the tree," Antoine yelled. He was pulling the horse, now, in a circle, even as the bull whirled to follow him. Antoine was holding Prince's speed down, allowing the bull to move closer, looking backward over his shoulder. Leland could see the horse was allowing passage for Antoine's thighs among the tree trunks, taking the mounds with no more rock than a skiff over the wake of a sailboat. As they passed Beau, the dying horse did not budge, did not even notice them or the bull behind them. Now that they were past Beau, Antoine allowed Prince to widen the gap, but not so wide that the bull would not follow.

"Away from the tree, Leland! Away! Ready yourself! Ready yourself! I'll pick you up!"

Now Leland realized he had been standing, gawking, immobile. Quickly, he moved away from the water oak, leaving room on either side of him for the horse to pass. Eagerly he watched Antoine weave among the trees and the mounds, Prince with utmost calmness obeying the reins to right and left, then in a circle, with the bull following as though tied to them by an invisible cord, but with distance lengthening. And the bull's fascination waned as though the invisible cord were being stretched and would soon snap. Until, finally, horse and rider bolted straight away at a gallop, then spun back and came toward Leland so swiftly that the bull was temporarily arrested, confused. But he quickly recovered and came, also, toward him.

Prince was still at full gallop when Antoine leaned with his weight in the right stirrup, to Leland's right as he faced them, Antoine's arm held diagonally toward the boy, the hand already cupped; then two miniscule tugs on the reins slowed the horse to a speed at which their arms could accept the shock. The bull gained ground. Leland knew where Antoine's arm would go, could anticipate the feel of it across his body, knew he would grab Antoine across the shoulders and swing behind him. The bull moved closer.

Now, in his peripheral vision, Leland saw the other horse and rider bearing down hard, and he knew Antoine would never reach him. Emile burst from the trees into the little ring of mounds, his horse at full gallop, the pistol in his hand held before him, pointed to the sky, at rest, the finger outside the trigger guard. He came down hard on Antoine, and Leland did not have time to yell. Antoine, leaning to the blind side of the horse, did not see Emile until just before impact, yet he straightened, dropped the stirrups, made a loop of the reins around the saddle horn even as Willy's shoulders struck Prince at the withers, Willy's head jarring wide-eyed in front of Antoine for an instant as Antoine grappled for the poncho, Prince going down, Antoine falling with him. In that same instant the two men's faces were not three feet apart, pale eye to pale eye.

Somehow Willy continued over Prince in a gallop, Prince rolling to his feet immediately and Antoine rolling across the ground, the poncho unfolding green and yellow around him, his arms swathing his head. But the bull went past him, now in pursuit of Willy and Emile. Leland dove for Prince's stirrup as the horse went by him, but missed, hit the ground, and looked up to see Emile's face contorted in a scream, staring straight down past Willy's rump into the face of the bull.

His left hand clutched the reins as tightly as the claw of a hunting bird on a windy perch and with his right hand he fired down point blank into the bull's face.

The bullet struck the nose and the bull jerked his head as if stung by a bee, but came on. The next three rounds went into the horse's rump. Leland saw the spurt of blood and the horse jump with each shot. Then one more shot and the horse went down, the hind legs rigid and extended and usless. The pistol sailed clear, but Emile was trapped, pinned beneath the horse as the bull drove in, hooked the horse's belly like a saber thrust and laid it open. Now the bull stood there and drove his horns into the prostrate horse again and again, punching like a boxer hooking down and low, and hit the heart with one blow because the blood burst forth and painted a horn almost black. The body of the horse bounced with each thrust.

Emile, now screaming, first kicked at the saddle and the horse's back to try to free his right, pinned leg, but could not. Then he kicked at the bull's nose as the animal came over the body to him. But then the bull could not see him because the poncho had whipped across his eyes.

Antoine was standing there, holding the poncho, wrapping it over the bull's face, then flicking it in front of him until he followed it away from Emile. Emile lay back against the ground in pain and Leland cowered close to the protection of a tree trunk as the bull came out after Antoine, the yellow-and-green poncho for protection.

He came into Antoine head up and galloping in an attitude of full confidence, his target having grown almost to the size of a horse by the spread folds of the poncho. Antoine continued to back away, the poncho fully open in front of him and held high with both hands spread wide and just enough room over the top to peer at the onrushing animal. He held the green side toward the bull, so that his thin body was outlined against the yellow from Leland's point of view. Backing away as the bull's pounding hooves ate up the ground between them, Antoine's boots made shuffling sounds in the moist soil. He moved awkwardly, at first, feet splayed outward as though he were trying to decide which way to run. Then, even as the bull's horns hit the thin, rubberized fabric, he half-turned, let the poncho swing on, and the bull ripped a patch from it as he went on past.

He came on toward Leland, but now Leland huddled against the thick tree trunk and did not move, and the bull did not discern him from the forest so turned quickly and faced Antoine, and without halting he charged again. This time Antoine held the fabric well ahead of the bull and swung it forward of him so that the horns did not actually touch it. And this time when the bull came out of the charge his head was oscillating confusedly. And he was facing Prince.

The horse, reins tied to the saddle horn, was a free agent. Many times in his training and his work, facing cattle with the reins gathered loosely behind his head, he had made his own decisions as to movement. So as the bull aproached he widened his base and lowered his head exactly as he had done thousands of times in the cutting pen, but this time his ears were flat against his neck, the one sure sign of venom in a horse.

The bull came on so swiftly and Prince held his ground so firmly that Leland thought in that instant Prince, too, was dead. Until Prince began to sway in his neck, his nose waving close to the ground and just as the bull reached him he darted in a sideward motion, like a crab chased by a frigate bird, and avoided the horns. As soon as the bull started toward Prince, Antoine folded the poncho into one hand and dashed toward Emile, who lay as still as he could with the pain. Now, as the bull paused ever so briefly, breathing hard, now, and spittle mixed with blood drooling to the earth, but with his eyes still on the horse, which had stopped and turned and faced the bull in the same attitude as before, Antoine slid his arm under Emile's shoulders and tried to slide him from beneath the dead horse.

Antoine continued to hold the poncho in one hand, but also continued to pull on Emile. They were half-hidden, crouched low behind the fallen animal, but enough of the movement was visible to attract the attention of the bull, who darted his gaze, now, between the horse and the men. He even shifted his weight, once, in the direction of the men. But Prince, for just a moment, his neck arched muscularly and his ears forward, now, like a parade horse, advanced a step, pawed the ground in front of him, and then turned toward the bull. At the charge, he reeled as lithely as dogs reel and dart in play and led the bull in two tight circles as he and Antoine had done earlier, widening the circles and the distance between them with each turn. Then, with the bull still in pursuit, he headed through the trees, away from Antoine and Leland, and Emile trapped in the little ring of mounds by one thousand pounds of dead horse.

Now Antoine laid the poncho across Willy's dead haunch and tried with both arms to free his brother. But as he began to twist, Emile began to scream a loud, high woman's scream of pain. Antoine ceased and squatted near his brother's head, his face strained and beaded with sweat, and pale, even paler with the fear.

"My leg, she is broken," Emile said. "I know she is broken underneath."

Antoine said nothing. He squeezed his brother's shoulder, picked up the poncho and ran to Leland. As soon as he reached him he formed a stirrup with his hands.

"Here," he said. "Put your foot in the stirrup. I can boost you to the first branch. In case he returns."

"I could do something, me," Leland said.

"Mais, you could hurry, you," Antoine said. "Get yourself safe, you. Mais, I need you safe, me, so I can think."

Leland put his boot into Antoine's hands and stepped up smoothly as Antoine stood and boosted him so that he reached the first thick branch quite easily and pulled himself with great effort up the gnarled skin of the oak and into the branches where he braced himself between a limb and the trunk.

"What will you do?" he shouted at Antoine, who was running again toward Emile.

"Mais, I'll have to kill him, me," he shouted back without turning.

"How?" Leland asked, but Antoine did not answer. He stopped midway across the flat circle. The dark, huge, shadowy hulk of the bull was knifing toward them through the trees. Now Antoine folded the poncho in half so that it made a half-circle of cloth curving from the straight edge held in both hands as the bull entered the sunlight of the clearing and paused, facing him. Now there was something else about the bull. He breathed hard, of course, from the long chase of the horse, but there was something of panic in the eyes. He teetered there, heaving and swallowing at the edge of the clearing. And Antoine stood perfectly still. From the one hit Emile had made with the light pistol, blood dropped slowly and mingled with the saliva that hung in thick strings.

Antoine, with the folded poncho held before him, stood without moving, but the bull had seen him and singled him out from the shapes around him, kept his gaze on him, and snorted as though thinking through a puzzle. At that moment Beau, his entrails now dragging behind him in a long train, began to give way weakly, his hind legs no longer able to support him. He did not make it to the ground before the bull hit him. The horse made no sound as the horn went in again and again, even as the body fell with a thud against the earth of the mounds.

Antoine made no attempt to draw the bull from the horse. He moved over slightly to see exactly how the bull got the horns in but was careful to keep well behind the animal's vision.

"Don't move, Emile," he said, now very calm. "Don't move. He sees too well from the side."

At that Emile lay back against the earth, his eyes wrinkled tightly shut and his mouth open and teeth bared in a grimace of pain. By the time the bull was through with Beau, the horse's barrel was riddled like a sieve. Nothing of the horse moved except the long neck on which the head from time to time reared serpentine. And now, looking somewhat refreshed, though still heaving for breath and draining saliva and blood, the bull turned back to Antoine. Antoine appeared to have been waiting for him as one waits for a child to turn its attention from a game. He took two sideward steps and the bull came on fast.

Antoine pulled the green-yellow poncho before him smoothly and when the bull had gone through he yelled for him to return. At first he yelled instructions. "Come back, you. You black bastard, come back. Come to your death, sweet son-of-a bitch. I'm here, can you not find me?" But then he yelled only sounds which seemed like words but were not French or English and sometimes only grunts and cries. He did not take his eyes again from the bull.

He got closer and closer to the bull before the animal charged. At first the charges were from distances of up to fifteen yards. But then Antoine began encroaching on that distance, and the bull let him come closer before charging. It seemed to Leland a great folly. Leland understood what Antoine was trying to do when he pulled the poncho back and made the bull turn swiftly, spin sometimes so fast and so much that his nose and his tail almost met. That was injuring the muscles along the back, it had to be. It might even injure the spine. Leland could see that.

But now Antoine was working very close to the bull and when the bull accepted the challenge and charged, Antoine jerked the poncho very high, so that the bull followed it, and sometimes his forefeet even came off the ground and the bull's eye was as high or even higher than Antoine's,

Antoine standing beside the bull as still and unprotected or unhidden as a post at a street corner. Again and again he did this, and afterward he would study the bull very closely, looking down, now, at the top of the bull's head, holding the poncho low, draped partially across the damp earth now churned with their feet.

Once, he even leaned forward, standing with his feet not a yard from the bull's down-hanging nose, and actually looked down at the bull's head leaning over the horns. Then the bull charged and Leland thought surely Antoine was dead. But the horns actually went on by beneath a part of Antoine's body and at that moment Leland saw Antoine's face clearly in a burst of sunlight and Antoine's features had the quality of the faces of nuns who prayed at early Mass in the front pew of the church, only the eyes of the nuns were always closed and Antoine's were open, heavy-lidded, pale irises looking down.

After that, he made the bull do it again and again, each time pulling the poncho higher and higher. And, though the bull no longer left the ground with his forefeet, he jerked his head after the fabric and each time seemed more and more willing to lower it before the next charge. Finally, Antoine faced him, squarely. He went in closer than he had ever been before, and Leland was aware Antoine had been holding his breath. He made this realization by watching the easy motion of Antoine's breathing through the shirt now stuck to his spare frame by sweat and, at the right forearm, blood. The wound had reopened.

Leland watched the red stain as the right arm glided smoothly forward, the left hand alone holding the poncho before the bull, the fingers of the right hand dipping downward ever so gracefully, as graceful as a woman dropping a handkerchief. Antoine kicked the fabric, then, and the bull's head jerked downward, the nose almost on the ground, but the bull did not charge and Antoine's fingers spat fire.

The bull dropped immediately, all four feet jerking straight out as though charged with electricity, the whole body rigid and stiff and dead at Antoine's feet even before the muscles relaxed. And then Leland heard the shot. He heard it echoing off the trunks of trees and the sides of mounds, and it seemed the sound of the shot would never die as Antoine raised his face toward the sky, his long, thin body dappled with sunlight and shadow, and filled his lungs so that Leland thought he would shout. But he did not shout. He stood there with the poncho dangling in loose folds from one hand and the silver barrels of the derringer from the other, face skyward, eyes closed and serene.

As the booming sound of the shot died, the profound and eerie silence of the island returned, broken only by Emile's groaning and then the sounds of Prince returning. Prince reached the edge of the clearing, now cut and plowed as though by a two-way disk, and walked gingerly to the corpse of the bull, sniffing and snorting at the hide and bobbing his head on a curved neck. Leland jumped to the ground and stood as Antoine went to Beau and lifted his head and held it against his thigh. He pressed the barrels of the derringer against him and discharged the second shot exactly where he had hit the bull, just behind the skull where the spine joins the brain through a passage to the vault of the cranium. The horse pitched once more with more life than Leland thought he had left in him. Antoine let the head fall dead before the blood spilled through the hole onto him.

Prince stood still though the reins were still bound to the saddle horn as Antoine unfastened the leather thong holding the nylon rope, made a clove hitch on the saddle horn and uncoiled the rope to Emile. He fastened the noose around Willy's saddle then tightened the foregirth and even the anchor girth of the roping rig. Then, with Leland leading him by a hand on the bit, Prince pulled the corpse off Emile's leg as Antoine slid his brother from beneath.

After Antoine had slit Emile's trouser leg and cut away the boot they could see the lump of bone bulging bluely against the flesh. It was a compound fracture, but the jagged edge of the bone had not broken through the skin. For this reason, Antoine walked beside the horse as Leland led him and Emile rode. Antoine hugged his brother's battered leg against his chest tightly with both arms, keeping it as still and straight as he could so that the loose bone inside would not swivel and cut. Leland found his sense of direction had returned and he led them exactly to where the marsh buggy and the others waited, on an exact line even before he heard the diesel rattle of the idling marsh buggy. He felt quite fine and in the first part of the walk there was only the groaning of the man on the horse behind him to temper the serenity of the island's silence.

Miraculously, no one had been killed. They had lost four horses and three others were severely wounded. Theophile Broussard had a bad horn wound in the groin, but it was not oozing blood any more and he was not in the medical kind of shock. Whitney had a horn wound to the buttocks, and even in the pain he could see the humor in it, and he kept repeating he had expected worse when he fell and the bull came on him swift and hurrying like a puppy in play but with absolute malice. The others were simply shocked, stunned.

They took the three wounded men in to the hospital in Abbeville and returned with high-powered rifles. The rest of the herd, except for a few very young calves and two starving old cows which never bred and died that fall at Pine Island, was shot from a distance and the horses were used to drag their corpses to limbs strong enough to hoist them with the block and tackle and the singletree so the men could go to work on them with Nose's sharp, brutal tools, butchering them and quartering them. Then the horses were used to haul the meat to the sled.

The calves they took alive were castrated on the spot and the tiny testicles scattered among the refuse of hooves and tails and heads with horns attached. It had not surprised them that the cows were as valiant as the bulls though not quite as dangerous by virtue of bulk and the male ability to abandon completely to aggression. What had surprised them, even frightened them, was the aggressiveness of the calves, the older calves, which charged the rifles just as readily as the bulls and cows.

And they were surprised at the size of the bull Antoine had killed with one shot of the derringer. Two horses labored to drag him to a limb heavy enough to bear him, his right horn plowing a small trench in the dark soil behind them. And it took six men to hoist his form with the block and tackle. When the skin had been flayed they found evidence of many old wounds in the meat, which shone whitely in the dappled sunlight. His testicles, too, they tossed randomly among the surrounding mounds though they were much more than large enough to eat.

So with the few small calves jammed against the rear of the sled and the men and the horses in the center and the meat piled in rows five feet high at the bow, they left the island. And it was as though the island's silence followed them, came with them for a while. For they did not speak, did not hold mouths close to ears to communicate in the surrounding marsh buggy noise. They were exhausted, it is true, but exhaustion had never kept Frenchmen from talking, and neither had noise, as far as Leland knew. But there was a definite silence covered by a blanket of diesel sound.

They had laid ponchos overlapping end-to-end on the deck of the sled on which to pile the meat. Then on top they had spread the remaining ponchos to protect the meat from spoiling in the sun, even though that sun, too, was nearly spent for one day, setting redly and tinting everything with its thinly burning hues. There was scarcely enough fabric to cover the pile, and between the folds and through the metal eyelets at the hems the meat showed pink and white and swollen.

V

E. J.'s eyes were still puffy red, raw, and with little blue crescents under them near the nose. The nun sat at her elevated desk above them so that their height standing was just beneath her height sitting. Behind them the empty classroom extended in rows of vacant desks with corners of books and sheets of paper occasionally protruding into the aisles from the pockets beneath the seats. She had asked a question Leland could not honestly answer. Perhaps E. J. could answer it, and Leland, like the huge nun who sat above them, was waiting for him to say it.

Some of the nuns sometimes screamed at the pupils to punish. Others, like Sister Magdalene with the third graders, simply ignored infractions in order not to punish. But this nun seemed to know everything and to be above screaming. In fact, the silence around her often had the effect of a scream. It made one terribly uncomfortable. Leland did not know how long they had been waiting, but it seemed a very long time. E. J. could not answer, at least not truthfully, because he had hit Leland first. Usually that was enough of an answer, who hit first. But this nun wanted to know what went on before that first hit. Only E. J. could answer that. Leland was bored. Outside, the clover was blooming. He wanted to lie in its coolness.

"He called me a name," E. J. said.

Leland felt his jaw fly open, but he closed his mouth and said nothing. Her eyes rotated to E. J. alone. She said nothing at first, then she leaned forward on the desk, and Leland could sense she knew this was a lie.

"Oh? And what was the name?" she asked.

"I can't say it in front of you," E. J. said. She sat heavily back in her chair, then, her hands still on the edges of her desk, the protective black cloth and brown floor-length scapular now bulging over her strong, authoritative breasts. Now Leland could sense this was even more boring to her, who was uninvolved, than to Leland, who felt uninvolved except that he knew some punishment would be extracted.

"Why not?" she asked, her forefinger and thumb pushing up the lenses of her glasses and rubbing her nose where the little saddle of the wire frame sat.

"Because you're a sister," E. J. said. Nun, coonass, and nigger were words never spoken officially. She continued rubbing her nose and did not open her eyes when she spoke.

"Well, if it's worse than you said to Sister Bonaventure last week when she caught you smoking, not only do I not want to hear it but I don't believe it exists."

E. J. said nothing and she said nothing. There was another long silence as she removed the spectacles and cleaned them with a man's white handkerchief she pulled from some pocket in the voluminous robes.

"You were both wrong for fighting for any reason, and you broke the school rules by leaving the grounds. I'll deal with that later. Go on, you'll miss dinner. Don't leave the grounds again."

E. J. smiled at Leland and eagerly went for the door.
E. J. obviously believed he had turned the tide of judgment against Leland. He left the door open as he darted
outside. But Leland, his hand on the knob, hesitated. Then
he closed the door. She still had her glasses off and her
eyes, even closed, seemed incredibly weak. She sat forward, one elbow on the desk and the fingers again pressed
against her nose at the juncture of her eyes. She had that
attitude of expression Leland had seen on nuns' faces at
mass and on his uncle at the killing of the bull at Outside
Island, and he believed she was praying so he said nothing and waited again before the desk. When finally she removed the hand from her face, sat hard back in the chair,
expelled a deep breath and opened her eyes she seemed
very surprised to see him there. She quickly took up the
glasses, inserting the temple frames between the immacu-
late white headdress and her skin, hooking them somewhere beyond, around hidden ears.

"Yes, L. D., what do you want?"

Leland took a deep breath. He was afraid and he knew
the best way to get through fear was to go ahead into the
act. When he spoke, he spoke French. At the sounds of
the first words she raised her head exactly like a horse does
to show an expanse of nostrils and surprise and sometimes
offense.

"I care nothing for your punishments," he said, "nor for
your humiliations. To me, the school itself is a humiliation
designed to give me nothing and only to take from me
what I already had. I can endure this. But what is intolerable to me is that you do not see me."

He paused, then, because he was certain by now she
would have interrupted him, and he thought by pausing
he could save himself that. But she said nothing. She sat
no longer looking down at him past her nostrils, but squarely

at him, a little lower in the chair, and with her head forward, the jowls bulging at the little white bow that joined the ends of the white headdress, their eyes even. Leland did not know if she understood him, but he felt much better speaking French so he continued in it.

"I am a man, now. I passed this during the winter, in the marsh. So I know I can endure your school if I must. But I wish to be seen for that which I am. Not simply a figure fourth from the front in the third row or one of a long line of grades in your book or one of the cattle you herd to dinner and benediction."

Now he was certain he had said too much, because it was possible she didn't know French and he was speaking only for himself. He could always speak inside his head, and French, after all, was forbidden. So he fell silent and stood there though he knew he could leave. He no longer felt the fear. There was the pause of silence as she seemed to be considering something, possibly the additional punishment for speaking French. But when she finally spoke it was Leland's turn to be surprised, and he felt his own head jerk back with an intake of breath like a horse will do. For when she spoke it was in French. And not the French of schoolbooks, but his own French.

"I am sorry for the humiliations," she said. "It is not my purpose in this life or the next to deal in humiliations. The worst of the Passion, I have always believed, was the humiliation Our Lord was made to suffer. Tell me, Leland, what humiliates you here?"

But he did not answer her. He had temporarily lost thought of school.

"Of where are you?" he asked. She smiled and did not hesitate.

"Loreauville," she said. He smiled.

"Do you know it?"

"No," he said, still smiling.

"It is near New Iberia," she said, using *nouveau* for new, not even yielding to the English word in the place name. She was speaking very softly. "It is a small town. There is a narrow wooden bridge over the Teche, there, which is quite beautiful. My father works in the mill. But, Leland, what humiliates you here?"

"Reading."

"Reading?"

"Reading aloud for everyone to laugh," he said.

"I understand," she said. "Anything else?"

"Small things," he said. "Things of no importance. Things that have nothing to do with you. Things everyone endures."

She thought, for a while, her chin in her hand. Leland guessed she was having a difficult time holding her head low enough for their eyes to meet, seated above him. If they stood to talk now it would be she who looked up at him, for all her bulk.

"Well, Leland, I will do something about that," she said. "But you must never leave the school grounds again. And fighting is wrong, Leland. It is very wrong to injure someone even slightly for whatever cause. And . . . and we must not speak French at school again, for we have broken the rule."

Things at school, then, began to change. He was never punished for the fight, and he believed E. J. had never been punished, either. For one whole week the nun did not use the usual order of reading aloud and instead called on students randomly. She never called on Leland, and, though he continued to follow the lines of words as closely as though his exposure was in jeopardy, he realized she would never call on him to read aloud again. This confused him until the next Friday when she kept him after the others had gone out to recess and gave him a book. She told him to read it in one week, a feat he was not at all certain he could do, and to discuss it with her at recess the following Friday.

It was the story of a boy who grew up in the woods of Florida and had a deer for a pet, which his mother killed. Leland did not know all of the words and did not look them up as he had been taught. But he understood the story, and the nun smiled when he related it to her. They exchanged books. The next one was much longer and harder. He was given two weeks to read it. It was supposed to be about the French Foreign Legion and some boys from England who grew up and joined it. But it had nothing to do with French, though he enjoyed it very much and often read it sitting or lying in the swelling bunches of dark green clover.

At lunchtime, the girls sat in the clover and made garlands from the green-stemmed, white-balled clover flowers, chatting and occasionally screaming about the bees that also enjoyed the clover. The boys played baseball, always, not having the courage to sit in the clover with the girls. So they teased Leland, but only about reading for a pleasant change, so Leland did not mind and, he not minding, the teasing stopped. Sometimes he was invited to join, and he found he could now hit a ball farther than anyone else in the class. Before, it had been E. J. who could hit the ball the farthest. But E. J. never played anymore. No one knew where he spent his time.

Most days the baseball did not attract Leland. He was swept with a wave of dazed laziness. The sunlight became a magnet he did not wish to resist. He would read on his belly in the cool, deep clover and turn over and use the book for a pillow when he was tired, feeling the cold of his front warm with the sun as the warm of his back cooled in the clover.

He enjoyed the bus ride home very much, now, seated mostly with Sandra Mestayer. Never before had he noticed how lovely was her skin, not pale nor dark, like the color of a paper-shelled pecan. Her brothers thought their sitting together was funny, but the ride to Esther beside her was very short.

Emile's leg took a long time to heal. Leland and Antoine handled the planting alone. They soaked the seed rice in the canal until it had time to begin to sprout, and Leland loaded sacks of soaked seed rice into the bag at the end of the boom until it was filled. Then he would climb the wings along the sparkling strip for traction to guide the opening, spilling seed rice swift and brown into the hopper. He did this from long before daylight until well after the sun came up as the planes made pass after pass. He did a good job. Everyone remarked on it.

And the field, well-prepared, came up quickly. First the tiny green leaves bristled the still, glassy water like an early morning beard. Then, almost overnight it was so thick you could not see the water. Thick and green, deep and dark and fertile so that Leland sometimes wished it would not head out and turn color and come to harvest but would last forever like this, a huge, long green, growing field. And yet, walking the narrow levees in the late afternoons, he would pause and pluck a stem and pry loose the tiny heads of rice, rub them between his palms and note with great pride their infinitesimal growth. He wanted the harvest, he decided. It was just that he wished everything could last longer so that he could hold it longer and understand it better. Like a book in which one could turn back the pages and take another look first hand, or stay on one page an hour before turning to the next.

The planting done, there was little to do until the fishing season except get the bateau rigged and Antoine always did that. Leland's mother hovered over Emile solicitously

at whichever chair he chose to prop his leg's long cast upon.
He was as proud of that cast as he would have been of a
Number Two rated rice crop. It was filled with names and
funny sayings because he insisted everyone who came
near him write on it.

But the names and funny sayings smeared and faded
because even before the cast was off he began hobbling to
the pickup truck in the mornings. And when he returned
each evening the cast and his boot and the sock of the foot
of his injured leg were all smeared with mud. So Leland
knew where he was going but said nothing. And if the
others knew, they said nothing, either. At first it was quite
difficult and then less difficult and finally quite easy and
natural to call Emile *Papa* again. There settled over the
house a great calm the likes of which Leland had never
known and did not understand.

Two mornings after the cast was cut away, Pa-Paw did not
come to breakfast. Neither did Ma-Mere. Leland's mother
prepared breakfast alone while Leland checked the pasture and Antoine fed the stock and Emile sat drinking cup
after cup of coffee. But when Leland and Antoine had finally come in, and all was ready, the biscuit and preserves
and all the rest, they could avoid it no longer. This had
never happened and could happen for only one reason.

Ma-Mere was seated on the bed when they entered the
room. Pa-Paw was dressed down to his shoes, lying very
peaceful and quite dead. Ma-Mere wore a black dress and
a long lace mantilla Leland had never before seen. She
wore it throughout the entire funeral proceedings, the
wake and the mass and the ceremony at the grave site. It
was very fine and very old and slightly discolored at the
edges of its folds.

Then it seemed time truly was suspended, but not exactly as Leland had dreamed. It was only that in the ar-

rangements and the sweet grieving, their routines had been interrupted. But the rice still grew green, Leland noted. And the days still grew longer and more bright and hot.

Emile got very drunk to be able to bear the funeral and wept openly at the wake, which was attended by hundreds of Frenchmen who rotated in and out of the funeral home. There was not enough room even in the largest of the salons for all of them, and outside they could smoke and talk about him, recounting many funny stories of him and his brother. Antoine did not arrive at the wake until almost nine on the morning of the funeral. He was wearing a black suit that was out of style and carrying a grass sack wrapped around some object. He had been gone all night, and Leland was afraid this was some sacrilege against some old custom, but no one in the family mentioned it, and he was welcomed with condolences and warmth by the other mourners at the funeral home.

The expression on the old man's face was one he used when giving some irreverent advice. Leland was struck by this as the family, alone, after the others had filed out of the room, took their final leave. The brothers kissed their father goodbye, but Leland could not bring himself to do it, and the coffin lid was sealed forever.

The mass was a short one and Leland paid little attention to what was said. He and Antoine took the forward handles, Antoine still with the bundle in his free hand, and Emile limped ahead to the hearse. Since it was by then illegal in Louisiana to bury in private cemeteries, they had purchased a plot at Esther, the closest Holy Ground to the gulf.

There was another ceremony there, more incense and words in the open air, and then the priest removed the crucifix from atop the coffin and gave it to Ma-Mere. Leland's mother supported her as they began to walk away, Emile at his mother's elbow but unable to give her physical support because of his leg. Antoine remained at the grave site, and when his brother and his brother's wife turned toward him he said he would wait until the tomb was sealed. She smiled.

"Wait with him," she said to Leland.

When they had all gone, filed away in their cars and pickup trucks, the masons asked permission of Antoine to begin. Antoine did not answer them. He walked to the coffin where it sat on boards across the sides of the cement tomb, which looked everything like a feed trough or a watering trough. He swept the flowers to the ground and unwrapped the parcel.

It was an aged, bleached, weathered, and pitted old conch shell. Exactly like those that had marked the graves at Cheniere au Tigre for generations. He placed it exactly where the crucifix had been, and the coffin was lowered, the shell growing less distinct in the gloom. Antoine and Leland then sat on two of the folding chairs beneath the canopy. The masons went to work.

"At Cheniere au Tigre, the beach is clearing," Antoine said softly, almost absently. "I think the Freshwater Bayou Locks has changed the current back to the way it was."

"It was so sudden," Leland said. "He was not even ill."

"He was never ill," Antoine said, "not one day in his life. It is a blessing, is it not, to die healthy?"

Then they sat silent in the sound of the wind in the canopy and the tiny scratching, grinding sounds of the masons' work.

"Emile, he expresses his grief loudly," Antoine said, then, with no hint of criticism in his tone.

"Yes," Leland said, "but, after all, he has *lost* his father."

"This is true," Antoine said, and there followed a silence charged with something not spoken.

"And he has not found the gold," Leland said finally, and Antoine turned to him and smiled.

"So this, too, you've discovered, ainh?" he said.

"Yes, but of course," Leland said.

"But how?"

"I followed him," Leland said. "He is not the Doctor, after all."

"No, the Doctor he is not," Antoine said. He silently watched the masons placing brick upon brick, building an angled arch like steps over the coffin. Then he turned with some eagerness toward Leland.

"Mais, you know what I think about the Doctor, me?" he continued in English.

"What?"

"Me, I think he went into the woods, him, to take a piss."

When they laughed it was conspiratorial, not for the impropriety in the presence of the old man's corpse, for the old man was a kinsman of humor, but because of the masons who were not members of the family and so would not understand. So they laughed softly and used their eyes to show their mirth. Then they settled and watched as the masons, with trowels and cement and bricks, sealed it shut.